FINAL CUT

FINAL CUT

Lin Anderson

WINDSOR
PARAGON

First published 2009
by Hodder & Stoughton
This Large Print edition published 2010
by BBC Audiobooks Ltd
by arrangement with
The Orion Publishing Group Ltd

Hardcover ISBN: 978 1 408 48699 3
Softcover   ISBN: 978 1 408 48700 6

British Library Cataloguing in Publication Data available

Printed and bound in Great Britain by
CPI Antony Rowe, Chippenham and Eastbourne

Acknowledgements

Thanks to Dr Jennifer Miller of GUARD, DCI Kenny Bailey (retired), Andy Rolph, R2S CRIME Forensic Services Manager, Tom Smith of Arboga, Sweden, stained glass artist and member of the Larkfield Gang (www.tomsmith.se), and the staff and regulars of the Beechwood, Glasgow.

To Detective Inspector Bill Mitchell

1

'They shall grow not old, as we that are left grow old,' he murmured.

It had been the recent televised Remembrance Ceremony that had prompted him to return. Watching five hundred primary-age children walk behind the British Legion flags, their poppies as bright as their little red mouths.

There was nothing to see now, especially in the winter twilight, but he knew they were there.

He smiled.

They were his.

They would always be his.

It was dark when he left the forest. Out of the sheltering trees, an icy blast met him head on. Snow swirled round him in a frantic dance.

When he reached the road he turned for one last look, promising himself he'd return soon. He braced his body against the wind, enjoying the pleasurable heat of memory as he stared back at the maddened trees.

2

'It's fucking freezing.' Private Fergus Morrison cupped his crotch, where his testicles had shrunk to the size of marbles. He'd have to get out of this wind soon or frozen balls would be the least of his worries.

The entry to the civic dump loomed out of the

darkness, lit by a single high-voltage beam. To his right a wall was graffitied with a Toryglen gang slogan, *You are now leaving Toi land*. In the distance, across a strip of darkness, rose the lighted mound of Hampden Park, graveyard of so many Scottish football hopes.

The gates to the site were closed, the vehicle barrier down. He slipped underneath it and took a run at the gate, easily hoisting himself up and over.

He landed with a dull thud and stood upright, listening. A rusty sign on the fence had told him CCTV cameras were in action. He doubted that. Who would bother protecting Glasgow's rubbish?

He narrowed his eyes against the thickening sleet. The nearest skips were for metal, wood and household waste. He glanced in at the pile of bursting bin bags. It would be warm in there, but he couldn't stand the smell. He wasn't that desperate.

When he located the skip he wanted, he climbed in, cursing as his shin caught the metal edge. He fought his way through the layered piles of flattened cardboard boxes to the back wall, glad to be out of the wind finally.

Once he'd built his cocoon, he settled down to drink the last can of strong lager. OK, he'd secured a place to sleep safely and something to drink. No food, but the six-pack had taken the edge off his hunger. Hey, two out of three wasn't bad. It was better than Afghanistan. There would be no one taking potshots at him here and any shit that smeared his face wouldn't be his mate's guts.

The memory of sudden death made his hand shake on its way to his mouth. He took a slug of lager, then wedged the can between his knees and lit a fag.

The arrival of a car didn't bother him. No one would be dumping at this time. He knew that prostitutes from nearby Govanhill brought their johns here. If it hadn't been so cold he might even have spied on them and jerked off alongside.

He took another mouthful of beer and blew lightly on the end of the cigarette. It was the nearest he would get to the warmth of a fire tonight.

3

'Is Granny going to die?'

'Yes, Granny's going to die,' said Claire, more sharply than she intended.

A small, choking sob came from the back of the car. Despite her stressed state, Claire felt a stab of guilt.

'I don't want Granny to die,' Emma wailed.

'Neither do I, Emma.'

Claire knew she was being blunt, but she couldn't pretend any more, even for the sake of a nine-year-old girl.

'Will Granny go to heaven?'

Claire didn't answer immediately. Instead, she flicked the wipers to fast mode and peered through the sleet-splattered windscreen. The road was pitch black, her beams the only lights for miles, but she knew this route like the back of her hand. Since her mum had been diagnosed with terminal cancer, she'd travelled it often enough.

The sobs in the back had dissolved to an

occasional whimper. Claire felt a rush of pity for her daughter. Just because she was beside herself with worry didn't mean she had to take it out on the child.

'Of course Granny will go to heaven,' she relented.

'You're sure?'

'I'm sure.'

There was a contented sigh as though a weight had been lifted from the small girl's shoulders.

'Why don't you have a nap? When you wake up we'll be home,' suggested Claire.

Silence descended in the back. Eventually Claire heard the soft sounds of sleep. Relieved of the need to worry about her daughter, she concentrated on the road and the worsening weather.

She turned on the radio, keeping it low. The local station was playing country music, interspersed with warnings about the wind and snow. According to the presenter, the Forth and Erskine bridges were already closed and all ferry sailings had been cancelled until further notice. Travel was not being advised.

'Too late for that now,' Claire muttered to herself.

As if in response, a sudden gust caught the car broadside, throwing it towards the left-hand verge. Claire yanked the wheel round, narrowly avoiding hitting a fence post.

'Shit!'

She would have to slow down, especially on the more exposed sections. When she'd regained her composure, she checked the rear-view mirror. Emma, thank God, had slept through the drama.

4

Claire consoled herself with the thought that they would soon be off the moor and in the shelter of the woods. She could speed up then and get them home as quickly as possible.

*   *   *

She entered the forest, the looming shadows of the trees swaying and creaking above her. Claire peered ahead, seized by a sudden fear that one of the creaking giants might come down and block the road or fall on the car.

A murmur from Emma brought Claire's head round.

'OK, sweetie?'

She waited for an answer, suddenly craving the sound of another human voice, but Emma was fast asleep.

Claire turned her attention to the rapidly whitening windscreen and tried to see through. The whirling snowflakes looked like fast-moving stars in the full beam of her headlights, so Claire dipped them.

Then she saw a figure standing in the middle of the road. She slammed on the brakes and spun the wheel.

Too late, she remembered that you were meant to turn into the skid. The car was on its own journey, ignoring her interference, slithering towards the steep embankment that dropped to the forest floor.

For a tortuous moment the car balanced on the edge, then Claire's world turned upside down.

*   *   *

Approaching consciousness brought a series of nightmarish images: an old woman; a sobbing child; dark shadows of trees bending and swaying above her. Then Claire's eyes flicked open and she stared into utter darkness. She realised she had no idea where she was, or even who she was. Her head was empty of everything except a searing red-rimmed pain.

She tried to shift her body, suddenly aware that the reason she could not draw breath was because of a seat belt biting into her chest.

The seat belt's sudden release sent her tumbling into a couple of inches of freezing water. A wave of panic hit as she imagined the car submerged and her trapped inside. There was air, but for how long? Taking a deep breath, Claire launched herself at the driver's door.

Air escaped her lungs as her shoulder met the inside panel. The door groaned in its frame, but shifted only marginally. Claire waited anxiously for the sound of incoming water. When she heard none she braced herself and tried again. This time it worked. The door jerked open and she heard the howl of the wind and the tortured creaking of trees.

Thank God. The car was upside down but it hadn't landed in water.

Claire inserted one shoulder into the narrow gap, realising almost immediately it would be too tight a squeeze. She retreated and struggled out of her jacket.

This time her exit was easier. She manoeuvred her upper body through. A sudden moan and shudder of the car sped up her efforts. She freed

6

her hips to land with a grunt on a boggy bed of moss and heather.

She lay there for a moment, catching her breath, then struggled to her feet. Out of the partial shelter of the car, a gust hit her head-on. She gripped the door to stay upright and stared into the darkness, listening for the sound of traffic, hearing nothing but the wind and the trees.

Which way should she go? Claire stared at the upturned vehicle in confusion. Why could she not remember who she was or what had happened?

She set off, panicking after a few yards when she realised she was heading downhill. She retraced her steps, or thought she had, then couldn't see the car. When the bulk of it eventually loomed out of the darkness Claire let out a whimper of relief.

This time she set off in the opposite direction. The sudden rise of an embankment brought her to her knees, but she knew she had found the road. She scrambled up and stood on the tarmac, the wind whipping her body.

No headlights punctured the swirling snow in either direction.

Claire suddenly remembered a radio presenter's voice advising against travel. Where had she been and where was she going? A shocking image of an old woman flashed through her mind. *My mother is dying.*

A sudden gust of wind unbalanced her. She stumbled backwards and rolled down the bank to land shocked and shaken at the bottom, tears of frustration welling in her eyes. The sound of an approaching car sent her crawling desperately back up.

On her right a distant pair of headlights

disappeared in a dip in the road, then reappeared. Claire waved her hands wildly, her shouts snatched by the wind.

What if the driver didn't see her?

Claire stepped into his beams. For a split second she thought the white van would plough into her, then it swerved and screeched to a halt. The near-side window slid down.

'Jesus, lady. You could've been killed.'

'I think there was an accident—my car went off the road.'

The middle-aged man leaned over and opened the passenger door, offering her his hand to help her climb inside. Claire sank back in the seat.

'Are you hurt?'

'I must have banged my head. I can't remember anything after I skidded.'

'Anyone in the car with you?'

'I don't think so.' There had been no one in the passenger seat. But something felt wrong. She could feel it, like a name on the tip of her tongue.

Emma! The name meant nothing at first. A disconnected word emerging from her addled brain. Then Claire knew with sickening certainty. Her little girl. Emma was in the back of the car.

'Emma, my daughter's in the car!' she screamed at him.

He jumped from the driver's seat, fighting the wind with the open door.

'There's a mobile in the glove compartment. Call 999 and tell them what's happened.'

Claire threw open the door and half scrambled, half fell out on to the road. The driver was already down the bank and fighting his way towards her car, which was clearly visible in his headlights, its boot crushed against a tree.

Claire stumbled after him across the boggy ground.

The back door hung open. He ducked his head inside.

She waited to hear him say the terrible words that meant her child was dead.

'There's no one here.'

'What?' she said stupidly.

'There's no one in the back.'

'But she was there.'

The man regarded her worriedly. Claire knew what he was thinking. The woman's had a bad knock on the head. She's concussed, confused. Now suddenly she's remembered a non-existent daughter.

'My daughter was in the back of the car,' she shouted at him, more certain with every second that passed.

He nodded as though he believed her.

'I'll call the police. If your wee girl managed to get out of the car, then she's not badly hurt.' He started back towards the van.

Claire began to shout Emma's name. Each time the wind snatched it and tossed it away. 'Please, God.' She stuck her head inside the car, desperate for some indication that Emma had been there. A doll lay face up in the brown puddle that was the roof. Claire picked it up and looked at its impassive, mud-smeared face.

The man was coming back.

'The police are on their way. An ambulance will take you to hospital.'

'No!' Claire yelled into the wind. 'I'm not leaving here until I find my daughter.' She shook his hand from her arm and started for the woods.

'You can't wander around in the dark. Wait for the police.'

His voice retreated as the trees enveloped her.

4

She wasn't confused any more. Now everything was hideously real. She had crashed her car. She had lost her precious daughter. Mad with fear and grief, Claire staggered through the wood. She could think only of the way she had talked to Emma. How cruel she had been. She had made Emma cry. Tears streamed down her face.

Her voice was hoarse from shouting, her calls making less headway than before against the wind. Now she began to imagine the terrible things that could have happened to Emma. Who was the man in the road? Had he taken her?

Claire stumbled and fell heavily as her right foot found a dip in the forest floor. Her head hit a stone, momentarily stunning her. She tried to draw breath. Tried to drag herself back to her feet. Her body was swaying, her limbs turned to water. The driver was right. She stood no chance. A strangled sob emerged from the rawness of her throat.

It was her fault Emma was lost and alone in the forest. It was all her fault. Claire slid to the ground, all strength gone from her body. Then she heard voices behind her. A strong beam of light caught her. A man's voice shouted, urging her to reply. The beam was followed by another. Claire lifted her head, stood back up and called in return.

A yellow fluorescent jacket emerged from the darkness. Claire gathered the last of her strength and stumbled like a drunk towards the man.

'My little girl . . .'

He caught her in his arms.

'It's OK. We'll find her. You need to get out of the wind.'

The officer put his arm about her shivering body and led her back the way she had come. An ambulance stood on the road behind a police van. The policeman helped her up the bank.

'Leave it to us. We'll find her.'

Claire was too weak to argue.

*　　　*　　　*

DS Michael McNab stared into the darkness. This was hopeless. They would find nothing until it was light, but for a missing child they had to try. In the open, exposed to this weather, the girl might not last the night. He had extracted a doll from her bereft mother before the ambulance had taken her away. The dogs had been excited by it, sniffing the ground round the car, taking off into the woods. These dogs were their only hope before dawn.

McNab stood, rain streaming from his hood on to his face. He rubbed his bristled chin. His eyes felt as if they were full of broken glass. Three nights on the trot he'd been called out. He was beginning to forget what sleep was.

The wind had dropped a little, but the upper branches still swayed with its strength. The woman had told him a story about a man appearing in her headlights. She'd swerved to avoid him and gone off the road. A bump on the head had left her confused, then she'd remembered her daughter was in the car. The driver of the van had found the car empty apart from the doll. McNab looked down at its dirty plastic face.

A child was out there somewhere, frightened and alone in the woods. Maybe hurt. Maybe even concussed. McNab consoled himself with the thought that she couldn't have gone far in the dark in this weather.

His radio crackled into life.

'We've found her.'

'Alive?'

'Alive. You'd better come.'

As he approached the lights McNab heard a sound like a twanging wire. The closer he got to the torches the more insistent the sound became. The trees eventually parted to reveal a small clearing. The search party stood near a pile of trimmed branches. McNab heard the excited panting of the dogs and saw their breath condensing in the cold air.

The handler pointed ahead to where a girl sat under a tall pine tree. Flakes of snow drifted down through its branches to settle on her hair. She was humming. McNab wondered whether that had been the noise he'd heard.

'She's scared. She didn't want us to go near.'

'Great.' Children were not his speciality, but he would give it a try. McNab put on his best child-friendly voice. 'Hi, Emma. My name's Michael. Your mum sent me to find you.'

The girl continued humming and didn't look up. The sound was eerily penetrating. McNab fought a rising feeling of disquiet. What was he worrying about? The girl looked OK. She was just a bit spooked, that was all.

'I brought your doll from the car.'

After a moment the girl lifted her head and looked in his direction.

'You've got Rosie?'

'Would you like me to bring Rosie over?'

McNab waited, judging when it would be OK to approach. He held the doll up to the light so that the girl could see it, then began to walk forward. That was when he noticed she was cradling something.

'What have you got there, Emma?'

McNab directed the torch on to the girl's hands.

The strong beam picked out a pair of hollow eyes, the curve of a cheekbone. Now McNab was spooked. Where the hell had the kid found a human skull? McNab heard the intake of breath behind him as someone else made out the shape in the torchlight. A metre away now, McNab crouched on a level with the child.

'Where did you find that, Emma?' he said softly.

She stared at him. 'I was lost. I heard them calling me.'

Something cold and claw-like gripped McNab's spine. Whatever was happening here, he didn't like it.

'Did you find it under this tree?' His eyes roamed the ground round the girl.

She pointed at the pile of brushwood. 'In there.'

'What if we exchange Rosie for . . . that?' McNab couldn't bring himself to say 'skull'.

Emma thought about it.

'Your mum's waiting at the hospital for you,' he tried.

'He killed them. They were small like me.' Her

13

eyes filled with tears.

His apprehension was growing by the second. 'What do you mean, *them*, Emma?'

The girl stood up and handed him the skull. Having rid herself of it, she seemed to crumple. 'I want my mummy.'

McNab put one arm around her trembling body.

'It's going to be OK. You've been a very brave girl.'

He waited until the small figure retreated hand in hand with a female officer before he took a proper look. He was no anthropologist but he could tell the skull was human, probably that of a child.

McNab approached the pile of brushwood. It stood three feet high and double that in width. He'd passed numerous similar mounds in his trudge through the woods looking for Emma. He ran his beam over the heap. It looked undisturbed apart from an opening in the right-hand side.

McNab was conscious again of the strange humming sound he'd heard as he'd approached the clearing. So it hadn't been the girl making that noise. He tried to pinpoint where it was coming from but couldn't.

He took a GPS reading of the site, then called the station to report the recovery of the missing girl and the subsequent discovery of human remains.

5

Despite the mask, the sickly-sweet smell of roasted flesh invaded Rhona's nose and mouth. Of all the scents of death, this was the one she found most difficult. She kept her breathing shallow and picked her way through the debris until she reached the back wall.

'A member of the public reported seeing flames at nine o'clock,' Bill said from the open end of the skip. 'When the engine got here ten minutes later, it was pretty well over.'

'When did they spot there was someone inside?'

'When they turned off the hoses.'

Once ignited, the fire had had the benefit of a confined space and a strong updraught. The result was both bizarre and horrific. The lower part of the victim was virtually unmarked, yet the head had apparently exploded, coating the nearby walls with fragments of bone and brain.

Rhona crouched next to the body and began to check for anything that might help with identification. Her thorough search produced an undamaged pack of playing cards from a back trouser pocket, obviously shielded from the blaze by the bulk of the body, and a dog tag round the remains of the neck. Rhona lifted it free and took a closer look. The flat metal disc was blackened with soot but she could decipher enough of the inscription to believe it might be genuine.

Rhona bagged both items and passed them to Bill. 'If it is a soldier, the tag will provide us with his identity.'

'OK, where's the fire?'

Rhona recognised the voice of Chrissy McInsh, her forensic assistant.

Chrissy stuck her head round the detective inspector's taller figure. She was already kitted up, only her face visible, her eight-month pregnancy hardly noticeable in the shapeless white suit. She took one look in the skip then swiftly raised her mask. Even for someone with her experience it wasn't an easy sight or smell.

'Jesus, how did that happen?'

'You tell me,' said Bill.

He gave Chrissy a leg-up. As she landed, flakes of drier ash rose to float around them like black snow.

'Who found him?'

'A fireman spotted something when he finished hosing. The guy who mans the site, Steve Fallon, took a closer look,' Bill said.

'Bet this caused a bit of a shock?'

'Fallon says he's found everything in these skips, including a newborn baby, but nothing as bad as this.'

'He should try doing our job,' Chrissy said grimly. 'Do we know who he is?'

'Possibly a soldier.'

'Gone AWOL?'

He wouldn't be the first to decide going on the run was better than going back to Iraq or Afghanistan.

Chrissy regarded the headless corpse with sympathy. 'So the poor bastard fried here instead of in a tank. Who's scene of crime officer— McNab?' Chrissy's tone softened. DS Michael McNab, once her sworn enemy, had recently been partially forgiven.

'A kid went missing from a road accident. McNab's at the scene,' said Bill.

'Please God, no missing kids. Not in the run-up to Christmas,' Chrissy echoed Rhona's thoughts.

Three hours later they were still ensconced in their well-lit skip. Chrissy had the worst job. Scraping the remains of someone's skull and brains from the inside walls was not for the faint hearted. Rhona concentrated on what was left of the body and its immediate surroundings. The smell of burnt flesh hadn't lessened although she had succeeded in temporarily blotting it out. That didn't mean the memory wouldn't come surging back when she least expected it. Rhona wondered whether that had been the trouble with the dead soldier. Too many memories, too awful to handle.

The wind was dying down, but the sleet had become heavy rain that beat on the metal roof and turned the skip into an echo chamber. The normal routine was to methodically grid the site then transfer everything to the lab section by section. It was laborious, painstaking work. Two SOCOs were already lifting the material near the open end while Rhona and Chrissy worked close to the body. The biggest headache for forensics was being pressured to allow the removal of the body too quickly. The ideal of twenty-four hours *in situ* was rarely achievable. The other headaches were where to find a toilet and how to get something to eat. For Chrissy in her present state, both were frequent necessities. It didn't take long for one of them to manifest itself.

'I'm starving.'

'How can you think of food in here?'

17

'I'm eating for two, remember?'

Chrissy stuck her head outside and shouted for the nearest yellow jacket. A policeman approached. The closer he got to the smell, the paler he became.

'Any chance of a chippie? We've been in here for hours.'

'You've got to be joking.'

'I never joke about food,' Chrissy said firmly. 'I'll have a double smoked sausage supper. What about you?' she asked Rhona.

'I'll wait until I get home.'

'*We* definitely can't wait that long.'

Chrissy sent him on his way with a tenner fished from below her forensic suit.

'OK, now I need the loo.' She set off towards the Portakabin.

Twenty minutes later the smoked sausage arrived. The strong smell of vinegar reminded Rhona just how hungry she was.

'Come on, take a break,' Chrissy suggested. 'Steve says he'll brew us some tea.'

'Steve?'

'My pal in the Portakabin.'

Rhona headed for the toilet first, glad to take off her mask and gloves and wash her hands and face. When she entered the cabin, Chrissy was already transferring a portion of her supper on to a plate.

'I knew you would want some once you smelled it.'

Rhona took a bite of the smoked sausage. It tasted delicious.

'We'll have to let them remove the body soon,' she said.

Chrissy took a slurp of tea and grimaced. She

helped herself to two sugars from an open bag on the table and gave the mug a quick stir.

'So, what do you think? Suicide, murder or plain unlucky?'

Rhona had been asking herself the same question. She'd found nothing so far to suggest foul play, but lab tests on the debris would confirm whether any accelerant had been used. The presence of an accelerant wouldn't necessarily mean murder, however. If the guy was troubled he could have set fire to the skip himself.

'Let's wait and see,' was all she would say.

'Spoken like a true scientist.'

Steve was proving to be a perfect host. He produced Jaffa cakes for pudding.

'I took a look at the surveillance tape while I was waiting for you lot to arrive. I spotted the young guy come in. There was also a car parked near the entrance for a while. I gave the tape to your boss.'

'Is there a recording of the fire?' asked Rhona.

Steve shook his head. 'The one camera's directed on the entrance gates.'

They reluctantly left the warmth of the Portakabin and went back to the skip. Half the debris had been cleared, leaving a free passage to the body. The duty pathologist had arrived. His job was to establish that a death had occurred, not difficult under the circumstances.

'Is he dead?' asked Chrissy with a straight face.

Dr Sissons' ability to deal with violent death in all its particular Glasgow forms would never be in dispute. How he managed to do that particular job without a sense of humour, black or otherwise, baffled everyone he met, including Rhona.

Sissons pointedly ignored Chrissy's joking

enquiry—cheeky young women didn't figure on his radar at all—and continued to study the wall behind the corpse.

Chrissy threw Rhona a look.

'I've never seen anything like this before,' he finally ventured.

'Me neither,' Rhona agreed.

Sissons was an experienced pathologist who'd studied more dead bodies than Chrissy had eaten sausage suppers. If he hadn't encountered this phenomenon before, few had.

'I'll deliver his brains later,' Chrissy promised as Sissons departed.

Rhona's assistant invariably had the last word.

*   *   *

When she and Chrissy eventually vacated the skip, Rhona went in search of Bill. He was standing near the entrance with a figure she recognised immediately. McNab's expression caused her heart to sink.

'No luck?'

'We found her. She's fine.'

'So what's wrong?'

'That's not all we found.'

The rain had lessened to a freezing drizzle. Despite the layers of clothing under her forensic suit, the cold was seeping into Rhona's bones. Her teeth chattered as she waited for him to explain.

'She was about half a mile from the car, sitting under a tree . . . holding a human skull.'

'What?'

McNab nodded. 'You heard right, a skull. Small. Looks like it's been there for a while.'

'A newborn?'

The discovery of baby remains was not uncommon. The public would be amazed to know just how regularly tiny skeletons were uncovered, hidden under floorboards, buried in gardens or abandoned in the open. Even nowadays, women still gave birth to babies they or their partners didn't want.

McNab indicated a measurement with his hands. 'About this wide.'

'A child or small adult,' agreed Rhona.

'The site's secured. You can take a look tomorrow,' Bill said.

They retreated to the Portakabin. Steve had left it open for them, urging them to make tea whenever they wanted. Chrissy had left with the other SOCOs, so it was just the three of them.

Bill slipped the tape in the recorder. The CCTV footage was grainy and grey but Rhona could make out the gates and the barrier. She saw a figure, blurred by snow, climb the wire.

'Note the time. Nine forty p.m.' Bill ran it on. 'Half an hour later the car arrives.'

The vehicle parked side-on, opposite the gate. In the subsequent few minutes the snow came on in earnest, whipping this way and that in a strong wind.

Rhona peered at the screen. 'Is the car still there?'

Bill paused the tape. 'Impossible to tell. We'll see what the Tech Department make of it.'

'You think the car might have had something to do with the fire?' she asked.

'I'd like to know why it was outside a civic amenity site at that time of night.'

'Illegal dumping?' suggested McNab.

'Nothing was dumped.'

'It's a secluded spot. They could have been here for other reasons? Sex, drug dealing. We're right on the line between Govanhill and Toryglen.' McNab attempted to smother a huge yawn.

'Let's call it a day before DS McNab swallows us whole,' Bill said.

When they emerged from the Portakabin McNab asked how Rhona was getting home.

'I'll cadge a lift from someone.'

'I could drop you?'

'OK, but straight home. I need a shower.'

*   *   *

The wind was dropping, but evidence of its strength was visible in the overturned bins and scattered rubbish. Now and again a sudden dying gust would catch the car, jolting it sideways. McNab said nothing on the way, waiting until they drew up outside Rhona's building.

'The boss is in trouble.'

'The Gravedigger case?'

McNab nodded. 'I thought I'd have been rapped over the knuckles by now. Maybe lost my stripes.' He smiled cynically. 'It would have been worth it.'

'And?'

'I told them the truth, that I assaulted the suspect during the interview. The boss, I believe, is telling them another story.'

'You want me to ask Bill?'

'He might tell you.'

Rhona wasn't so sure. She and Bill went back a long way. He was her mentor and her friend. If she had been in trouble, he would be the first to know. But the Gravedigger case was different. The killer had made it personal, threatening those Bill loved.

'What if they take the boss to court?' said McNab.

Prisoners brought accusations of assault on officers all the time. It was a hazard of the job. A conviction for assault, if proven, could end a career. Rhona didn't want to think of that as a possibility.

'I'll have a word with him.'

'Thanks.'

McNab looked disappointed as she opened the car door and said goodnight. Rhona understood what he was feeling. At times like this it was difficult to let go. Only those who did what you did understood what you were feeling or thinking. Most nights after work, she and Chrissy would have a drink together, come down from the high their work required.

'Go home. Get some sleep. I'll see you tomorrow.'

McNab graciously accepted her dismissal. She got the feeling that, like her, he was going home to an empty flat.

6

Rhona turned on the shower and stepped beneath the jet. A stream of sooty black water streaked her body. She tipped up her face and rinsed out her mouth. This must be what firemen felt like all the time, she thought—blackened inside and out.

Tom the kitten was mewing just outside the cubicle. She could see his silhouette through the glass. She had fed him as soon as she'd arrived home, so it was company he was after.

A shower, food, drink and a seat by the fire was what Rhona herself craved. Company she could do without, although she would make an exception for Tom.

Dried off and wearing a dressing gown and slippers, Rhona opened the freezer compartment. She was down to two ready meals. Chicken and vegetables or vegetables and chicken. She stuck the plastic container in the microwave and checked in the fridge for wine. An opened bottle of white stood in the door.

Rhona poured a glass and headed for the sitting room. The central heating had come on some time earlier. The room wasn't cold, but it wasn't warm either. Rhona shut the curtains and lit the gas fire, watching the flames lick at the coals. She rooted about on the sofa, found the remote and switched on the TV, flicking through channels for a news update. There was plenty on the storm, but nothing about the skip fire.

A ping from the microwave sent her back to the kitchen. She heaped the hot food on to a plate and took it back to the fireside. Tom curled up on her lap as soon as she sat down, so Rhona held the plate above his purring body and ate with a fork.

She would have to write up her notes after the meal. She usually liked to do it in the incident tent. It was well lit and nobody interrupted her there. Chrissy thought the practice weird—sitting writing next to a dead body—but Rhona found it strangely peaceful. There had been no opportunity to do that in the skip.

The flat settled into silence, with only the faint hiss of the gas fire. She gently transferred Tom to a cushion and began her notes.

She clicked through the series of digital photographs she'd taken for her own use. To an untrained eye, the sequence of images looked like the work of a twisted mind. Grotesque pictures of discrete parts of the body, burned and broken. The gaping neck, the claw-like hands. Rhona studied the neck images first, then moved to the hands. The lower part of the body was virtually unmarked, protected perhaps by layers of cardboard.

Rhona switched to video mode and ran through the clip she'd taken of each hand. She paused then replayed. A characteristic feature of bodies exposed to intense heat is heat-stiffening, the pugilistic attitude caused by coagulation of the muscles, giving the impression of a boxer.

Death by fire was not a popular suicide method—too slow and painful. Dousing yourself with petrol was faster but no less agonising. Homicide by fire was also unusual, but using fire to disguise a death wasn't.

Rhona went back to the photographs taken of the neck region. She downloaded them to her laptop and magnified them. Now she could make out the hyoid bone amid the burnt muscle and flesh. There was what looked like a fracture on the left-hand side of the horseshoe shape. Rhona flipped through the other images, looking for confirmation. Another told the same story. The hyoid was the only bone in the skeleton that didn't articulate with another bone. It was supported by

25

muscle only. For the bone to break would take intense pressure, such as that applied by a ligature. Maybe the soldier hadn't died accidentally after all.

The final photograph she'd taken was of the upper body. Here the clothes had been burned away, leaving raw skin exposed. On one shoulder was what looked like the remains of a tattoo. Rhona magnified the image. It wasn't the usual girl's name or motto. If she were to take a guess, she would have said it looked like a rose.

*   *   *

Rhona forced herself awake and lay frozen, her heart hammering, bile filling her mouth. This was what sleep had become. The smothering fear, the taste of his coated tongue, the weight of his body pressing down on her, preventing her from breathing.

She stared into thick darkness, knowing she should have left on the light, that it was inevitable that this would happen.

'I am alone. I am safe.' Rhona repeated the mantra, waiting for her body to respond to the whispered words. Eventually her semi-paralytic state began to ease. She sat up and reached for the light switch.

The room sprang into life in front of her. Rhona took her time, absorbing its comforting familiarity before swinging her legs out of bed and heading for the shower.

She switched on the water and stepped under before it had time to warm up, gasping as the icy needles hit her head and shoulders. She reached for the nail brush and began to scrub her arms and upper chest methodically. Her skin reddened in angry protest at the onslaught, but the pain brought a form of absolution. Her heart began to slow. Her chest loosened its tight grip on her lungs and she was able to breathe more easily.

The water was warmer now. Rhona took the soap and smothered her body in lather, breathing in the strong scent, replacing *that other smell*. She knew that the scrubbing and washing were becoming obsessional, but it was the only thing that worked.

The final stage of the ritual was the mouthwash. Rhona poured a capful and took it into her mouth, holding it there until her tongue burned. Only then did she creep back into bed and huddle beneath the duvet.

*　　*　　*

Her mobile woke her at seven. It was McNab.

'OK to pick you up?'

Rhona had fallen asleep at around four, which felt like five minutes ago.

'What?' She struggled to get her brain working.

'The deposition site. The skull?'

'It's not even light yet.'

'The snow's melted but there's more forecast. I'd rather get going while the ground's clear.'

'OK. Give me an hour.'

'You don't need that long. You don't even shave.'

'Who says?'

They compromised on forty-five minutes. McNab was there in forty. Rhona was on her second cup of coffee when the buzzer sounded.

'I'll be right down.'

'I'm on a yellow line.'

'You're OK until eight thirty.'

Rhona grabbed her camera and forensic case and hurried downstairs. She could sense McNab's agitation as she slipped into the passenger seat beside him.

'I planned to spend today in the lab. All the stuff from the skip fire . . .'

He cut her off. 'Chrissy can do that.'

'Is Bill coming down?'

'He's been told to stay at the station,' McNab said sharply.

Which probably meant the super was planning to talk to him. Rhona decided to return to the original subject. She was aware how concerned McNab was but nothing they said here could help the DI anyway. She waited until McNab had drawn into the traffic then asked him about the skull.

'The kid said she found it in a pile of brushwood. The area is a managed forest, a mix of natural and planted trees. Mostly pine but some birch and larch. They trim back and stack the offcuts together to rot. There was a pile of the stuff next to her.'

His jaw was set. Rhona had a feeling there was something he wasn't telling her.

'Old photographs of the area would help,' she said. 'If it's managed woodland there would probably be some available from around the time they started to plant. Did the skull have mud inside?'

'Is that important?'

'It might indicate if it had been moved.'

McNab gave her a funny look.

'What's wrong?'

'The kid kept saying *them*. Like there was more than one. She said she heard *them* calling her.'

'*Heard* them?'

'She was frightened and her mother said she had a vivid imagination.' McNab sounded as though he was trying to convince himself. 'But there was a strange noise.'

'It was blowing a gale,' Rhona said, then relented when she saw him scowl. 'What kind of noise?'

He shrugged. 'I don't know. It just sounded weird.'

They had left the city and were passing through moorland, patches of it still white with snow. Completely exposed, it must have been a difficult road to negotiate in a storm. Even now in daylight it looked desolate. Last night it must have seemed like the end of the world.

The wood was a welcome relief. Stark grey skeletons of silver birch stood among more mature evergreens. A steep bank on the left-hand side dropped to the forest floor. On the right the trees climbed towards an escarpment. A mile in, Rhona saw R2S's Mobile Response Unit parked by the side of the road.

'The cavalry have arrived,' said McNab.

* * *

Rhona supervised the sectioning of the site into metre squares while McNab worked out a way to protect it from the elements.

The MRU had the camera set up to take a 360-degree spherical image of the area. The result would be fed into software that would dynamically

29

integrate all crime scene information—maps of the area, forensic notes, post-mortem findings, DNA and fingerprint results. McNab and his team would have twenty-four-hour access to the material via phone or PDA. Results on DNA or fingerprints would be texted to him if or when they were identified.

Despite the high-tech equipment, this would be a slow, laborious job. A body left above ground could be scattered over a wide area. Wild animals tended to attack the soft tissue first, especially for winter food—fingers, toes, cheeks and lips. Once defleshed, the skeleton was liable to be broken up. Larger animals went after the marrow from the long bones and smaller creatures would drag bits down holes.

An initial search of the area under the tree had revealed nothing. Rhona was now concentrating on the pile of branches where Emma claimed she'd found the skull.

The brushwood had definitely been there for a considerable amount of time. It was partly rotten and woven together with dark green moss and pale lichen. There was an opening near the right-hand side, as if someone or something had disturbed it. Rhona called Roy over and asked for a 3D recording before she started to dismantle it.

Roy Hunter was a former DCI who'd discovered that golf and sailing weren't enough to occupy him in his retirement. A keen interest in computers had resulted in the creation of Return 2 Scene, the kind of investigative software only a serious police professional could have developed. He was also an old friend of Rhona's, having been in charge of forensic support services for a decade.

'How come you look younger every time we meet?' Rhona laughed.

'There is life after retirement.'

'But you're still working.'

'Yeah, but I'm my own boss.'

'Maybe I should try that?'

'I can get you plenty of work if you do.'

Rhona acknowledged Roy's offer with a smile, then knelt by the rotting branches. 'The kid says she found the skull in here. I need a full recording before I take it apart.'

'No problem.'

Rhona stood aside while the camera captured the structure from all angles. When she was satisfied they had enough footage, she called McNab over.

'The tent will have to be low to get under the tree,' he said.

'I can cope.'

Once the tent was up, Rhona set to work. Inside the blue cocoon she felt at ease. On jobs like this time passed by unnoticed. Patience was essential. If there were remains, it was important they weren't disturbed.

In the confined space, shielded from the elements, Rhona could smell the pungent aromas of wet wood, earth and rotting vegetation. It was a pleasant scent with nothing sinister about it, even though this place could turn out to be someone's grave.

Lying alongside it, Rhona directed her torch into the hole. The structure appeared to be supported by the crumbling remains of a thicker log. Below lay the detritus left by decay. Among it, the concentrated beam picked out what looked like

31

fragments of bone.

Rhona began to grid the structure. When taken apart and recorded correctly, the heap would reveal a great deal about what had happened in this wood since the body had been dumped here. Each layer would tell its own story. Mosses, grass seeds and species of tree would indicate how the mound had been constructed over time. It might also reveal traces of the person who had dumped the body in the first place.

She carefully began to remove branches, taking before and after photographs from all angles. Rhona liked this sort of work. She loved the quiet, concentrated attention to detail. It was like opening a multi-wrapped present, each layer as interesting and enticing as the last.

The only sound in the tent was her breath against the mask. The wind had dropped, and in the shelter of the trees there was no movement of air.

She was at the lower layers now. More heavily rotted, their underlying sides thick with moss, they crumbled under her touch, forcing wood ants to abandon their honeycomb of passages to run over her latex gloves.

Rhona switched to trowelling, sieving each portion of wood mulch for smaller items before bagging it for further investigation in the lab.

Looking at the emerging collection of bones, Rhona was in no doubt that they formed part of a small human skeleton. She began ticking off each bone on the skeleton recording sheet, already knowing it was incomplete, unsurprisingly given its relatively exposed position. When she had completed her check, she knelt in a moment in contemplative silence before she called for McNab.

He entered the tent and stood next to her, his tall frame bent under the low roof.

'A child?'

'Looks like it.'

'How long do you think it's been there?'

Rhona shook her head. 'I'll have to take a look at the vegetation cover before I hazard a guess. Above ground like this a child's skeleton would deteriorate quickly.'

'A private estate apparently passed ownership of the wood to the local council twelve years ago, to be used as amenity woodland.'

'That could help with the time frame.'

'You're sure there's only one?'

Rhona showed McNab the recording sheet. 'We're missing a few bones, but there are no duplicates.'

A sudden breeze plucked at the tent, rippling the plastic. Rhona heard a faint humming noise amid the creak of branches overhead.

'That's it,' McNab said animatedly. 'That's the sound I heard last night.'

They ducked outside. The wind was coming in gusts, swaying the upper branches of the circling pines. Rhona could hear a high-pitched whine.

'D'you hear it?' asked McNab.

The sound rose and split into something resembling a musical chord. It was eerily compelling. Rhona looked up, searching the branches for whatever was making the increasingly familiar sound. She had definitely heard something like it before.

Then she remembered. When she was a child on

Skye, a New Age enthusiast, escaping from city life, had come to live near by. She'd been fascinated by a large wooden structure he'd built in his back garden. It had been designed like a tunnel. Standing inside, listening to its music, was weird and unsettling, yet at the same time magical.

'I think it's a wind harp.'

McNab looked perplexed.

'A structure that resonates in the wind to make a kind of music.'

Now that she knew what she was looking for, it was easier to spot.

'Up there,' she told McNab.

The tree was an ancient pine that had survived from some earlier forest. In its uppermost branches was a wooden construction, smaller than the one Rhona's neighbour had made. Paler in colour than the bark, it was narrow with holes at various positions.

'Who put that there?'

'Maybe the local council, as part of the woodland experience. Maybe just someone who likes wind harps.'

As the wind lifted, the sound rose to pulsate around them. 'I think Emma probably followed that sound,' said Rhona.

McNab looked relieved that the girl's story might have a logical explanation, which surprised Rhona. She hadn't taken McNab for the superstitious kind. They had worked together on a voodoo case and McNab had openly ridiculed the notion of witchcraft. Rhona suspected that finding a lost child in this wood nursing a skull would have spooked anyone, even him.

'I'd check with the council. See if the wind harp's

theirs,' Rhona suggested. 'If it is, they'll have a record of its installation. Might help again with our time frame.'

Rhona returned to the relative silence of the tent. Now the skeleton was exposed and recorded, she could lift it and transport it to the lab. After that she would concentrate on excavating below the remains until she reached the undisturbed layers. Rhona set to work.

7

'Is there anyone who could keep an eye on you?'

'I've got good neighbours.' Claire didn't mention the fact that the nearest was a mile and a half away. 'But I'm not sure how we'll get home.'

'You could wait for an ambulance, but that might take a while.' Dr Spence looked apologetic.

'It's OK. We'll manage.'

'I'll let your local GP know. He'll want a look at that head wound in a couple of days.'

Free of the consultant, Claire checked her wallet for the emergency breakdown number. Thank God someone had thought to remove her handbag from the wreck and send it in the ambulance with her. Claire had a suspicion it had been her rescuer. She silently vowed never to talk disparagingly about 'white van man' again.

Her mobile proved useless, either damaged by the crash or out of battery, so Claire asked the nurse whether she could use the ward phone.

The emergency number rang for a long time, and Claire was glad she wasn't on a cold lonely road in the middle of a storm. When a woman finally responded, Claire explained the situation. The woman tutted sympathetically.

'Our garden shed blew down. It was a terrible night.'

Claire gave her the whereabouts of the car.

'We'll pick it up and supply a replacement.'

If the woman had been in the room, Claire would have kissed her.

'Can someone bring the car to the hospital? My daughter isn't well enough for me to come to you.'

It wasn't strictly true, but it worked. The car would be with her in half an hour. Claire thanked the woman profusely and rang off.

She dressed slowly, conscious she was putting on the clothes she'd soaked and muddied the night before. Someone had done their best to clean and dry them, and she was grateful. Without anyone to bring fresh clothes to the hospital, Claire had little choice.

When she went in search of Emma, she found her sitting on her bed reading a book. She was wearing something from the hospital's store of children's outfits, a bit too big for her. It made her look like a refugee.

'Hi.'

Emma studied her mum's expression. 'Can we go home now?'

Claire smiled. 'I've organised a car.'

Emma slid off the bed and came for a hug.

'I promise to stay on the road this time,' said Claire.

She had a fleeting recollection of the figure that had caused her to swerve, and a shiver ran down her spine. The detective had listened to her explanation as to why she'd left the road, but although he'd taken down a description, he hadn't looked convinced. Claire decided not to think about it or mention it again. Especially not to Emma. One thing she was sure of, the figure on the road had not been Nick.

A shadow crossed the little girl's face. 'Gran's dead.'

'What?' Claire had been so busy worrying about getting Emma home, she'd almost forgotten her mother.

'When I fell asleep in the car, I dreamt she died.'

Claire hugged the girl to her and kissed the top of her head.

'I'll call the hospice.'

*   *   *

'Your mother passed away at six thirty p.m. last night.'

It was, almost to the moment, the time she'd turned on the radio to listen to the weather warnings.

'We tried calling you . . .'

'I was in a car accident. My mobile was damaged.'

'Oh, I'm sorry. You're all right, I hope?'

'I banged my head and lost my memory for a bit.'

The hospice nurse murmured a few more condolences, then added: 'Your mother made all the arrangements for her funeral when she came to us. You don't have to rush over. Give me a call tomorrow.'

Her mother had made all the arrangements, probably even written the funeral invitations. It

37

was so like her. 'I don't want to be a burden' was her motto.

Emma looked up as she re-entered the room. Claire had expected tears, but her daughter didn't look upset. Not the way she'd been the previous night.

'Gran's OK, Mummy. She told me.'

'When did she tell you?'

'When I was in the woods.'

The look of conviction on the child's face made Claire uneasy, but she decided to play along.

'Granny will be in heaven, bossing everyone about.'

'She's not there yet,' Emma corrected her firmly, 'but she says she soon will be.'

*   *   *

It was difficult to believe they were travelling the same route. In broad daylight the moor looked unthreatening, even pretty in its patchy cloak of white. As they entered the wood Claire saw a line of police vehicles parked close to the spot she'd gone off the road.

'Stop the car, Mummy.'

It was the last thing Claire wanted to do. 'I don't think that's a good idea.'

'Please.'

'But why?'

'I can hear them.'

'Emma, this is silly.'

Emma began to cry so Claire reluctantly pulled in behind a police van. An officer immediately approached to wave them on, and Claire rolled down her window.

'I'm sorry, miss, you can't stop here.'

'That's my car. I went off the road here last night.'

'This is a crime scene now. No one is allowed to approach.'

'I found them,' said a small voice from the back of the car.

Claire explained. 'It was my daughter who found the . . . remains.'

The policeman was spared making a decision by the arrival of the plainclothes officer Claire had met the previous night.

'Mrs Watson. How are you?'

'DS McNab. Thank you, I'm fine.' Claire paused, unsure how to continue.

Emma got out of the car. 'You told me your name was Michael.'

'Detective Sergeant Michael Joseph McNab.' He held out his hand and Emma solemnly shook it.

'I want to go back to the tree.'

'I'm afraid that's not possible.'

'They want to talk to me.'

Claire grimaced apologetically at McNab, who squatted down in front of the child.

'Thank you for finding the bones, Emma, but you have to leave it up to us now.'

Claire watched her daughter's face. The girl could be very stubborn.

'If I write down what they say, will you read it?'

Claire and the detective exchanged glances.

'Of course I will,' he replied.

Emma looked appeased, for the moment.

'Why don't you go with one of my officers and bring anything you left in the car?'

Claire waited until her daughter was out of

hearing.

'What does she mean, they? Is there more than one?' Claire was horrified.

'We're examining the site, that's all I can say.'

'I don't want this to prey on Emma's mind.'

The detective gave her an understanding look.

'Here's my card. There's a phone number and email address. Let Emma get in touch if she wants to.'

'You're sure? She does have an active imagination.'

'Mum, you forgot these!' Emma was running towards them, waving a bunch of keys.

'I keep the house keys on the same ring as the car key, otherwise I lose them,' Claire told McNab.

Emma seemed to have forgotten her earlier request in her delight at saving them from being locked out.

'Do you have far to go?'

'Another twenty minutes or so.'

The detective crouched to speak to the child. 'If you remember anything else about last night, your mum has my email address.'

Emma nodded solemnly.

*　　　*　　　*

Fifteen minutes later, Claire left the main road for a narrow track that wound into the nearby hills. From here you could see Chapel Mains farm and its outbuildings, but not the farm cottage that nestled in the glen behind.

Coming here had been the best thing she'd ever done. For the first time in months she felt safe, hidden from Nick's sight.

40

'Can I put the Christmas tree lights on?'

'Of course.'

Emma burst through the door ahead of her and made for the small sitting room, while Claire headed for the kitchen. She opened a bottle of red wine and poured herself a glass. She could hear Emma talking to Toby, the cat who'd taken up residence almost as soon as they'd moved in. According to the farmer, Mr Jenkins, Toby had belonged to Mina, the old woman who'd lived in the cottage before them from childhood to the grand old age of ninety-two.

'If Toby's stayed, he must like you.'

The farmer's words had pleased Claire, helping reassure her that she'd made the right decision. The move meant a new school for Emma, but they could worry about that after the Christmas holidays.

Her jangled nerves beginning to steady, she set about making them something to eat. A few flakes of snow fluttered past the kitchen window, but the prospect of more snow didn't worry her. She'd stocked up well, and Emma's presents were already hidden on top of the wardrobe. Being alone here over Christmas would be a blessing. At least they wouldn't be travelling back and forth to the hospice. The thought made Claire feel momentarily guilty, before she reminded herself that that was what her mother had wanted. 'Let the child have her Christmas without coming here.' It was as though her mother had decided it was time to go.

Claire wondered about the funeral. She would call the hospice in the morning and discuss the arrangements with them.

41

When the pasta was ready, she went in search of Emma and found her upstairs in her bedroom at the computer.

'What are you doing?'

'Sending Michael an email,' Emma told her brightly.

She resisted the desire to read over her daughter's shoulder and tried to keep concern from her voice. 'Tea's ready.'

'OK.'

Emma ate with gusto, appearing none the worse for the ordeal of the last twenty-four hours. Claire broached the subject of the email over the ice cream.

'So, what were you telling the detective?'

Emma gazed at her levelly. Sometimes Claire thought her daughter had been here before.

'There are two of them.'

'How do you know that?' Claire tried to keep her voice steady.

'I hear two voices.'

'Voices?'

'Just whispers.'

Claire's heart was pounding. She told herself that Emma had a vivid imagination; that finding the skull had upset her. The best thing was to say nothing and let nature take its course. Emma would soon forget all about it when the excitement of Christmas took over.

Emma was waiting for her response. She mustered herself. 'More ice cream, or have you had enough?'

Emma shook her head. 'Can I watch TV?'

Claire had never been so glad to hear her daughter ask that question.

'Good idea. I'll clear up and come and join you.'

She quickly rinsed the dishes, then took her refilled glass through to the sitting room and sat on the couch next to Emma.

'Would you like to sleep in with me tonight?'

The little girl didn't turn. 'It's OK, Mum, I'm fine. Honestly.'

Claire tried to relax into the sofa and let the wine do its job. Emma was right. They were fine—no, they were lucky. Very lucky. They had survived a bad accident with little more than a few cuts and bruises. And, she reminded herself, her mother was at peace at last.

She made up her mind that this would be a good Christmas. The best they'd had for years.

8

She saw me. The bitch saw me.

He flicked channels, his hand shaking with rage. The news programmes were full of reports of storm wreckage, but nothing on a car going off the road.

Maybe the bitch was dead?

The car had turned over. He'd watched it slide down the bank, heard the crunch when it hit the tree.

If she wasn't dead, she was badly hurt.

He hoped she was dead.

He'd parked his own car well out of sight of the road. Same place he always used when he went back. She'd appeared out of nowhere just as he was crossing the road, blinded by snow, thrilled by memories.

The bitch had seen his face.

It doesn't matter if she saw me. She doesn't know why I was there. Nobody knows why I was there. No one but me.

But the truth was the bitch had messed things up. She had given him grief.

He would have to deal with her.

9

'These cards are marked.' Chrissy was flicking through the pack Rhona had taken from the soldier's pocket. 'Watch.'

The cards flew from one of Chrissy's hands to the other.

'Where did you learn how to shuffle like that?'

'I had a boyfriend who was a magician.'

'A magician?' Chrissy never failed to amaze Rhona.

Chrissy placed the pack in her right hand. 'OK, in technical terms I'm not shuffling, just springing the cards from one hand to another without moving their place in the pack. When I do it this time I want you to watch for dots of light.'

The cards whizzed from one hand to another. She was right. There was a faint line of light.

Chrissy extracted a card and placed it under a microscope.

'Take a look.'

Rhona focused on the magnified image.

'There are two holes in the card.'

Chrissy replaced that card with another. There

44

were two holes pierced in it too, although in different positions.

'Every card's like that,' she said. 'A hole for the suit and a hole for the card's position in that suit.'

'So our soldier cheated at cards?'

Chrissy raised an expressive eyebrow. 'If the corpse is our soldier.'

'What d'you mean?'

'While you were at the deposition site, I checked the blood sample you took against the grouping indicated on his dog tag. They weren't the same type.'

The information on the cleaned metal tag had been easily distinguishable under the microscope —name, identity number, blood type and date of birth. The MOD had already confirmed that Private Fergus Morrison had gone AWOL after returning from Afghanistan.

'Any chance of a fingerprint?' Rhona asked.

Her assistant showed her what she'd succeeded in lifting from the burned hands. The partial print was too warped to be of much use.

'We can DNA him, that's not a problem, but if he's not the blood type on the tag, he's not our soldier.'

'What about evidence of petrol?' asked Rhona.

'I'm just about to start on the debris.'

'So, we have a corpse carrying a false identity?'

'Looks like it.'

'I'm going to the mortuary,' Rhona said, standing up.

'Why?' Chrissy had gone back to shuffling the cards.

'I need to ask Sissons something.'

You needed a strong stomach to work in a mortuary, or no sense of smell. Similar attributes were required in Rhona's own profession. The headless corpse was laid out on a metal table, and Dr Sissons had already begun the post-mortem procedure and was talking into his overhead microphone. The chest had been sliced open and the various organs removed. The stomach contents were in a receptacle awaiting analysis, which would be done in Rhona's lab.

Sissons carefully finished his sentence before switching off the microphone and regarding her quizzically.

'I wondered if you'd got to the stage of examining the hyoid bone yet?'

'The fracture, you mean?'

She nodded.

'You suspect foul play?'

'I thought the fracture odd.'

'If the brain boiled and caused the skull to shatter, that might account for a fracture in the hyoid.'

Rhona had come to the same conclusion herself until the result of the blood sample. 'He was wearing a dog tag that wasn't his.'

'You can buy fake dog tags in any army surplus store, or so I'm told.'

'The dog tag was real. The soldier it came from is missing. The MOD have reason to believe he's gone AWOL. His name is confirmed as Fergus Morrison.' Rhona looked down at the blackened corpse. 'But this isn't him.'

46

*   *   *

When she got back to the lab, Chrissy had forsaken the cards and was tucking into a cheese-and-tomato panini. Rhona was struck by how well she looked. Being pregnant suited Chrissy, so her tales of being chatted up in spite of the bump didn't surprise Rhona.

'So?' demanded Chrissy.

'The hyoid bone was fractured.'

'He was strangled before the fire?'

'It's a possibility.'

'Maybe he cheated at cards once too often?'

It would be up to the Procurator Fiscal to decide whether this was a murder inquiry, but going on what they'd discovered up to now, it had begun to look likely.

'Are you not due in court this week?'

Chrissy's casual enquiry gave Rhona a split second of panic. Two major incidents in the space of forty-eight hours acted on the brain like jet lag. 'What day is it today?'

'Tuesday.'

Rhona breathed a sigh of relief. 'I'm in tomorrow.'

Court appearances, though a vital part of her work, could be long winded. Sitting around waiting for her turn to enter the witness box drove Rhona to distraction.

The case in question—the killing of an elderly woman—was particularly nasty. The old lady, Mary Healey, had been in her eighties and well liked by her neighbours. Brought up in Govanhill, she'd never left the area of streets she'd known as a child, then a wife and mother, and eventually a

47

grandmother. She'd continued with her life as she'd always done; her door kept open for her neighbours. Last Christmas Eve, someone had entered Mary's flat uninvited. When she'd challenged the man in her hallway, he'd bludgeoned her to death. The shock of Mary's murder had reverberated round the community and brought the decent folk together to mourn her loss.

Rhona wanted to stand up in court and fight for Mary. She wanted to present the forensic evidence that laid the blame firmly on the suspect the police had apprehended—a twenty-five-year-old heroin addict who was willing to do anything for money to feed his habit. Mary had been old-style Glasgow, solid, hard working and friendly, and some creep had ended her life in an instant.

Rhona left Chrissy in charge of the lab work for the skip fire while she concentrated on the material brought from the wood. Cold cases had to be run alongside current work. They cost more and took longer, but the discovery of a body, if identified, could bring closure for relatives tortured by never knowing what had happened to those they loved.

Rhona began by making up the skeleton as it had lain in the deposition site, placing the bones in their appropriate places, double-checking against photographic records and her recording sheet.

As she worked, she recalled the first time she'd really understood what lay beneath skin and flesh. It had been a revelation and the beginning of an insatiable desire to know more; a desire that had eventually led her to the job she did now.

It had been during one of those long summer

holidays from school, when you forgot the wet days and remembered only the sun shining and the tar melting beneath your feet. She'd been ten years old. A keen swimmer, she'd walked to the nearest outdoor pool every day, sometimes with her friend Alison, sometimes on her own.

The incident was as crystal clear now as it had been then. The footpath to the pool ran along the edge of a field a couple of metres from the road. A group of boys, one from her class, had been clustered left of the path, throwing stones at an object in the near distance. Their movements had been determined, the look on their faces cruel. Rhona had been watching for some minutes before her classmate had turned and spotted her. He'd stared defiantly back, as though challenging her to say something. She remembered being suddenly afraid of him. After a few moments' stand-off, he'd called to the others to move on. As they'd run away, catcalling, towards a nearby wood, Rhona had had a burning desire to see what they'd been doing.

She'd caught the smell first, rancid and nauseating, then, on moving closer, watched as a buzzing cloud of flies had risen at her approach to settle again moments later on what looked like the corpse of a cat. Repulsed and fascinated at the same time, Rhona had stepped nearer. The greyish body had been indented with the force of their stones. Scattered tufts of fur had lain strewn around in the blackened remains of its blood. Then Rhona had noticed that the dead cat was actually heaving with life. Squirming mounds of maggots had been feeding in the open wounds, exposing the underlying skeleton.

So this is what a cat is below the fur, she'd thought. This is what we are, too. Bone and flesh covered with skin.

She'd gone back every day, observing the various stages of decomposition until there was nothing left but a whitened skeleton. It was then she'd spotted the ligature. The thin wire had been wound so tightly that the noose was half the circumference of the neck. The cat hadn't been run over and thrown there from the road. Someone had deliberately strangled it.

Now Rhona looked down at the small skeleton slowly taking form under her hands. Establishing how the cat had been killed had been easy. Establishing who this child was and how he or she had died would be far more difficult.

There were many gender differences between male and female skeletons. The clearest indicators were found in the pelvis and the skull. In females the pelvis was flatter and more rounded, proportionally larger to allow a baby's head to pass through. Women usually had narrower ribcages, smaller teeth, less angular mandibles. Their brow ridges were less pronounced, their chins less square and the small bump at the back of the skull less prominent.

All of this helped identify gender, but only when dealing with an adolescent or adult skeleton. Bone morphology couldn't sex this age group either. The truth was, she had no idea whether the dead child was a girl or a boy.

If she had been asked to hazard a guess, she would have said female. There were two reasons: first, she had come across no evidence of clothing and suspected the body had been naked when dumped, suggesting a sexual motive; and second, statistically speaking, more little girls were abducted, assaulted and murdered than boys.

Rhona wrote up her report, seated next to the remains. Her work with the skeleton was over. A forensic anthropologist would need to examine it as an expert witness. Rhona's next task was to carefully examine the wood mulch and soil to try to establish how long the child's body had lain in its woodland grave.

10

The woman was attempting to give him detailed instructions on how to find Fern Cottage but McNab's pounding head, the result of too many whiskies the previous evening, was refusing to take it all in.

He cut her short. 'I'll find it.'

'OK,' she said dubiously. 'If you get lost, give me a call.'

McNab managed the road south out of Glasgow no problem. It was when he entered the wilderness (as he thought of it) that it threatened to go pear shaped.

How many roads can a man walk down, before he admits he's lost? When he and Rhona had been together she'd liked to tease him about his reluctance to ask for directions. McNab briefly lingered on the memory of that time before reminding himself that he'd ceased to obsess about Dr MacLeod. Even as he silently repeated this mantra, McNab knew the empty whisky bottle from the previous night was evidence to the contrary.

The car crested yet another hill and McNab looked out on more white fields dotted with desultory sheep grazing on turnips. He decided he'd rather live in Glasgow any day. At least there you only had to worry about getting lost in the one-way system.

Five minutes later he reluctantly reached for his mobile. The number rang for a few moments before she answered.

'Tell me what you're looking at.'

'White fields and sheep.'

'You'll have to be more precise. Imagine you're at a crime scene.'

'You mean where one sheep murdered another over a turnip?'

She laughed. It was a nice sound.

'Can you see any windmills?'

He examined the skyline and spotted a blade due east. He told her so.

'OK, you need to turn round and come back for about a mile. You'll see a narrow entrance on your left. There's no sign, but if you're in the right place you should look back and see two turbines on the brow of the hill.'

They were the same directions he hadn't listened to earlier.

'The cottage is half a mile down that track. It has a blue door and the fire's on, so there will be smoke from the chimney.'

He came on it minutes later. Even to McNab's jaundiced eye, the setting looked beautiful.

Mrs Watson was at the door as he drew up.

'You found us, then?' she said as he climbed out

of the car.

'No problem.' He grinned ruefully.

There was a squeal of pleasure as Emma came clattering down the narrow staircase behind her mother.

'Michael!' She grabbed his hand. 'I've something to show you.'

'I think Detective Sergeant McNab needs a coffee first.' Mrs Watson looked to him for confirmation.

McNab suspected she'd observed the evidence of his hangover and felt slightly uncomfortable.

'I'll wait for you in my room,' Emma told him firmly, before heading back upstairs.

Her mother led him along a narrow hall and into a small sitting room, where a wood fire burned and a real Christmas tree stood in the corner.

'It's nice out here,' he admitted grudgingly.

'We like it.'

'You used to live in Glasgow?'

'The accent's a giveaway?'

'You can take the girl out of Glasgow . . .'

'We used to live in the West End. I take it country life doesn't appeal?'

'No one to arrest. I'd have to retire.'

She disappeared into a small kitchen off the sitting room. McNab caught glimpses of her as she moved about; filling a kettle, switching it on. He saw her lay out mugs, sugar and milk on a tray. While he waited, he wondered why he was here.

The child had sent him an email. He hadn't picked it up right away, because he was spending so much time at the deposition site. In the email, Emma had stated she thought there were two bodies because she could hear two voices. McNab

53

suspected this was nonsense, particularly since Rhona had found the wind harp, but although it didn't follow protocol, he felt he had to talk to the kid about it. She had taken a shine to him, that much was obvious, and useful under the circumstances.

There was another reason, of course. Everyone knew he'd messed up on the Gravedigger case. Anything he did on this one had to be an improvement. The girl was a little strange, but he was afraid of missing something vital if he didn't go the extra mile and question her about what she professed to know.

Mrs Watson reappeared and laid the tray down on a coffee table. She was dressed casually in jeans and a sweater, her long brown hair caught up in a clip. She looked pretty and much more relaxed than when they'd first met. She handed him his coffee.

'I never got the chance to thank you properly for finding my daughter.'

McNab decided it would be churlish to argue, even though it was the dogs which had found her.

'Emma talks about you a lot. About wanting to help you find the . . . other one.' She couldn't disguise the mixture of worry and embarrassment on her face.

'It's OK,' McNab reassured her. 'I told you to contact me if Emma remembered anything else about that night.'

'I keep hoping it will stop, this obsession.'

'Maybe if I talk to her, it will.'

She didn't look convinced.

'Mrs Watson . . .'

'I'm not married, DS McNab,' she snapped.

'Please call me Claire.'

McNab had clearly touched a sore spot. 'OK, Claire, but only if you call me Michael.'

She nodded, relaxing a little.

'So, can I talk to Emma now?'

*   *   *

The girl was sitting cross-legged on her bed. The room was in shadow, the weak winter sunlight barely lifting it out of darkness.

Claire switched on the light, breaking Emma's trance-like state. She looked round at them.

'Hi, Emma.'

Her solemn face broke into a smile and she bounced off the bed.

'Michael. Have you found him yet?'

'Him?'

'The other one.'

'I came to talk to you about that.'

She glanced at her mother, then back at him. McNab wondered how much the girl was aware of Claire's fear.

'Why don't we take a walk in the snow?' He surprised himself with the suggestion, but he suddenly wanted to talk to the child on her own. 'Is that OK?'

Claire looked puzzled but nodded her agreement.

Downstairs, Emma chatted animatedly as she pulled on a hooded coat and wellington boots. Her mother handed her a pair of mittens.

Outside it was cold and crisp, the sky a pale blue. Emma led McNab to a stile leading into a snowy field. He thought briefly of his city shoes before following. They crunched through the snow in companionable silence.

She led him to the bank of a river, where they spent ten minutes throwing stones at the frozen eddies on the far side. Emma wasn't a bad shot for a nine-year-old girl. McNab told her so.

'Nick taught me how to throw stones.'

He was momentarily nonplussed. The girl had to have a father, but since Claire had said she wasn't married McNab had assumed there was no man in the picture.

'Your dad? I bet he was worried when he heard about the crash.'

'Nick isn't my dad.'

McNab decided not to enter the minefield of single-parent relationships. He broached the subject of the skull instead.

'It looks like there was only one body hidden beneath the brushwood, Emma.' He did his best to sound certain.

She picked up another stone and threw it. It bounced on the thicker ice and plopped into the water.

McNab carried on. 'We found a wind harp in a nearby tree. It makes a sort of music when the wind blows. I expect that's what you heard that night.'

The child's face was impassive.

'I think you should try and forget what happened. Look forward to Christmas.'

She turned and gave him a searching look. 'Then why can I still hear his voice?'

He was beginning to feel out of his depth. If the kid was hearing voices she should be talking to a psychologist, not a detective.

'When something frightening happens, it can make you imagine things.' It sounded like something his own mother would have said to him. Something he wouldn't have believed.

'I've asked him to tell me where he is, but he won't.'

McNab examined her small, pinched face. Jesus, no wonder Claire was so concerned.

'Mum doesn't believe me. I thought you would.' Emma looked sad. 'I want to go home now.'

Claire must have been watching for them, because the door opened as they approached. She looked enquiringly at him.

'We went to the river and threw some stones. Emma was very good at it.'

'I'm going upstairs, Mum.' Emma had already discarded her coat and boots.

'OK, I'll call you when lunch is ready.'

McNab waited until the child had disappeared before he spoke.

'I told her about the wind harp, and that there's only one body.'

'She didn't believe you, did she?'

He cleared his throat. 'Shock does strange things to people. Give it a few more days. Let her keep writing to me, if it helps. I think Christmas will soon take over.' He hoped he was right.

On the return journey, he pondered the relationship between Claire and her daughter. It reminded him of his own childhood. Brought up by his mother, he had never known his father. He'd been born illegitimate, back when it had mattered. He'd been ashamed. Hid the fact by telling tall tales of his soldier father, always away on duty. He'd cut a photograph of a soldier from a

57

magazine, a young man with dark auburn hair like his own. He was handsome and smiling, the dad McNab wanted. For a while he'd believed him to be real, and the soldier's imagined bravery had made him brave. Brave enough to face the bullies and their taunts.

The discovery of the skull had made Emma the centre of attention. Maybe she didn't want that to end.

11

DI Lane of the Complaints and Discipline Department didn't like the job he'd been given, and McNab didn't blame him. A complaint against a senior officer was a serious matter, especially when it was scum like Henderson who had made it.

Lane laid out the photographs of Henderson's injuries, taken by the duty officer that fateful morning when McNab and DI Wilson had confronted Henderson in the interview room.

Looking at a photo of the man's bruised balls made McNab wish he'd kicked him even harder. If he'd had a knife in his hand when the bastard had talked filth about Bill's daughter, McNab would have sliced them off.

'I kicked him under the table.'

'That's not what DI Wilson says. He says he pulled rank on you to interview Henderson after he'd been ordered by Superintendent Sutherland not to do so. When Henderson bad-mouthed his daughter, he lost his temper and attacked him.'

'That's not the way I remember it.'

DI Lane shuffled the photos together and put them back in the folder. If a criminal assault had occurred, then the case would have to go before the Procurator Fiscal. It would be the Fiscal who would decide whether the case should go on to the Sheriff Court. If the DCS decided it was a breakdown in procedure rather than assault, it would go down the police disciplinary route. McNab was well aware DI Wilson was trying to protect him from the fallout of their interview with Henderson, but he wouldn't let his boss take the blame for what he'd done in that room. Given the opportunity, he would do it again.

'What does Henderson say?'

'He says DI Wilson kicked him.'

'The bastard!' Anger darkened McNab's face. 'He knows it was me. He's just trying to get at the DI. Christ, the guy sexually assaulted Bill's daughter.'

Lane frowned sympathetically.

McNab got himself under control. Surely if he stuck to his story they couldn't prosecute the DI? 'So where do we go from here?'

Lane was already on his feet. 'I pass everything to the DCS and he decides.' This was Lane's get-out clause. He carried out the investigation, but he didn't have to make the final decision.

'How long?' McNab was already thinking about going directly to the super to give his version of events.

Lane shrugged, indicating that he had no idea.

'You realise Henderson's trying to stitch the boss up?'

Lane didn't respond.

'I kicked the bastard and would do it again if I

had the chance. You can tell the DCS I said that.'

McNab thought frantically that it didn't matter what he said. It didn't matter that he was the one telling the truth. The fact that Henderson backed up DI Wilson's version of events meant that his boss would pay the price for McNab's anger. As though he hadn't paid enough already.

When he emerged from the room, Clark was waiting for him. She read his expression and gave him a compassionate look.

'The strategy meeting's just started. The boss said to go in.'

*   *   *

Rhona paused in her delivery to allow McNab and DC Clark to take their seats at the back. McNab didn't look happy. Bill had picked up on it too. The two men exchanged glances before Bill indicated that Rhona should continue.

They were tackling the cold case first. On the screen was the video footage of the deposition site. Rhona explained how the various levels of decomposing wood had been removed and a child's skeleton located.

'It's not possible to tell the sex of the skeleton, but I can say that it is a child and that there is only one. If I was to hazard a guess, I would advise looking for minors who disappeared around ten years ago, but I hope to be more exact once I've studied the material in detail.'

After confirming that the remains had been sent to a forensic anthropologist for study and digital facial reconstruction, Rhona handed over to McNab to give his version of events.

He repeated the story of a young girl going missing from a car crash and the dogs locating her unhurt in the nearby woods. The fact that she'd been found sitting under a tree, nursing a human skull. The story had been circulating in the office, but this was the first time most of the team had heard it in its entirety.

'She found the skull on the ground?' Bill asked.

McNab shook his head. 'She says she took it from beneath the brushwood Dr MacLeod spoke about.'

'How did she know it was there?'

'She says she heard it calling to her.' McNab paused as disbelieving murmurs broke out. A stern look from Bill resulted in quiet, allowing him to continue.

'She was quite adamant about that, sir. She said the sound led her there. Dr MacLeod later pointed out that a construction in a nearby tree, called a wind harp, may have produced the noise the girl heard.'

Bill digested this. 'We're in contact with the girl's family?'

'I visited Emma this morning at the request of the mother, Claire. The child is showing signs of distress since the event. She claims she can hear the voice of another victim. A boy. But she doesn't know where he's buried.'

The murmurs grew louder. Bill called for silence.

'OK, I want as much background as you can find on the Watson family. If the kid comes up with anything else, I want to know about it. It's pretty unorthodox, but it's all we've got.'

'There's one more thing, sir.'

'Yes?'

61

'Claire Watson says she swerved off the road that night because a man appeared in front of her.'

'There was another car in the area?'

McNab shook his head. 'Not when we got there, apart from the van driver who stopped to help.'

'And he is?'

McNab checked his PDA. 'His name is Keith Walker, fifty-six, works for the gas board. He was on his way to a broken-down boiler. Walker says Mrs Watson stepped out in front of him. She was confused, knew she had been in an accident, but didn't know who she was, then she remembered her daughter was in the back of the car. Except she wasn't.'

'OK, our first priority is to try and identify missing minors that might fall into the frame. Let's keep the press release low key. Just "human remains found in wood". Nothing about it being a child. Nothing about how they were discovered. We don't want to raise hopes that we've found someone's missing child until we know more. And we don't want the Watsons hounded by the tabloids.'

'Sir? Maybe we should bring in someone professional to talk to Emma. There might be stuff she hasn't told us.'

'You think her mother would agree?'

'She believes her daughter's been traumatised by what's happened. I think she might.'

'OK, get in touch with Professor Pirie. Ask him if he's willing to get involved. If he is, run it past the mother. Let's get the coffees in, then we'll take a look at the skip fire case.'

Rhona saw McNab's horrified expression. Magnus Pirie wasn't a name he'd wanted or expected to hear, despite his request for professional help with the girl.

He told Rhona as much when they met at the coffee machine.

'Magnus was cleared of any wrongdoing in the Gravedigger case,' she reminded him.

'Unlike the boss.'

'That's not Magnus's fault.'

McNab threw her a look that spoke volumes. 'The boss is lying to the inquiry.'

'What?'

'I found out that he gave a statement saying he had been the one to assault the suspect.'

'But you've told them the truth?'

'Of course, but Lane doesn't believe me. And guess who also says it was him? Christ, the Gravedigger is stitching him up and I can't stop it.'

Now she understood the suppressed fury on McNab's face when he'd entered the strategy meeting.

'What the fuck do I do? It's two against one.'

Rhona was running the worrying scenario over in her mind. 'They'll have to take into account the mitigating circumstances.'

'It'll still mean a disciplinary charge, even if it doesn't go to court. You have to talk to the boss. Get him to tell the truth.'

'I'll try after the meeting,' Rhona promised.

She never got the chance. She was halfway through her contribution on the skip investigation when Bill was called from the room. There was an uncomfortable silence as the door closed behind him. The entire team knew the DI was likely to be up on a charge.

McNab indicated that she should continue. If the

DI walked back in and they were discussing him rather than the case, then there'd be hell to pay.

'As Dr Sissons reported, photographs taken at the scene and the subsequent post-mortem identified a break in the hyoid bone, suggesting that the victim could have been garrotted before the fire occurred.'

She brought up the collage of photographs she'd taken at the scene and flicked through them. Crime photographs always looked worse away from the locus. When you were there, you were surrounded by the horror. Here in the normality of the meeting room, the individual images had an obscene quality.

'Blood tests on the body indicate the victim was not Fergus Morrison as stated on the dog tag. So this guy is not our missing soldier. We're still testing the debris for accelerant.' Rhona handed over to McNab, who seemed distracted.

'The boss thinks a car on CCTV around the time of the fire could prove significant. The dog tag could indicate we were expected to assume the victim was the soldier. If that's the case, Fergus Morrison could be involved, so priority number one is to find him.' McNab brought up the squaddie's picture. In the photograph he looked about fifteen, though his details said he'd passed his nineteenth birthday.

'OK, let's get on with it.'

McNab came over to Rhona as the team filed from the room. 'What about the deposition site?'

'I've got a mountain of mulch and soil to sift through. Unless anything else turns up out there, I won't go back. Any luck with possible missing minors?'

'Nothing yet. DC Clark's working on it.'

She put her hand on his arm. 'I'm sorry I didn't get an opportunity to talk to Bill.'

'I've a feeling we're too late, anyway.'

12

It was on the lunchtime news. Human remains had been discovered in woods south of Glasgow. He realised he had been anticipating this moment for a decade. He wasn't afraid. He was angry. And not with himself.

He sat on the sofa, his body rigid, his eyes fixed on the screen. Details were scarce. Nothing about who had found them. Nothing about what exactly they had found.

He felt violated. Choking anger prevented him from breathing. He imagined their graves being defiled. Their remains being removed, examined. Bile rose to his mouth. *How dare they*.

He channelled his rage into cold, calculating anger. He would find out how they had been discovered. It wouldn't be difficult with his connections.

He took out his mobile and began going through the list of names. He paused, knowing that any call, no matter how casual, might be questioned later.

He put the phone down and went out into the garden.

The trimmed grass and ordered wintering flower beds calmed him. He took the path that led to the wooded area. The starkness of the bare birch trees reminded him of the other wood. He should have laid them to rest here, like the others.

He would have needed no markers, no wind harp to guide him. He knew every inch of this garden, every plant, every tree, every secret thing. He sat down on the wooden bench he'd placed in his favoured spot and closed his eyes, feeling the weak warmth of the sun on his face.

It could not be coincidence that the remains had been discovered shortly after that woman had swerved off the road and crashed her car.

He pondered this. Through closed eyes, he relived the moment when the blue Peugeot had appeared from nowhere—the startled face at the windscreen, the mouth open in a scream.

He channelled his anger towards that face.

If she'd died in the crash, he had nothing to worry about. There was nothing else to link him to that wood.

If the bitch had survived, then the sooner he found her the better.

13

McNab sat down at his cluttered desk. The double shot of coffee he'd fetched from the machine was doing its job, but not fast enough. He surreptitiously added a nip of whisky from the half-bottle in his drawer. Everything was going arse up and he couldn't stop it. He knew the boss was in with the super. It had to be about the assault case.

He swallowed the whisky-laced coffee quickly

then got himself online. There were twenty emails waiting. He skimmed through them, hardly registering the titles, until he spotted one from Emma. It had an attachment alongside. McNab braced himself, then clicked to open. He had planned to offload the kid on the DI, but that no longer looked like a possibility. He would have to keep the contact going himself. He liked Claire. He liked the kid, even if she was a little strange, but he didn't have the time to spend nursing either of them.

The message read:

I wanted to show you this when you were here, but Mum wouldn't let me. This is what I dream. This is what I hear.

McNab opened the attachment.

It was a simple drawing of a tree done with a kids' software program, the branches bare of leaves. Under the roots, a small naked body hung suspended as though in the air. An attempt had been made to draw the genitals, making it a boy.

'Jesus.' McNab found himself repulsed by the image.

Below was the message *Don't leave me here alone.*

The kid's sick, he thought. Maybe she was sick before this happened. Claire had seemed frightened, but he'd assumed it was just the effect of the accident. He realised he should have asked more questions, but then he hadn't been there to interview or interrogate either of them. Claire had asked him to come.

McNab's first instinct was to ignore the email. If Claire contacted him about it, he could pretend he hadn't checked his mailbox because of pressure of

67

work. If in doubt, do nothing. A mantra that had served him well in the past.

What the kid was suggesting was nonsense anyway. As far as the investigation was concerned, they had one set of remains. They'd searched the area surrounding the deposition site and turned up nothing else. His job now was to check the records and find out which kids had gone missing a decade ago. Around that time he'd been intent on practising law. Had someone told him he would end up becoming a policeman and working in CID, he would've laughed in their face. No money and no respect in police work, he would have said. He'd been right back then. He was right now. At least if he'd become a lawyer he might have been able to help the DI, something at which he was failing spectacularly as a cop.

He selected 'print' and went to pick the page up. Only then did it register that the drawing was in colour. The tree printed out in black, the body in a lurid red. The message had been written in purple. All this seemed to reinforce his earlier suspicion that the girl was an attention-seeker. It was a game to her, a way of keeping her mother on her toes, or perhaps punishing her in some way.

McNab had an uncomfortable memory of the variety of ways in which he'd subtly punished his own mother for failing to produce his father. For years he'd secretly convinced himself that his dad was trying to see him and being prevented from doing so. It had taken a long time to register that his father didn't care that he existed at all.

Claire had been quite adamant about not being married. Angry, even. So who the hell was Nick?

McNab didn't want to go there.

He screwed up the drawing and went to toss it in the bin then changed his mind and stuck it in his pocket. He had enough to worry about without taking on childcare duties, especially a problem child.

He abandoned his desk and went looking for DC Clark.

'Hey.'

Janice's sympathetic look didn't help. McNab had told everyone he'd been responsible for the assault. It didn't make any difference. If the boss went down, the team would hold him responsible.

Janice handed him a list. 'That's UK-wide. D'you want to extend it to Europe?'

'Is there anything here that might match?'

'Hard to say with what we've got on the remains so far. In truth, it could be all or none of them.'

'Better extend it to Europe.'

Barriers had been down for a while, the flux of immigrants from the Eastern Bloc steadily increasing. Rhona had said that a child's remains didn't last long above ground, even with the covering such as these had had. Her guess of a decade or so was just a guess, until she concluded her study of the detritus from the deposition site.

McNab took the list back to his desk. Janice had identified twelve possibilities. Eight girls and four boys. Over half of the list were believed to have been abducted by an estranged parent and taken abroad. One girl was thought to have been taken to California by her Russian father.

A child being abducted by a parent was often the most likely explanation for their disappearance, especially when custody had been awarded to the other parent. Most people who ran off with their

69

children were never found. If your partner took your child abroad, the UK government could not bring them back, only offer you legal advice. But estranged parents rarely murdered the children they were fighting so hard to keep.

McNab concentrated on the others.

Four girls, two boys. All would have been between six and ten at the time of their abduction. All had disappeared south of the border, and the abduction sites were varied: London, Birmingham and the North of England. McNab stared at the photographs. Little faces, frozen in time. He thought about his first sight of Emma sitting under the tree. His elation that they'd found her alive— every mother's dream—then his horror when he saw what she was holding.

One of the photographs was of a smiling, elfin-faced girl with light-coloured hair, cut so short she could have passed for a boy. She'd last been seen in the company of a middle-aged man in St Pancras station in London. The second girl was dark haired and older, of Indian extraction. She'd disappeared in Birmingham on her way home from school. One boy had a freckled face and ears that stuck out like the handles of the Scottish Cup. He was from Sunderland. These three disappearances had taken place over a two-year period.

The road where the accident had happened ran from Glasgow to the village of Muirkirk. The village itself wasn't remote. It lay on the A70 between Edinburgh and Ayr, just ten miles from the M74 motorway, the main artery between Scotland and England.

McNab fished out a map. On his way to the scene of the accident, he hadn't passed a single car on that road. True, it had been a bad night and folk had been warned not to travel, but even on his subsequent visits to the site vehicles had been scarce.

He thought about Claire's conviction that there had been a man on the road. She'd insisted McNab take his description down on his PDA. He suspected believing in the figure was one way of convincing herself she wasn't to blame for the accident and its consequences.

The man was short, Claire had said, and wore a dark, heavy coat. Initially his back had been towards her. That was why she hadn't seen him. He'd turned and her headlights had lit up his face. He was middle aged and bald.

When McNab asked whether she'd hit the man, she'd shaken her head. 'I wrenched the wheel round to avoid him. That's why I went off the road.'

He logged into the incident files and had another look at the photographs. The team had taken a whole series from multiple angles showing where the car went off the road, the marks on the bank indicating how it had overturned and slid down. The one of the wreckage against the tree was pretty scary. Claire was lucky to have climbed out of that unscathed. As for the rear of the car crushed against the tree—Emma's survival was little short of a miracle.

McNab replayed the geography in his head. Claire had said the figure had his back to her. So where was he facing? McNab rotated the 3D image on the screen, placing himself in the picture where Claire said the man had stood. Why had the mystery man been standing in the middle of the road looking towards the wood?

14

The majority of foods are plant based, and food remains undigested after death until the body starts to decay. Digestive erosion and volume of food can also help identify the time elapsed since the last meal. The body in the skip had been damaged by fire, but the food in his stomach was as it had been at the moment of death.

Sissons had sent through the stomach contents, retrieved at the post-mortem. They made an interesting study. Rhona was used to examining the remains of various Glasgow eating habits; McDonald's and Burger King, pizza and chips, kebabs and curries.

These were more interesting.

Beetroot soup with dumplings was not a Glasgow speciality. Assuming the victim didn't have a mother at home preparing his favourite meal, he must have eaten at a restaurant that served this type of food.

It didn't take long to find a possibility. There were several restaurants that had borscht on their menu, but only one that claimed to be authentically Russian, so Rhona decided to try them first.

The phone rang a couple of times before it was picked up. Rhona could hear violin music and chatter in the background. Lunchtime at the restaurant sounded popular. The voice that answered was female with an accent, possibly

Polish. When Rhona asked to speak to the manager, the girl called out a name that sounded like 'Misha' and a man came on the line.

Rhona explained who she was and why she was calling. His voice was deep and slightly accented. 'Beetroot soup with dumplings. A speciality of ours.' He laughed. 'By all means come and try some.'

*   *   *

Mikhail Grigorovitch was younger than Rhona had envisaged on the phone. She'd always imagined Russian men as elderly, stocky and Cossack-hatted, watching tanks roll past, as in newsreels taken at the height of the cold war. Mikhail was the exact opposite.

He offered her a warm handshake and urged her to call him Misha.

'You will eat, of course?'

'I really came to take a sample.'

'It's important to taste what you sample.'

Misha called over a small, dark-haired waitress with eyes darkly rimmed like Amy Winehouse's.

'Borscht for the lady.'

He waved Rhona to an old church pew with the number 207 carved on the back. As she waited for her soup to arrive, she took in the rest of her surroundings. The place was simply furnished but stylish, the accent on colour and all things Russian. On a nearby wall was a painting of hens in a wintry birch wood, a setting sun bathing the scene in an orange-red glow.

The soup arrived, accompanied by Misha, who slipped into the seat opposite. Rhona liked

73

beetroot, at least the pickled variety. She wasn't so sure about beetroot soup with fat little dumplings floating in it.

Misha gave her an encouraging smile. 'Try.'

She took a spoonful. It was surprisingly good.

He raised an eyebrow. 'Well?'

'Delicious.'

'And the dumplings?'

She broke open a dumpling. It tasted light and savoury. 'I like them.'

Misha sat back, satisfied by her response.

'Finish,' he encouraged, 'then we talk.'

On the last spoonful, Rhona made an excuse and escaped to the toilet. The interior was decorated with the music of famous Russian composers. She chose the cubicle papered with the work of Rachmaninoff. Then she washed her hands and checked her mouth for beetroot stains, slightly disconcerted that it seemed important to look good.

Misha was awaiting her return. He eyed her appreciatively.

'You should finish with a shot of vodka. I recommend Stolichnaya.'

'A bit early in the day for me.'

'You're driving?' He looked disappointed.

'No.'

'Then what is the harm?'

The vodka bottle arrived, accompanied by two shot glasses.

'You like whisky?'

Rhona nodded.

'This is smoother. No burning of the throat.'

He filled both glasses and lifted one, encouraging Rhona to do the same.

'*Na zdorovie!*'

Rhona watched him swallow, then followed. Misha was right. It was smooth.

'Good?'

'Yes.'

'Another?'

'Definitely not.'

Misha shrugged, accepting defeat.

'So, you are a forensic scientist, like in *CSI*?' His brown eyes sparkled.

'Not quite. I don't wander round crime scenes dressed in my best clothes, looking like a movie star.'

'Tell me why a forensic scientist wants to sample my food.'

Rhona chose her words carefully. 'A man died in suspicious circumstances. I believe he ate soup like this shortly before that happened.'

Misha looked horrified. 'You think we poisoned him?'

'He didn't die of food poisoning,' Rhona reassured him.

'Then why are you here?'

'It might help us trace his movements in the time leading up to his death.'

'We are not the only place to serve borscht in Glasgow. All eastern European people eat this soup. Polish, Ukraine . . .'

'I know.'

'You have a photograph of this man?'

Rhona shook her head. 'There was a fire.' She didn't elaborate.

'When did this happen?'

'Sunday night.'

Misha sat back in the seat and observed her

75

closely.

'And you cannot describe him?'

'Not his face, no. I can tell you he was a young man, slim build, just under six feet tall.'

Misha thought about that for a moment, then shook his head. 'There are many customers that might fit that description.'

'It's better that I try and establish if he did eat here.'

'Come, I will take you to the kitchen.'

Rhona followed Misha behind a shawl curtain and along a corridor into a large bright kitchen. He introduced her to two young male chefs and gave them instructions in Russian, which brought a burst of laughter.

'I told them to give you whatever you want.'

I bet you did, thought Rhona.

The menu on Sunday night had featured the famous soup. Their beetroot soup was, according to Vanya, the younger chef, a recipe unique to this restaurant.

'We make it exactly the way Misha tells us. It is his family recipe.'

'May I have a list of the ingredients?'

'Misha says we must give you what you want.' He smiled widely.

Rhona went about her sampling, keenly aware that the rapid Russian conversation going on behind her was more likely to be about her than the next meal.

When she escaped the confines of the kitchen, she found the restaurant empty and the dark-haired waitress sweeping the floor. Misha was seated at a table near the back, a pile of papers in front of him. He stood up at her approach.

76

'You have what you need?'

'Thank you, yes.'

'So what happens now?'

'The police will want to talk to you and to the other members of staff who were around on Sunday night.'

Misha shuffled the papers. It was the first time Rhona had sensed a nervousness about him.

'If you cannot show us a photograph, then how can we help?'

'There was one thing that might help identify him.'

'Oh?'

'A rose tattoo.'

He looked momentarily startled.

'Is that a Russian thing?' Rhona asked.

He shrugged. 'Not that I know of. Perhaps his girlfriend was called Rose.'

'Maybe.' Rhona thanked him for his help.

'My pleasure.'

Misha walked her to the door.

'Do you get time off from this work of yours?' he said.

'Occasionally.'

'Come again and I will treat you to a full Russian meal on the house.'

'With vodka?'

'Of course.'

'I may take you up on that.'

15

'Again.'

Chrissy obligingly shuffled the cards and offered them up to McNab.

He pulled one free and checked it. 'OK.'

Chrissy thought for a moment. 'Seven of spades.'

There was an intake of breath.

'No way can you have known that.' McNab shook his head in disbelief.

'Another lucky guess?' Chrissy suggested, keeping her face straight.

The battle had been going on for ten minutes. Rhona suspected marked cards were in play again. Chrissy certainly had McNab worried.

'Show me.'

Chrissy laughed. 'No chance. Then you'd know as much as me.'

McNab was like a terrier. He couldn't, or wouldn't, give up. 'One more time.'

Chrissy's expression implied she thought him a sucker. 'Only if you bet on this one.'

Rhona kept quiet. If McNab wanted to throw his money away, that was up to him.

'How much?'

'You stand drinks for myself and Rhona. Whatever we want.'

Rhona decided her drink would be a bottle of champagne. God knows what Chrissy was planning. She couldn't drink alcohol at the moment but that didn't mean she couldn't save it until after the birth.

McNab was swithering. He was one of life's

gamblers and he didn't like being beaten by a woman.

'OK, but if I lose you show me how you do it.'

It was a difficult call for Chrissy, who didn't believe in giving ground.

Rhona pretended to study her notes, keeping half an eye on the proceedings. McNab had been at the lab when she'd got back from the restaurant. He hadn't made it plain why, though Rhona suspected it might be about Bill.

'OK,' Chrissy conceded.

'And these are definitely not the marked cards from the skip.'

'Hey, I wouldn't tamper with the evidence.'

McNab nodded at her to go ahead.

Chrissy sprang the cards from left to right, showing off, then shuffled and laid out a fan. McNab pondered for a while, faking a choice then changing his mind. Chrissy showed not the least concern. Rhona wanted to laugh, but didn't dare. Two red spots marked McNab's cheeks. He was taking this seriously.

He made a big thing about choosing a card, then switched his allegiance to another and quickly withdrew it from the pack.

'OK, what is it?'

Chrissy tried to look puzzled. 'Mmmm, difficult one.'

McNab began to look more confident. Rhona could have wept for him.

'Not sure. Maybe the jack of hearts?'

He stared at the card, perplexed. 'You are such a shite, by the way.'

Chrissy smiled the smile of the victor. 'Yes, but I'm very good at it.'

McNab began turning the cards face up, as though that would somehow reveal the secret of Chrissy's success.

'Mine's a bottle of Remy Martin.' Chrissy smirked at Rhona.

'I'm partial to a glass of champagne.'

McNab's relief was short lived.

'But I prefer a bottle.'

Chrissy laughed. 'We can make champagne cocktails.'

McNab seemed to be accepting defeat with unusually good grace. They discovered why almost immediately.

'Do you play poker?' he asked Chrissy.

'Do *I* play poker?'

'The guys have a card night every second Wednesday. Fancy joining in?'

'You let women play?' Chrissy's voice was heavy with sarcasm.

'Not normally.' He raised an eyebrow. 'But then you're no normal woman.'

'You want to shaft your mates?'

'You just shafted me.'

'True.' She contemplated the offer. 'OK, if you promise to take me to hospital if I go into early labour.'

'That won't happen, will it?'

Chrissy looked wordly wise. 'With first babies you never know. Especially as I'll be excited about winning.'

*   *   *

McNab waited for Chrissy to depart before he produced a crumpled piece of paper and handed it to Rhona.

'What's this?'

'I got it in an email today from the kid in the crash.'

She spread out the drawing on the table.

'You've shown this to Bill?' she said.

He shook his head. 'Not yet. I'm beginning to think this second body is just a ruse by the kid to get attention.'

Rhona looked up at him. 'From you?'

'I did give Claire, the mother, my contact details. Told her to get in touch if Emma remembered anything else about that night.'

'What's the mother like?'

'Mid-thirties, attractive. Made a point of telling me she wasn't married.'

'Really?'

'Not like that, she was angry I called her Mrs.'

'You think the kid's trying to pair you off with her mum?'

'Maybe.'

'Drawing dead bodies and sending them to a policeman to get a new dad sounds a bit over the top to me.' Rhona took another look at the drawing. 'The girl must have wandered around in those woods for a while before you found her. Maybe she did see something else, but can't remember now what it was. I could go back. Take another look.'

'The dog sniffed every pile of brushwood in that wood and didn't detect any more human remains.'

Rhona looked again at the drawing. 'The body here is buried.'

'We can't dig up the entire wood just because a kid draws a picture.'

'Have you talked to her mother about this?'

'Emma said in the email that her mother didn't want her to show me the drawing.'

'I'm not surprised. The woman's probably as freaked as you are by the kid's story.'

McNab said nothing.

'What if I contact the mother?' Rhona suggested.

This was obviously what McNab had been hoping for. She studied the drawing again, registering the classic shape of a Christmas tree.

'Pine needles are very acidic. A small body buried under a pine tree would be subjected to a constant trickle of acidic water, enough to dissolve even the bones.'

'So there would be nothing left?'

'After a decade, maybe some fabric, plastic things like buttons, gold items like a ring.'

'Did you find anything in the material from the deposition site?'

'Not yet. I suspect the body had been stripped before it was left there.'

'Meaning the killer was forensically aware?'

'Ten years ago he was probably just being careful. Hoping if it was ever found, it couldn't be identified.'

'He might be right.'

'Hey, *we* don't give up that easily.'

McNab was suitably chastised.

'On a different note. The dead guy in the skip might be eastern European. He had a meal of beetroot soup and dumplings before he died, possibly at the Russian Restaurant.'

'Beetroot soup?'

Rhona found herself defending the borscht. 'It's

very good. I tried some.'

'You went to the restaurant?'

'The manager's name is Misha Grigorovitch. He invited me back for a Russian meal.'

'Hope you're not planning on fraternising with a suspect?'

'He's hardly that.'

'He might be.'

'So might Claire Watson.'

That made them both think.

'You're suggesting the girl or her mother knew there was a body in those woods?'

Rhona hadn't really considered the idea until that moment. It would certainly explain how Emma 'found' the skull.

'Maybe we should take the story of a second body more seriously,' she said.

'I could take you down there tomorrow,' McNab offered.

'I have a court appearance in the morning and so do you.'

'We do?'

'The old lady, Mary Healey? We're going to put her killer behind bars.'

'Oh yes, I remember. What about a visit to the Watsons' afterwards?'

'Possibly, if we don't have to sit around waiting to be called. Give me the contact number. I'll talk to the mother.'

When McNab left, Rhona tidied up before dialling the Watsons' number. The phone rang out four times then a small voice answered.

'Is that Emma?'

'Who's speaking please?'

'My name is Dr Rhona MacLeod. I'm a

83

colleague of Detective Sergeant McNab.'

The voice brightened. 'Michael?'

'Yes, Michael. May I speak to your mum?'

The phone went down with a clatter. She could hear Emma's voice calling for her mother, then footsteps before the receiver was picked up.

'Hello.'

Rhona repeated what she'd said to Emma.

'How can I help you?' The woman's tone was guarded.

Rhona explained her role in the inquiry then said, 'DS McNab showed me a drawing Emma sent him.'

There was an intake of breath. 'I told her not to send that.'

'I know you must be worried by all this.'

'I am.'

Rhona chose her words carefully. 'There's a remote chance Emma did register something odd on her way to the place we found her. Something that's preying on her mind. I wondered if I walked with her through the woods, I might be able to both check it out and put her mind at rest.'

Rhona could sense controlled anger in the response.

'I don't think . . .'

'Detective Sergeant McNab has already spoken to his commanding officer about Emma's claims to know of a further body. It's likely he'll ask a psychologist to speak to her.'

'A psychologist?' Claire Watson sounded panicky now.

'It's nothing to be concerned about. A trained person is more likely to ask the right questions.'

'I think she's making it all up,' said Claire. She

84

sounded exasperated.

'Why would she do that?'

There was a pause. 'I recently broke up with my partner. Emma misses him.'

'I see.'

There was a pause then Mrs Watson said, 'I suppose it'll be all right, but I don't want Emma upset.'

When she rang off, Rhona contemplated that McNab might not have been far off the mark when he'd suggested Emma was intent on setting him up with her mother.

16

'Is Michael coming back?'

Claire took Emma tightly by the hand. 'Why did you send that drawing?'

The child tried to disengage herself from her mother's fierce grip, but Claire hung on.

'Why, Emma?'

The girl's expression grew stubborn. Claire had seen that look before.

'Answer me.'

Emma raised her chin defiantly.

'I can hear his voice. He's alone.'

'Stop it!' Claire's voice was shrill.

Emma cringed away from her.

'If you keep bringing the police here, we won't be safe any more.'

'Michael will look after us.'

Claire felt her throat constrict. Maybe her daughter was right. Maybe that was the best solution. Play to the policeman. Make him desire her, a lone woman in need of help and protection. DS McNab had been totally professional, but she'd sensed he might respond, if she played him the right way. A policeman for a lover. Would that keep them safe?

She looked at Emma's tight little mouth. Sometimes she almost wanted to slap the child, see the stinging hurt redden her face. Punish Emma for her own fear.

'Go to your room.'

After Emma had stomped up the stairs, Claire went to the phone and pulled out the lead. She didn't want any more emails leaving the house without her say-so. Thank God she hadn't been like most parents and given Emma her own mobile. She had been terrified that the girl might contact Nick. Even now she wasn't sure her daughter understood why they were hiding from him.

Her hand moved to her throat, remembering Emma and the policeman walking together across the snowy field. How pleased Emma had been to go out alone with the detective. Claire had questioned her closely after the policeman had left. She'd wanted to know whether Emma had told him about Nick, but hadn't dared ask outright.

Sometimes, she realised, she was afraid of her daughter. Afraid of the intensity of her stare. Of the humming she could hear coming from her bedroom. Of the sight of the small figure sitting in darkness when she opened the door.

She returned to the kitchen to find that the pasta had boiled dry in her absence. She rescued what hadn't stuck to the bottom of the pot, tipped it into an oven dish and poured over the sauce. Her hands were trembling with anger or fear, she didn't know which. She slid the dish in to the oven, then fetched the open bottle of wine, poured herself a glass and sat down with it at the table.

Claire didn't want her daughter to talk to the forensic woman, but realised she couldn't refuse. Not after Emma had sent the policeman that drawing. She lifted the glass to her mouth. The liquid struggled to make its way down her tightened throat. She felt like crying, but wouldn't let herself. If she started, she knew she would never stop.

A suffocating blackness began to press down on her, taking her breath away. A familiar pain grabbed her chest. She pulled open the cutlery drawer, selected a small sharp knife and pressed the point into her wrist, willing all the pain to concentrate on that spot.

The problem was she wasn't sure whether Emma knew what had happened—back then. She thought about the drawing and wanted to scream. The image of that small boy's body below the ground. The words *Don't leave me here alone.* All too terrible to contemplate.

The knife point had finally broken the skin. Claire watched as a trickle of blood ran over her wrist, then released the blade and threw it into the sink.

She would not go back there. She would not walk through that black tunnel again. She had not been to blame. She swallowed the rest of the wine in the glass, then washed the knife and put it back in the drawer. The wound on her wrist was barely visible.

Claire set about making a salad. They would eat

87

the meal in front of the television. She didn't want to sit opposite her daughter at the kitchen table and worry about what Emma was thinking.

When the news came on, Claire tried to switch channels, but Emma protested loudly enough for Claire to relent. There was very little on the remains. Just that they had been confirmed as human and were those of a child. No gender had been established. Forensic experts were studying material taken from the site to try to establish how long the body had lain there.

The next story involved a soldier gone AWOL and the possibility a body found in a burned-out skip might be that of Private Fergus Morrison. The police were looking for any information relating to the incident at a civic dump on Sunday evening.

Claire switched channels, looking for anything that didn't involve violence or death.

'Can I go upstairs now?' Emma gave her a pointed look.

'It's warmer down here. Why don't you put on a DVD.'

The girl was staring at her again.

'I'd rather go upstairs.'

Claire decided to tell her about the woman on the phone.

'She's coming to see me?'

'She wants you to walk through the woods with her, in case it helps you remember anything more.'

Emma's face lit up. 'Will Michael be there?'

'Probably.'

The girl stood for a moment, a small smile playing on her lips, then regarded her mother. 'Would you like to watch *Pirates of the Caribbean* with me?'

'I'd love to.' Claire tried to keep the relief from her voice. 'I'll clear up and come straight through.'

As she rinsed the dishes and stacked them, she watched the reflection of her daughter in the darkness of the window. Not for the first time, she wondered what her relationship with Nick had done to Emma. She couldn't take that time back, no matter how much she wanted to. It was over now and they would both have to live with the consequences.

She refilled her wineglass, then corked the bottle.

'Hurry up, Mummy.'

Claire checked that the back door was locked, then did the same at the front. They were miles from anywhere, she reminded herself. No one knew they were here. No one that mattered.

Claire entered the warmth of the sitting room and nestled down on the couch beside her precious daughter.

17

He got lucky on the third phone call. The scrapyard did have a Peugeot Estate, blue, just in.

'Went off the road and hit a tree, back's smashed, but it's got some nice pieces on it.'

He thanked the guy and said he'd be round in an hour.

'No problem, mate, but if someone strips it before you arrive, it's not my fault.'

He bit back a sharp reply and rang off. He could feel his temples throb as the blood rushed to his head. This had to be the one. It wasn't the nearest salvage yard to the crash, but it was close enough.

He took his time getting ready, ignoring the warning from the idiot on the phone. Stripping the car of its hubcaps and badge was not the purpose of his visit.

He chose a black waterproof hooded jacket with multiple pockets, a hat and a pair of leather gloves. With the hat pulled down and the hood up, there wouldn't be much of his face to see. On the way to the front door, he lifted the route map from the printer. He entered the workshop and headed for the small room at the back where he picked up evidence bags and a couple of pairs of latex gloves.

Outside, the wind cut through him like a knife.

He checked in the boot of the car for the toolbox and selected a couple of screwdrivers. He wanted to look the part. He slid into the driver's seat. The distant hills were frosted with white, but the sky was clear of the promised snow.

He switched on the radio and flicked through for news bulletins, but there was nothing more on the human remains story. He reminded himself that a child's bones lying that long in the open would be fragmented. They wouldn't even be able to tell whether it was a boy or a girl. He prided himself on knowing these things, although even he was amazed at what had developed in the last few years. That was the problem. The measures he had taken to protect himself then might not be enough to shield him now.

The street outside the salvage yard was lined with cars. He drove past and went looking for a space farther on. After spotting a CCTV camera, he ignored the parking on the main street and drove round until he found a space in front of a row of tenements.

It took ten minutes to walk back to the yard. He hung around outside then followed another two men on their way in. He made a point of not asking for the location of the blue Peugeot. Better to find it for himself. He followed a younger bloke who eventually veered off towards a black Fiat Punto with fancy hubcaps, just short of what looked like the Peugeot.

The man on the phone had been right, the car was a mess. He checked the number plate first, making a note of it. The back was completely bashed in, the roof dented where it had flipped over. He pulled open the driver's door and manoeuvred himself inside, then replaced the leather gloves with the latex ones. This was the moment he loved. It would have been even better had he been in a position to wear a forensic suit. He'd considered passing himself off as a SOCO who'd come for another look at the car, but had decided against drawing attention to himself. As far as the yard were concerned, he was just another punter looking for cheap rip-offs from banged-up cars.

He sat for a moment breathing in the scent of the car's interior. It smelled of female with no hint of cigarette smoke. That pleased him. When he got up close to her he didn't want her stale breath taking the enjoyment away.

A wave of pleasure rippled through him when he spotted dried blood above the windscreen. So she'd been hurt. He checked for more, finding what looked like splashes on the dashboard and the door, but not enough to suggest the bitch had been seriously injured.

He swivelled round to inspect the back and spotted the child booster seat for the first time. For a moment the breath left his body. When he'd seen the startled face in the windscreen, there had been no one in the passenger seat, but that didn't mean there hadn't been a kid in the back.

He ran his eyes over the seat, chastising himself for not bringing a kit with him to test properly for blood. There was a darkened spot on the side wing. He hesitated for a moment, then rubbed his latex finger across the stain and licked it, tasting the crusty metallic flavour.

There had been someone else in the car when it went off the road. A child. His heart sped up to match his rising excitement. So there were two of them to deal with. He contemplated the seat. It was the type made for older children, say five to ten.

He felt around under the seat and found a plastic hair clip in the shape of a flower with a few strands of white-blonde hair attached. He sniffed the clasp, catching the scent of shampoo. He took an evidence bag from his pocket and slipped the clasp and hair strands inside. The bitch had a daughter. This was getting better all the time.

He began to go systematically through the various compartments, dashboard first, then door pockets. The car hadn't been cleaned for a while. He pulled out a newspaper dated a month earlier from under the seat and two empty crisp bags, cheese-and-onion flavour. The glove compartment held crumpled tissues. He extracted these and dropped them into an evidence bag. Below was a lipstick called Pink Spice, a brush bound around with medium-length brown hairs and a map of the Glasgow area. He put the make-up and hairbrush in separate bags.

At the very bottom of the glove compartment was the instruction book for the car. Two phone numbers were written on the front page. He made a note of both.

He slid over to the passenger seat and directed his search under it, where he found half a packet of Loveheart sweets and a Tesco receipt for £63.24. He ran his eye down the list of groceries, which included a bottle of decent red wine. She'd paid the bill with a debit card and had amassed 346 points.

His last find was a pair of well-worn black slip-on shoes with a small bow. He eye-measured the shoe size against his own and decided she was probably around a UK six. He extracted a larger bag from his pocket, put the shoes inside and popped the sweets in with the crisp packets. The receipt he put in his wallet.

Through the windscreen he spotted the young guy approaching carrying a pair of hubcaps from the Fiat Punto. He slipped on the leather gloves and busied himself with one of the screwdrivers. His concern was unnecessary. The guy passed him by without a second glance.

He waited for a moment before pocketing the leather gloves, then began systematically going through every compartment and door pocket one more time, just in case. He was running his hand along the underside of the driver's seat when he felt a piece of paper jammed beneath the metal frame.

He eased it free and pulled it out, his heart

beating wildly.

Bingo.

The crushed Christmas card envelope was addressed to a Mrs C. Watson.

He allowed himself a smile.

He had found the bitch.

18

The thing you noticed first about Ivan Solonik were his hands. Disproportionally large for his squat, broad-chested body, they seemed to possess a life of their own.

Solonik's hands were what worried Brogan, that and his tiny brain. Brogan would be the first to admit that in most circumstances the pea-brain didn't matter. It was the hands that counted. Stories abounded about those hands and what Solonik could do with them. Snap a neck like a dry twig. Gouge out your eyes with those thick, blunt-ended fingers. Beat your kidneys to a pulp.

Brogan believed Solonik's hands capable of doing all those things and more. His own men, born and brought up in the less salubrious areas of the city, possessed many skills suited to Brogan's line of work. The Glasgow underworld was a good training ground, but couldn't compare to being a member of a Russian mafia gang.

The hands hung at Solonik's side like haunches of red ham. Brogan had witnessed them punching a head until the skull cracked and splintered, then snapping the neck just to make sure. He could hear the sound even now in his own head. Jesus, nothing could survive those hands.

Brogan hadn't wanted Solonik around, but the pea-brain had been part of the deal. He was there to keep an eye on Brogan, make sure the 'partnership' went smoothly. Prokhorov's words, not Brogan's. Brogan wondered once again whether he had got in above his head. But hey, this was the new world. If you didn't cooperate with The Organisation you didn't do business.

Brogan tried to focus his attention on the latest shipment details laid out on his desk, but Solonik's presence made it difficult. The guy had this quality of silence. He could stand next to you like a statue for hours on end. You couldn't hear him breathe. Christ, the bastard didn't even fart. Brogan wanted to tell Solonik to take an hour off, go eat, fuck one of the girls, but he didn't speak any Russian.

He made an eating gesture at Solonik, then a sexual one, the same in any language. Solonik just stared through him. Brogan gave up and poured himself a drink from the open bottle on his desk. Vodka. Sixty per cent proof. One small and powerful compensation for having Solonik around.

Brogan ran his eyes over the list of munitions. It was just like old times in Northern Ireland before peace broke out and put him out of business. Assault rifles, grenades, missile launchers, automatic rifles. Just one small part of the burgeoning Russian–Scottish enterprise. Weapons, prostitution, drugs, extortion, gambling—the money was rolling in. Developing ways to launder it was the real challenge. It was easier now for the police to confiscate the proceeds of crime. The drug barons kept their bank accounts empty and no money stashed under the bed. They invested it instead: property, expensive restaurants, chic nightclubs. The nouveaux riches of the Merchant City liked to spend their money and they needed places like the Poker Club to spend it in. Glasgow was the new Dublin, upwardly mobile, looking for fun.

To keep control of the business, Brogan needed munitions. With the Russians moving in, the knife was no longer the weapon of choice. Brogan had set up a nice little business to supply his troops courtesy of Her Majesty's forces. A couple of disgruntled soldiers from the Royal Regiment of Scotland, pissed off at being shafted by the government, had decided to stash away a nest egg for their retirement, if they reached it alive. In the mess that was the current supply chain in the British Army, it was easy to remove some weapons from use and send them north of the border.

He poured another shot of vodka. Solonik's massive bulk shifted almost imperceptibly. Was it a warning gesture to indicate he was watching Brogan's alcohol consumption? Brogan swallowed the shot and rose from his seat, indicating he was going for a piss. Solonik lumbered out of his way.

Brogan closed the cubicle door behind him. This was the only place he could escape Solonik's beady eye. Christ, even when he was fucking, the man mountain stood outside the door.

'For your protection,' Prokhorov had told him. 'People want me dead. You work with me, so they want you dead too.'

Brogan didn't buy that. Solonik wasn't his bodyguard, he was his minder, making sure he didn't get too big for his Glasgow boots.

His piss hit the pan in a cloud of steam. He

imagined it hitting the big Russian's face after he'd stuck a knife through his kidneys.

Solonik was in trouble. He just didn't know it yet. Brogan pulled the tabloid newspaper cutting from his inside pocket. AWOL soldier burned to death in skip. The tabloids always got things wrong.

With the inside information he had, it wasn't hard to figure out why. Someone had found the body at the dump and used it to try to cover their own disappearance. Clever, but not foolproof. Still, if it worked it meant Solonik was off the hook for the killing and Brogan didn't want that. He wanted that hook right in the bastard's gullet. He wanted Solonik reined in and disposed of, off his back for good.

He just hadn't decided how to go about it—yet.

19

Rhona glanced at the clock. McNab had left the lab two hours ago. She swivelled her head, trying to relieve the tension in the back of her neck. If Sean had been here, he would have massaged her shoulders to help her relax. But he wasn't here. Rhona tested her reaction to that, much as she had been doing for months, and decided she liked being on her own—most of the time.

The routine of sieving soil could be therapeutic. A bit like gardening, she thought. Her father had been a keen gardener. As a child she'd taken the well-tended garden for granted, assuming its beauty would be there for ever. But nothing lasted for ever. Her father's garden in Skye was grassed over now, a victim of her neglect.

She lifted another bag of soil, noting the details on the label which indicated the grid location and depth of the sample. She emptied the material into the sieve and began to agitate it. She had returned to this job on McNab's departure. The discovery of human remains was a cold case that could last for months or even years. The skip fire should take precedence, yet talking to McNab and then to Emma's mother had served to make this case feel more immediate.

The initial sieving of soil normally identified larger items, but in this case there had been none in the top level. No bottle tops, ring-pulls or the other debris you found in more urban settings. Worm action often resulted in the redistribution of items in the soil, so the depth of an object didn't necessarily indicate when an item had been deposited.

The finer soil had percolated through. Rhona examined the remnants that lay on the fine mesh, spreading it out with her latex-covered finger. There was a fragment of glass, so small as to be almost invisible. She extracted it and took it over to a high-powered microscope.

Under magnification she could make out the orange-red colour and the splinter-like shape. As trace evidence went, glass could be useful. Perpetrators of crimes, particularly burglary, didn't realise that they carried microscopic particles of the glass they'd shattered on their clothes and in their hair.

An analysis of the chemical content and refractive index of the glass could give an indication of what it had been used for. Coloured glass tended to be more identifiable than ordinary glass owing to the mineral content that produced its colour. Glass manufacturers each had their own glass recipe, just as paint manufacturers created their own unique paint.

Rhona's stomach was reminding her just how long it had been since she'd eaten the borscht. She decided to finally call it a day and go home. The prospect of another microwave ready-made meal didn't appeal, so she bought a pizza on the way.

Tom met her at the door, winding himself round her legs, nearly upending her and the precious cardboard box. She quickly fed him, feeling guilty at how long she'd kept him waiting. She would have to buy one of those bowls with a timer, set to release food at regular intervals.

Rhona walked through the flat, putting on lights and turning up the heating. This was the moment in her day when living alone didn't appeal as much. She allowed herself to remember how it had been when Sean was here—the scent of cooking when she'd opened the front door, the sound of a human voice calling out to her—then recalled how often she'd welcomed the realisation that Sean had left for work and the flat was empty.

'There's no pleasing you,' she muttered to herself. She shoved the pizza in the oven to keep it warm while she showered and changed.

Eating alone at the kitchen table had become something she'd avoided since Sean had left. These days she preferred to eat in the sitting room with the TV for company.

She fetched her notes for next day's court appearance and read them while she ate. It seemed an open-and-shut case. Mary had heard a noise in her hall and gone to investigate. Her attacker, a young man high on drugs and alcohol, had beaten her to death. His defence was that he had stumbled into the wrong flat and in the darkened hall had been attacked by the flat's occupant. He'd hit her only in self-defence. Not a bad attempt at getting off with murder. He wasn't denying that he'd entered the flat. He was just denying that he'd attacked Mary on purpose. The problem lay in his assertion that the hall had been in darkness throughout, preventing him from realising how badly hurt the occupant was.

When the first SOCO arrived, they'd filled in the usual checklist, which included the question *Was the light on or off?* The light had been on, which meant the accused was lying. Along with the details of the forensic report on the body, this meant Mary's killer would be going away— hopefully for a very long time.

Rhona set the notes on one side and laid her head back on the sofa, overcome with tiredness. She thought about sleeping right there on the couch, knowing once in bed she would likely end up staring at the ceiling for hours before the nightmare took over. She fetched the duvet and draped it over her, then reached for the remote.

The late news had already begun. As far as she knew, Bill still had a blackout on Emma Watson's role in the discovery of the skull, so she was surprised to hear the newsreader reveal that it had been discovered after a car had gone off the road in the recent storm. A description then followed of a man believed to have been in the vicinity at the time, who the police urged to come forward. There was still no direct mention of Emma or Claire. It

100

looked as though Bill was taking Claire's story about a man on the road seriously, unless something else had come to light that Rhona didn't know about.

She lowered the sound on the television to a background murmur and nestled down, leaving the table lamp on. Tom had come to join her, and the steady rhythm of his purring began to lull her towards sleep.

*   *   *

She was wakened by the alarm. Her initial reaction was confusion as she heard the murmur of early morning television. Then she was absurdly grateful that she had slept through the night, something that hadn't happened for some time. She rose, her limbs stiff from the confinement of the couch.

Claire Watson phoned while she was eating breakfast.

'I'm afraid you won't be able to see Emma today. My mother died last Sunday and I have to go to the nursing home and finalise arrangements for her funeral tomorrow.'

McNab had never mentioned that the child's granny had just died, in fact had died the night of the crash. Rhona wondered whether he knew.

'What if we meet with you after the funeral?' Rhona suggested. 'I could check out the wood with Emma on her way home.'

The silence that followed was long enough to convince her that Claire had changed her mind about allowing the excursion at all.

Finally she answered. 'If Emma is distressed . . .'

'Then of course we won't go.'

Claire, sounding mollified, gave Rhona a time and a place.

'We'll be there,' Rhona promised.

*   *   *

The old and the new High Courts of Glasgow sat side by side at the foot of the Saltmarket, both pillared entrances, the new version reflecting the grandeur of the old.

Behind the court Shipbank Lane housed Paddy's Market, Glasgow's legendary flea market. Started by Irish immigrants in the nineteenth century, it still sold second-hand clothing to the poor of Glasgow. Recent reports suggested the end of the two-hundred-year-old market was nigh, as the City Council had announced plans to lease the site and turn it into a showcase for aspiring artists. Rhona felt a stab of sadness about this. The gentrification of the city was intent on wiping out its past.

McNab was waiting for her in the lobby.

'I've done my bit. Apparently forensic testimony is next up.'

'Good.'

'So we can head south after that.'

Rhona told him about her early morning conversation.

'Shit. I had no idea the granny had died.'

'Claire never said?'

He shook his head. 'No wonder the kid's screwed up. OK, so when do we go?'

'I got her mother to agree to tomorrow after the funeral.'

The clerk emerged from the court and beckoned Rhona over.

'Will you be here when I come out?'

'I'll get a coffee and wait for you.'

*   *   *

'So?' McNab said when she re-emerged.

'I think he's fucked.'

'That's what I like to hear.'

McNab had gone to Mary Healey's funeral. Him and most of the residents of Alison Street. He was a Govanhill boy himself. 'Brought up in Govanhill Street in a top-floor tenement,' he told Rhona. Hence his desire to see the old woman's killer go down.

'Fancy a real coffee?' McNab made a face at the polystyrene cup in his hand.

'Definitely.'

An early morning frost had combined with freezing fog to blanket the city in white and grey. It was still an improvement on a howling wind and snow. Rhona wound her scarf tightly round her neck and stuck her gloved hands in her pockets.

'Central Café?'

She nodded and hurried to keep up with him. When they reached the café, he pushed the door open to let her enter first. The contrast in temperature made Rhona's cheeks burn. McNab stopped for a word with Rocco, the proprietor, while she headed for a window table.

The Central Café was one of those places you hoped would be there for ever. Some felt it already had been. McNab remembered it from his childhood, as did people twenty years older. It was one of the old-style cafés, of which there had once been many. No longer an ice-cream parlour, it was

103

now better known for its fish and chips.

Rhona recalled a similar establishment at the top of Byres Road when she'd been a Glasgow University student. The proprietor had made the best Horlicks ever, substantial and creamy enough for a poverty-stricken student to use as a lunch substitute.

McNab arrived with a large mug of black coffee, just the way she liked it. It was at times like this she was reminded just how well he knew her.

'I saw the bit on the late news. You're sure there was someone on the road?' she asked when he'd settled himself opposite.

'I had a look at the R2S video of the crash location. If there was a man there and he was facing like Claire said, then he was staring back at the wood in the direction of the deposition site.'

'Really?'

'I decided that merited trying to find him, if only to eliminate him from the inquiry.'

Rhona told him about the glass fragment. 'I'm checking out the constituents, but it looks like it might be stained glass.'

'As in a stained-glass window?'

'Yes.'

McNab considered this. 'It's not much to go on.'

He was right. On its own the glass wasn't a lot of use, but it might be if they came up with a suspect.

'I did a trawl of unsolved cases,' he said. 'There are twelve missing children during the period we're focusing on.' He handed Rhona a printout.

She ran her eye over the pictures.

McNab pointed to a smiling elfin girl. 'She disappeared from St Pancras station nine years ago. She was with her big sister one minute, gone

104

the next. Only one possible sighting of her later that day with a middle-aged man getting into a red car, no make, no registration number.'

'I don't think it's her.'

McNab waited for an explanation.

'The skull Emma found didn't have that overlap on the front teeth.'

'That simple?'

'Teeth are unique and last a long time. Obviously we'll check out the dental records of all the missing kids against the remains, but at a first glance I would say that isn't our child.'

They sat in silence for a moment.

'What if the dead child was never reported missing?' she suggested.

They both knew that was a possibility. For a minor to be registered as missing, a parent or guardian would have to inform the police. Social services weren't interested in your child unless you were on their radar. Kids joined and left schools in the urban areas with monotonous regularity, especially those with itinerant workers for parents. As for those in the care system, recent high-profile cases showed how easily they could disappear, especially ten years ago.

They both contemplated the thought that the skeletal remains would never be identified and the killer never found.

Rhona broke the silence. 'I've got to head back to the lab.'

'What about tomorrow?'

'The funeral's at eleven.'

McNab's brow darkened. 'The meeting with the super is at nine. I'll call you when it's over.'

Rhona left him at the table, staring into his

coffee. He looked terrible, hollow eyed and haunted. She suspected the disciplinary inquiry wasn't allowing him much sleep. Whatever the outcome, it didn't bode well for him. If Bill took the rap, McNab would never forgive himself. If they believed McNab's story, then he was in trouble. Either way was bad news. They might have caught the Gravedigger, but he'd left his mark on them all, including Magnus, the psychologist they'd called in to help. Rhona contemplated calling him and asking his advice on her meeting with Emma. She'd promised to get back in touch. Maybe now was the time.

20

Magnus looked different. It took a moment to register that his long hair had been cut off. He no longer resembled a Viking warrior. Rhona felt a little saddened by that.

She stood back to let him enter. Tom covered the initial awkwardness by coming running to see who the visitor was. Magnus scooped the kitten up. 'What's your name?'

Rhona told him.

'Hey, Tom.' Magnus rubbed the ears and was rewarded by a rolling purr. When he set Tom down, the kitten scuttled off towards the kitchen. Rhona hesitated in the hall, not sure which room to use. She opted to follow Tom. In the kitchen they could sit with the table between them, which seemed appropriate somehow. She waved Magnus to a seat and offered him a whisky. 'It's Highland

Park.'

He smiled. 'I converted you, then?'

'I like the taste.'

Magnus had championed the Orcadian whisky at one of their first meetings, using it to illustrate Rhona's sense of smell. His own highly developed sense of smell had played a large part in the search for the Gravedigger.

She poured two drams and offered him a jug of water. He added a little and swirled the mixture round the glass. Rhona did the same. They took a sniff before tasting.

'So, how have you been?' Magnus got the question in first.

'Fine,' Rhona lied. She had no intention of telling anyone about the nightmares, particularly him. She caught him studying her expression. He would know she was lying. She waited for him to delve further and was glad when he didn't.

'What about you?'

'Fine.' He looked down. She suspected they were both being minimal with the truth. 'The university gave me some time off. I spent it in Orkney, as you know.'

Rhona nodded. She had visited him there, staying a few days in his house overlooking Scapa Flow. In those surroundings things had been easier between them. The mutual attraction had still been there, but neither had acknowledged it and they'd parted amicably.

'It's good to be back at work.'

Things got easier after that. Rhona explained about the car crash, Emma's disappearance and reappearance nursing the skull. Magnus was obviously shocked by the story.

'The news never mentioned a child was involved in finding the remains.'

'McNab didn't tell you?'

Magnus looked puzzled. 'I haven't spoken to McNab.'

So McNab hadn't followed Bill's orders and called in the psychologist. Rhona decided not to elaborate on that.

'There's more,' Rhona went on. 'The skeleton was well concealed under a pile of branches but for some reason Emma poked her hand in and retrieved the skull.' She paused for a moment. 'She says she heard it calling her.'

Magnus's brow furrowed. 'Calling her?'

'I know it sounds daft, but there it is. Now she insists there's another body doing the same.' She handed him the printout McNab had given her.

He studied it for a few moments. 'You've searched the wood for other remains?'

'Bill sent in specially trained dogs. They're not totally reliable but in this case they didn't show any more interest in the wood, apart from the deposition site. The child is obviously distressed by this and insists she's right.'

'So where do I come in?'

'I have permission to take Emma back to the wood tomorrow morning. She was wandering about in there for some time before they found her.'

'And you thought she might have seen something that's preying on her mind?'

'Yes.'

'I suppose it's possible. There's a fine line between imagination and reality, especially with children as young as Emma. Is the girl under stress at home or school?'

'The mother left her partner recently. That's all I know. McNab's been dealing with the family. It seems Emma's taken a liking to him.'

Magnus contemplated this.

'What if I come with you? Would that help?'

Rhona had considered this option before calling Magnus and decided it might be more productive than just asking his advice. There was, however, the issue of McNab.

'I'll have to run it by the mother first and . . .' Rhona decided to come clean. 'DS McNab will be going down there with me.'

'And he won't want me around?'

Rhona explained about the disciplinary investigation. 'McNab blames himself for Bill's predicament.'

'As do we all,' Magnus said grimly. 'Check with the DS first. If he's willing, I'll come along.'

They made small talk after that, both keen for the meeting to end. They said goodbye at the door. For a moment Rhona thought Magnus would embrace her, the way he had done in Orkney, dispelling the awkwardness between them. Part of her wanted him to, but she folded her arms.

'You'll let me know, then?' Magnus looked sad, as though he had been reading her mind as well as interpreting her body language.

When she closed the door on his echoing footsteps, Rhona realised just how nervous she had been that seeing Magnus again would serve only to feed the nightmares.

21

'Do I have to come in?'

'I don't want to leave you in the car.'

Emma made a face and opened the door.

Claire reached for her daughter's hand and they walked together towards the entrance. The hospice looked over the river. On sunny days the view from the garden was quite beautiful. Today a freezing mist clung to the sluggish, oily water.

Claire hesitated for a moment before she pushed open the glass door, aware that this time there would be no welcoming smile from her mum. She wished once again that she'd stayed overnight at the hospice the previous Sunday. She'd turned the offer down, anxious to end the day as normally as possible for Emma's sake.

Susan Richards looked up as she approached the reception desk. 'Claire.' She opened her arms and gave her a big hug, then stood back and looked at her. 'I'm sorry.'

'I should have stayed.'

'She didn't want you to, you know that.'

Susan was right. Her mother had insisted she take Emma home. Let the child sleep in her own bed.

'I think she knew,' said Claire.

The nurse nodded in agreement. 'Carol called me in after you left to give me her instructions in the event of her death.' She chuckled. 'I get the feeling she's keeping an eye on me to make sure I carry them out.'

Claire felt Emma's little hand tighten in her own.

'I have Carol's things in my office.' Susan bent to speak to Emma. 'Your gran left something special for you.'

They walked along a familiar corridor. Through open doors, Claire saw groups of visiting relatives. She wished she could turn back the clock and be like them again.

Susan ushered them into a room where a large picture window gave a view of the nearby suspension bridge. Her mum had had the same view. My bridge to the stars, she'd called it.

She handed Claire an envelope. 'A list of the six people she invited to the funeral. She joked that there were only six left alive she liked, apart from you and Emma. She asked me to post the invitations as soon as I knew the date. I understand you were an only child?'

Claire nodded. 'Mum didn't have me until she was forty. I was a bit of a surprise. She'd been told she was unlikely to have children.'

Susan handed Emma a cardboard box. 'Your gran asked me to give you this.'

Emma laid the box on the table and removed the lid. Inside was a photograph album.

'Your gran spent a long time on that. She said it was a record of your family's history. Photographs and stories. She told me some of them.'

Emma replaced the lid and clasped the box to her. Claire felt her own chest tighten.

'I'll see you tomorrow,' said Susan.

'You're coming to the funeral?'

'My name's on that list.'

*   *   *

Claire sat for a moment in the car park, watching pedestrians cross her mum's bridge to the stars. This would be the last time she came here. She felt suddenly bereft, as though losing this place was the same as losing her mother.

'OK?' she asked Emma.

A small voice answered yes, the tone upbeat.

Claire glanced in the driving mirror and saw the album, now out of its case, being hugged to the girl's chest.

She took the route alongside the river. The mist had lifted and the opposite bank was no longer a mysterious place on the other side.

'I'm going to call in at Granny's house. Make sure everything's all right.'

They'd been checking on her mother's house once a week since she'd moved into the hospice. Their visits had been swift and perfunctory. Devoid of her mother, the house had taken on a different guise, its emptiness almost threatening.

*   *   *

Claire stood shivering in the small hallway. She had left the heating on to avoid burst pipes, but not set it high enough to warm the place. She turned up the thermostat and was heartened to hear the boiler roar into action.

Emma followed her in, still clutching the album, heading upstairs to the small room she'd called her own when they'd stayed over. Claire made for the kitchen. Past midday in midwinter, the room was already darkened by shadow. Claire switched on the light and busied herself filling the kettle and spooning loose tea into the pot. Her mother had always insisted on *real tea*, as she called it. None of those floor sweepings in a paper bag. The fridge stood open and unplugged. On her earlier visits Claire had brought milk with her, but today she would have to drink the tea black.

Seated at the table, she sorted through the mail. There were three condolence cards which she set to one side, a couple of circulars and an invitation to join the postcode lottery.

She turned her attention to the large brown envelope Susan had given her. It contained an order of service, which included the Twenty-third Psalm, a favourite of her mum's, and her chosen eulogy:

Death is nothing at all.
I have only slipped away into the next room.
I am I, and you are you.
Whatever we were to each other, that we still are . . .

Claire slipped the poem back in the envelope, unable to read any farther. She took a deep breath and picked up the list. There were only three names she recognised on it, including Susan. Her mother had been a keen member of the lunchtime club in the local community hall, so she assumed the extra names had been her erstwhile companions there.

The last item was a smaller envelope addressed to her. Claire studied the old-fashioned handwriting, the swirling 'C', the intricate 'r'. It was from her mother. She put it in her handbag, unable to read its contents.

She had no idea how long she sat there, listening to the silence, noticing the film of dust that lay

113

over everything, knowing that it was now too late to tell her mother the truth.

When she felt the familiar darkness begin to press down on her, Claire rose and walked to the window. Dusk was claiming the day, the horizon bruised in red and blue. A trick of the light on the dirt-smeared window split her reflection. There were two faces now, hers and the other Claire's. The one that told lies, the one that could do what she had done.

She felt a sob rise in her throat. She swallowed it back, desperate to hold on to what fragments of sanity she had left. She shifted her position and watched as her two selves began to merge, gradually becoming one again, reminding her that she had once been whole.

A cry from Emma broke the spell. Claire took the stairs two at a time. The door to the child's room lay open.

'What is it? What's wrong?'

'Someone's been in my room,' Emma said crossly.

Claire looked round quickly. The room appeared exactly the same as it always did.

'What do you mean?'

Emma gestured to the window. Claire went over to check. The window was firmly shut.

'There's nothing here.'

'Look!' The girl pointed.

Immediately above the radiator, the lower pane had steamed up, leaving a zigzag pattern on the glass.

'I wrote my name on the window in real writing, the way Gran showed me.'

Her daughter's face was indignant.

'It's not there any more. Someone's rubbed it out.'

Claire felt her fear turn to irritation. She did not have the time or inclination for another one of Emma's games. 'You must have touched the window. You've just forgotten you did.'

'I did not,' said Emma stubbornly. 'I always rewrite my name every time I come, for Gran. Someone's rubbed it out.'

'Don't be silly.'

'I'm not being silly. Look.'

Emma breathed on the glass and the shape took a clearer form. Claire could make out part of a capital 'E' written in the old-fashioned way, but the rest of Emma's name had been obliterated.

'See, Mummy.'

She didn't know what to say. 'I'll check the rest of the house.'

It was an excuse to get away. She left Emma staring at the window and went on to the landing. Part of her wanted to ignore what the child had suggested, but another part felt uneasy.

She checked the spare room first, the one she used when staying over. It looked exactly the same. No open drawers, no scattered possessions, no suggestion that anyone had been there.

She made her way to her mother's room.

She opened the door and breathed in the familiar scent of lavender. A pile of clothes sat folded on the bed. Claire had laid them out the last time she was here, in case her mother might ask for them. Too late now, she thought. The room was as undisturbed as hers had been. Yet the sense of unease was growing. Why? Claire went to the dressing table and opened the drawer. It was filled with small items, bits of jewellery, Christmas cards, birthday cards. Claire picked up a school jotter, loose at the seam. She opened it and saw a drawing of a teapot with a flower on the spine. Beneath were the words 'My mum's teapot' written in a childish hand. She realised with a start that it was one of her early jotters from primary school. She began going through the other contents of the drawer, finding her swimming certificate, a poem she'd written, even a note left behind when she'd gone out as a teenager against her mother's wishes. Claire sank down on the bed and stared at the store of memories, the reason she'd begun looking far from her thoughts.

The radiator clanked as a rush of hot water expanded the metal. The wooden tallboy, a relic of her grandparents' house, creaked as the wood absorbed the change in temperature. Claire remembered her mother telling her that wood lived on even after it was cut down and made into things, provided it was cared for. After her grandfather had died, they'd planted his walking stick in the garden and it had sprouted, just as her mother had said it would.

A rising breeze hit the window, rattling the glass and reminding Claire why she was there. She closed the drawer and went to check. The window was firmly shut, the lock in place.

She examined the downstairs rooms, knowing it was pointless but not wanting to tell Emma all was well without making sure. In the kitchen she lifted the junk mail, planning to put it in the bin. She unlocked the back door and went outside. It was on her return that she noticed that the porch window to the right of the door was clean.

She stopped in her tracks.

The rays of the sinking sun showed up the accumulated dirt on every window on the back of the house, except that one. Claire went for a closer look, the sense of unease flooding back. The window was about three foot square and made of plain glass. The putty worked round its edges looked fresh and much cleaner than its neighbour on the other side. This pane of glass had been replaced, and recently.

Her mother had been in the hospice for a month. This glass couldn't have been here for that length of time. Claire stepped forward, hearing a faint crunch beneath her feet. She crouched down for a better look. Something glistened among the gravel. She licked her finger and pressed down on what looked like a splinter of glass. She went into the kitchen and examined it in the brighter light. There was no doubt about it, someone had cut out the old window and replaced the glass.

She shut and double-locked the back door, her hands trembling, and looked wildly round the kitchen. Her mother had moved into the hospice well before Claire left Glasgow. There was nothing here that could possibly lead Nick to the cottage. Only the hospice had her contact details, and they would never give out that information without her permission.

Claire suddenly didn't want to be there any more. What if Nick were watching the house, waiting for her to come back? Unease had become panic. She shouted for Emma.

'We have to go now, or we'll hit the teatime traffic,' she added, trying to keep the tremor out of her voice.

117

The child appeared at the top of the stairs.

'What's wrong?'

'Nothing,' Claire lied.

'You checked everywhere?'

Claire forced a confident smile. 'I remembered I asked Mrs Craig next door to take a quick look in last week, when we couldn't make it. I expect she rubbed out your name when she was checking the window locks.'

Emma was examining her expression. Not for the first time Claire realised how astute her daughter was at reading mood and thought.

Emma came downstairs, carrying her album.

'I'm going to read more when I get home.'

'Good. I'd like to look at it too, if that's OK?'

'Some bits are just for me.'

'Well, you can show me the other bits.'

Claire took a swift look about as she exited the drive, but saw nothing unusual. Still, she drove round the small estate three times. If someone was following her it might be easier to lose them here, in a maze of streets with similar names, than on the main road. Emma said nothing about their strange route, just sat hugging her album.

The more she thought about it, the more convinced Claire became that Nick had broken into her mother's house. Nothing had been stolen, nothing wrecked. The intruder had made it look as though he had never been there. If Emma hadn't got cross about her name on the window, Claire would never have discovered the changed pane of glass at the back door.

Women didn't leave Nick. That was what he'd told her. 'It's a big bad world out there, especially for a woman alone with a kid. You never know what's going to happen.'

His words still rung in her head. Why had she imagined for a moment that he would give up on her?

Nick didn't give up on anything.

22

He'd lost her in the maze of bungalow-lined streets.

His car now sat in a cul-de-sac, engine running, while he regained his composure. Already a curtain was twitching at a nearby window. He swallowed his anger, feeling it fall like a hot stone to the pit of his stomach.

As he turned the car an elderly man appeared at a nearby door to watch. He swore under his breath and crunched the gears in annoyance. Keeping his face out of view, he finally drew out.

On the journey home, he kept his rage in check and focused his attention on what he knew. The woman who'd seen him on the road didn't live in that bungalow. There was a child's room but it was not occupied all the time. Of the other two rooms, one was obviously that of an older woman. The other bedroom he suspected had been used by the woman he sought. He glanced at the three evidence bags on the seat beside him. He'd been selective about what he took. Two items belonging to the woman, one to the child, whose name he now knew.

Emma, Emma, Emma.

He savoured the name, attached a face to it. A

119

face framed by long white-blonde hair. It helped calm him down.

When he arrived home he headed for the kitchen, boiled the kettle and made a mug of tea, before pulling on a fresh pair of latex gloves and opening the evidence bags.

The woman's room had held little belonging to her. A change of clothes and some underwear, a few items of make-up, some perfume and a selection of earrings. He'd removed a single earring, three small black pearls on a fine gold chain. Very nice. Dressy but not showy. He'd already formed a picture of the woman but the earring and her underwear now added to this. He knew her bra size was 36C, her taste in undergarments feminine but not provocative.

He turned his attention to Emma's bag. He'd been careful in his selection from the child's room. There had been a number of items on the windowsill he'd liked but had decided they were probably treasured, so he took something from the drawer instead. It was a pencil with an eraser on the end.

He lifted the last bag, his mouth moving in a smile. Now he understood why he'd been mistaken with the Christmas card envelope. Both women had first names beginning with a 'C'. The woman he sought was called Claire Watson, her mother Carol.

The card had been behind the front door. It was one of several items of mail, consisting of a bundle of circulars addressed to Mrs C. Watson, plus four white envelopes, all addressed to Claire Watson. He'd decided to open one. Inside was a sympathy card on the death of her mother and a message from someone called Una saying she would be at the crematorium to say goodbye to her friend Carol.

He smiled.

It wouldn't be difficult to find out which crematorium was disposing of Mrs Carol Watson within the next few days. If that failed then he would return to the house to wait. Claire would have to deal with her mother's effects sooner or later.

The heat of anger had dissipated. He had lost Claire for now, but he knew where he could find her.

23

McNab added a nip of whisky to his coffee, then waved the half-bottle at the old man at the next table, who'd been watching him intently. When he nodded, McNab tipped a fair measure into the old guy's mug.

'Thanks, pal.'

'No problem.'

They each took a swallow, registering the improved quality of their beverages, before McNab went back to wondering what to do about his DI's designs on self-destruction. In twenty-four hours he suspected it would be a fait accompli. His boss would be charged with assault, his career in ruins.

McNab pulled out his mobile and punched in Henderson's lawyer's number. Henderson had a woman representing him, which seemed rather rich considering the nature of his crimes. His brief's name was Sandra Morris. She was in her early thirties with naturally auburn hair. It was the only thing she and McNab had in common, apart from height. As well as being tall and something of a looker, Ms Morris was also known as a ball-breaker to some of Strathclyde's finest. The men who called her this were of course the ones who stood least chance of getting anywhere with her. McNab didn't like Ms Morris, but that didn't mean he didn't fancy her. He was only human.

It wasn't a direct number, so he had to get past her secretary. She listened to his name, rank and request to speak to she-who-must-be-obeyed and advised him to wait. McNab suspected Ms Morris would refuse and was therefore surprised when he heard her husky tones on the other end. Her voice was one of her greatest assets in court, its pitch, its power and its melody almost hypnotic qualities. McNab was sure that even the most hardened of jurors, if subjected to Sandra Morris reciting nonsense, would be inclined to accept it as the gospel truth. Even judges had been spotted looking mesmerised by her magic tones.

They were a bit harsher today. 'What d'you want?'

'He's telling porkies. *I* kicked him in the balls, not the DI.'

There was a significant pause.

'I'm not at liberty to discuss my client's case with you.'

McNab bulldozed on. 'We were seated across the table from Henderson. Me on the left, the DI on the right. For the DI to connect with Henderson's balls he would have had to kick with his left foot.

Possible, but improbable. The DI has a metal plate in his left knee. Broke it badly playing football for the police team years ago. It works, but not much strength in it. Now my right leg was beautifully lined up for Henderson's balls. And one of my hobbies is kick-boxing.'

Ms Morris had listened in silence to his story. McNab awaited her response.

She spoke slowly and carefully, as though he might be going deaf. 'DI Wilson says he did it. Henderson says it was him.'

He spat out his rejoinder. 'Henderson's a bastard and he's out to get the DI.'

She considered this for a moment.

'I understand your concern.' Her voice had softened. 'But I think it would be better if . . .'

McNab ended the call without letting her finish. He couldn't listen to another platitude about letting the investigative officer do his job. Seething with barely controlled anger, he tipped another shot into the remaining coffee. When his neighbour looked over hopefully, McNab handed him the bottle.

'Help yourself to the rest.'

The old guy's face split in a grin that showed a set of false teeth that sat loose from the gums. 'Aye, you're all right, son.'

McNab threw back the coffee and stood up to go. Outside, the wind had strengthened and was rattling signs and blowing plastic bags and empty polystyrene boxes along the gutter. Coming towards him was a motorised street sweeper, a guy perched on the back. It manoeuvred its way along the gutter.

McNab joined the other pedestrians walking

123

head down into the wind, hailstones biting at his face. His phone rang as he reached the Trongate heading west towards the Russian Restaurant, and he took refuge in a doorway to answer.

'McNab?' a voice said.

He tried to put a name to the refined west coast accent. It wasn't difficult.

'Paddy Brogan.'

'The same.' Paddy lowered his voice a little. 'I heard there was a wee fire at Polmadie?'

'You know something about that?'

'Maybe. How about you come along to the club and check out our gambling licence?'

McNab snapped the phone shut and changed direction, heading back towards the river. If Brogan had asked him to come calling, he had something to say.

Paddy Brogan's father, Billy Brogan, otherwise known as Poker Billy, had left school at sixteen. He'd gained no formal qualifications but had a brain like a calculator, only faster. If he'd been in at the computer revolution they would have used his brain as a model.

He could also play any card game and win. He could read players' faces like crib sheets, work out odds in nanoseconds. He'd used this ability in a number of ways, all of which made him vast sums of money and most of which were illegal. Billy had married Paddy's mother, Ida, when they were both eighteen, and he stayed married to her until the day he died. He lived all his married life two streets away from where he was born, drove a Jaguar Mark II and spent his holidays on the Costa del Sol. His son Patrick had been enrolled in the best fee-paying school in Glasgow and from there went to Glasgow University, where he gained first-class honours in Business Studies. McNab remembered him well. They'd played five-a-side football together. Paddy was good at that, too. He had gone on to the London Business School to study for an MBA, after which he headed for the South of France, only reappearing when his old man kicked the bucket. Now he looked like the well-educated gentleman he was, and was expanding his father's empire in new and interesting ways.

The Brogans' club was imaginatively called 'The Poker Club'. It lay just south of the river, its impressive pillared entrance a monument to Glasgow's glorious architectural past. Vast glass doors led into a marble-lined hall that could rival the City Chambers. To the left was a classy bar that served quality food, a tribute to Paddy's time spent sampling French gastronomy.

Soft green carpeted stairs led up to a variety of smaller rooms where the average punter was welcomed in from 3 p.m. to midnight. Special games were kept for select people and held in the penthouse suite with a view of the river. McNab was not one of the special people. Brogan had said to keep it official, which meant he wanted him to enter as a policeman on police business, as though Brogan hadn't invited him there.

McNab flashed his ID and asked to speak to Mr Brogan. He was shown into the bar and offered a drink or a coffee. McNab ordered a five-year-old malt. He was sipping whisky from a very nice cut-glass tumbler when Brogan appeared.

In his mid-thirties, with just a sprinkling of grey, Paddy Brogan looked every inch the proprietor of

125

a classy Glasgow gambling establishment. His entrance would have rivalled that of George Clooney. As he approached the table, he nodded and McNab caught the tiniest wink from his left eye.

Following this cue, McNab did well to prevent his mouth falling open. The man accompanying Brogan was built like a whisky barrel, his head sitting squat on his shoulders, three rings of fat taking the place of a neck. But it was the hands which had caused McNab to momentarily gape. They reminded him of the gammon roast his mother used to bake at Christmas time—thick and pink. McNab had a sudden image of one of those fists firing towards him and almost flinched. After glancing round the room and giving McNab the once-over, the man took up his stance at the door.

'Where the hell did he come from?' McNab muttered under his breath.

Brogan's voice was low and angry. 'Let's say Solonik doesn't speak English apart from *fuck you, ya bastard* and *vodka.*'

'Russian?'

Brogan nodded.

'Legal?'

'A student on a gap year who's come to Scotland to learn the language.' Brogan raised his voice a little. 'Another drink, Officer, while we discuss the licence?'

McNab acquiesced. After all, it wasn't often he got to drink free whisky of this quality.

Brogan nodded at the barman, who'd been awaiting his command. There was a flurry of activity behind the counter followed by the swift

126

delivery of another whisky for McNab and what looked like the same for Brogan.

Brogan tasted it then brought out some folded papers from his inside pocket and pushed them across the table. McNab glanced at them long enough to note that they were part of a licence agreement.

'By all means take them with you. Study them at your leisure, Officer.'

McNab glanced at the minder to find his blank stare focused on Brogan's back. He had no idea what the fuck was going on here, but whatever it was had generated fury and caution in Brogan in equal measure.

'Haven't seen you for a while,' Brogan said. 'Given up playing poker?'

'I heard there was a lot of vodka being drunk here. I'm a whisky man myself.'

'As am I,' Brogan said with conviction.

McNab finished his drink and rose to go, pocketing the papers. The huge man watched as he made his way into the marble entrance hall. His eyes felt like bullets chasing McNab to the exit. At any moment he expected their impact to shatter his spine.

He was glad to hear the heavy glass doors close behind him and step into the wind and the freezing rain. What had Dylan sung? 'The times they are a changin' '. If Brogan was under the influence of Mother Russia, then things definitely were changing. For a fleeting moment McNab hankered after the time of Poker Billy, when the villains spoke English, or at least a Glasgow version of it. Where the knife was the weapon of choice and power was kept in the family. Paddy Brogan's career, he feared, was nearing its end, much like his own.

24

From the back of the chapel Rhona and Magnus could see that, apart from Claire and her daughter, there were only six mourners, and all bar one were over seventy. Claire stood tall and straight at the front, as the pensioners' thin voices trembled through the Twenty-third Psalm.

Beside Rhona, Magnus joined in, providing a strong and confident tenor. At the start of verse two, the child turned to look with interest at who was singing at the back.

As the curtains opened to accept the coffin, Claire clung tightly to her daughter's hand. Then it was over. The others waited as she exited first with Emma, followed by the younger woman. Claire looked tired and distracted as she walked past, but she did acknowledge Rhona's presence with a nod. The one elderly man stood aside to let all the ladies pass, then followed, leaning heavily on a stick.

Rhona and Magnus hung back until the various mourners had paid their respects and headed for their cars. Already the next funeral cortège was winding its way into the chapel.

Rhona approached Claire and introduced herself.

'I know who you are.' Claire's manner was curt, but there was none of the anger Rhona had sensed in the phone call.

Claire turned to Magnus, waiting to be introduced.

'This is Professor Magnus Pirie.'

He offered Claire his hand. For a moment Rhona thought she would refuse to shake it.

'Thank you for allowing me to come,' said Magnus.

Claire nodded stiffly then turned to Emma, who was staring at him in fascination.

'You've got a funny voice.'

Claire made a move to remonstrate with her daughter but Magnus stopped her with a smile.

'I'm from the Orkney Islands. Do you know where they are?'

Emma shook her head.

'You have to drive right to the top of Scotland then take a ferry across the Pentland Firth.'

Claire interrupted him. 'Remember I told you about Dr MacLeod? Well, this is her and this man is a colleague of hers.'

Emma thought about that, her small brow furrowing. 'Where's Michael?'

'He couldn't come today,' replied Rhona.

Disappointment clouded Emma's face, and Claire looked quizzically at Rhona.

'DS McNab sends his apologies,' Rhona lied. She hadn't received the promised phone call this morning and had been unable to reach McNab. When she'd checked with the station she'd been told he and the DI were currently in a meeting. 'He hoped you would look after the professor for him,' she said to Emma.

'Orkney has no trees, so I'm not used to walking in the woods,' Magnus explained.

'That's OK. I'll look after you,' promised Emma.

Claire reached into her handbag and produced a piece of paper. 'Instructions on how to get to Fern Cottage. We're a bit off the beaten track, DS McNab got lost when he came down. Emma will keep you right. I'm going to take Mum's friends to lunch then I'll head home. I should be there by three, but Emma knows where the spare key is.' She gave them a searching look. It was clearly difficult for her to render up her daughter to them like this. 'I spoke to Detective Inspector Wilson this morning. He assured me that Emma is in safe hands.'

'She is,' said Rhona.

Emma seemed unperturbed as her mother gave her a goodbye kiss and urged her to help Dr MacLeod as much as she could. Rhona had the impression the child was revelling in the attention and was not in the least perturbed by what she was being asked to do.

Emma chatted happily to Magnus on the drive out of town, asking him what kind of professor he was and whether he knew how to sail a boat. Magnus described his house in Orkney, where water lapped three sides at high tide, and told her about the sailing dinghy he kept moored at his jetty. They also discussed cats. Magnus told Emma tales of Olaf, the cat that sometimes came to stay, while Emma explained how Toby had decided to be their friend when they'd moved into Fern Cottage.

Rhona joined in with her story of Tom the kitten. Emma listened carefully, then asked her what a forensic scientist was. Rhona explained that she looked for evidence that was mostly invisible to the human eye. Criminals didn't realise this evidence had been left behind.

'Like invisible ink?' Emma asked.

'A bit.' Rhona laughed.

When they pulled in by the side of the road adjacent to the crash site, Emma was first out of the car, her small face lit up with enthusiasm. Rhona fetched her forensic bag and a video camera from the boot.

*   *   *

The sky was heavily overcast, the breeze bitterly chill. They had made a point of coming prepared for the weather, Claire supplying Rhona with a warm coat and floral wellington boots for Emma to cover her more formal funeral wear.

They'd been walking now for ten minutes. Rhona felt as though they were wandering in circles, but Magnus seemed content to let Emma lead while they followed.

This part of the wood was populated with older trees; Scots pines with thickly layered trunks, spindly rowan and birch dotting the areas in between. Directly below the wider-spreading pines, the ground was drier and scattered with needles, their acidic quality making it hard for other plants to take root. In the more sparsely wooded areas, dwarf heather and blaeberry bushes flourished.

They had been moving constantly downhill, aligning themselves with small streams, little more than trickles intent on reaching the valley floor. A few steps ahead of Rhona, Emma and Magnus appeared to be in constant conversation. The child looked animated, her cheeks flushed, her eyes

131

bright.

Her instant friendship with McNab, followed by her rapport with Magnus—two entirely different characters—suggested that Emma did hanker after a father figure in her life. Rhona wondered whether the girl had lost her own father, through death or separation, and was constantly trying to replace him.

McNab had mentioned someone called Nick that the girl had seemed fond of. Nick had apparently taught Emma the art of throwing stones accurately and far, but Emma had stated categorically that Nick was not her father, in much the same way that Claire had told McNab she wasn't married.

Despite the continuing conversation between Magnus and the girl, which Rhona could only partially hear, they hadn't stopped at any particular location, although Emma paused at times to glance about intently. It appeared to Rhona that the pair were walking randomly, looking for some stimulus that might remind Emma of that fateful Sunday night when she'd found the skull. Rhona was beginning to suspect that McNab was right, that Emma was trying to make herself the centre of attention while introducing her mother to possible future partners.

Rhona was so deep in this thought that she didn't notice that the pair had suddenly veered from the downhill path and cut across the hillside. Here the vegetation pattern changed, lush undergrowth replacing trees. The canopy opened and they were looking up at a sky so heavy with moisture that the cloud cover appeared to touch the surrounding treetops. Rhona shivered in the cold damp air.

Magnus and Emma had come to a halt next to a small lochan, little more than seven metres long and six wide. The northern side was a wall of rock, over which a small stream cascaded into the pool below. On the remaining three sides the forest floor dropped abruptly to the water's edge with no evidence of a shoreline.

Rhona joined them beside the dark, deep peaty water. Emma's face was no longer animated, but pale and frightened.

'Are you OK?' she asked the girl.

'In there.' Emma pointed to the water.

Rhona looked to Magnus for guidance.

'What's in there?' he asked.

'The voice I heard.'

'You think there's another body?'

'I heard it that night but Michael wouldn't believe me.'

Rhona put her arm around the girl. 'It's OK, Emma, we believe you.' She glanced at Magnus. *Did they?*

'This is the body in your drawing?' he asked.

'I heard *him* crying when I was here. The drawing's different.'

'How is the drawing different?' asked Rhona gently.

'I drew it before this happened.' Emma's face creased tearfully.

'I think we should walk back now,' Rhona suggested.

Magnus nodded silently above the child's head.

The return to the car took no time at all. In their wandering they had followed a loop. The lochan lay parallel to the road, south-west of the forensic circle they'd drawn round the original remains.

133

Emma walked in silence, her face pinched and white with tiredness, her small hand encased in Magnus's larger one.

Minutes after they got into the car, the child was asleep.

'Out of the mouths of babes and sucklings . . .' Magnus said quietly.

'You believe her?'

'I think you should trawl that lochan.'

'The dogs didn't pick up anything in that area,' Rhona countered.

'If the remains are under water, that's not surprising.'

'You don't think she's making it up?'

'Children tell fewer lies than adults. We choose to forget that.'

Rhona had recorded Emma's reaction at the lochan. It would be up to Bill to decide whether he wanted to take the matter farther.

'The drawing she sent McNab didn't look anything like that place,' she said.

'She claims she drew the picture before this happened.'

'Then why did she send it now?'

Magnus glanced in the back. Emma was sound asleep, her body relaxed, her breathing steady.

'I think maybe something bad happened to Emma. Something that the discovery of the skull brought back. Emma doesn't remember what it was but it haunts her, through her dreams and through her drawings. I'm not sure Claire Watson has told us the whole story.'

*　　　*　　　*

134

Claire was waiting as they drove up the rutted track to the cottage. She greeted them in an upbeat manner, but her quick, searching glance at her daughter showed how worried she really was.

Emma, on the other hand, apparently refreshed by her sleep in the car, shot into the house with barely a backward glance and immediately called for Toby to come out and meet Magnus.

'How did it go?' Claire asked.

'It went well,' replied Magnus.

'Emma found something?'

'She indicated a place we should look,' said Rhona.

'And you believe her?' Claire sounded dismayed.

There was a noise from above, footsteps running over bare floorboards and Emma's voice calling Toby's name.

'Emma's a bright little girl and very perceptive. All her senses are highly developed, especially her hearing. She remembered hearing falling water when she was lost that night. She led us to a small lochan with a waterfall.'

'Are you going to search this place?' Claire asked Rhona.

'I have to run it past the officer in charge, but I will recommend we do.'

By now they were in the sitting room, where a bright fire burned in the hearth. The curtains were shut against the gathering dusk. It should have been a comfortable and safe domestic scene, but Claire looked even more drawn than she had at the funeral. She had obviously wanted the excursion to end her daughter's involvement in the case and was now faced with the opposite outcome.

135

'I hope Emma's not wasting your time,' she said sharply.

'I think you did the right thing in letting her go with us,' Magnus assured her.

Claire didn't look as if she agreed.

'The drawing she sent to DS McNab . . .' Rhona began. Claire's head jerked up, her expression fearful. 'It doesn't match the location she took us to.'

Magnus said, 'Emma's a little confused about this and we didn't question her on it, but I wondered if there was something else troubling her. Something that the discovery of the skull brought back.'

'Of course there is. Her granny just died.' Claire sounded exasperated.

'Emma says she drew the picture before all this happened.'

'What?' Claire's voice had risen in pitch. 'I don't understand.'

'I wondered if there was something traumatic in Emma's past . . .'

'No. Nothing happened that would have made her draw such a horrible picture.' Claire stood up. 'If you don't mind, I'm very tired. It's been a long day and I want to get Emma's tea ready.'

Rhona and Magnus rose to join her.

'Of course,' Rhona said. 'And thank you for letting us speak to Emma.'

They heard the front door being locked behind them as they headed for the car. Glancing back, Rhona spotted Emma's small face peeking between the curtains at an upstairs window.

*   *   *

136

In the gathering dusk, Rhona concentrated on finding her way back to the main road. Beside her, Magnus sat in deep contemplation. As they neared the outskirts of the city, he asked whether she wanted to get something to eat. Rhona readily agreed. Breakfast seemed like a lifetime ago.

'I could fix you something at the flat?' offered Magnus.

Rhona hesitated before answering. She hadn't visited Magnus's place since the Henderson case and wasn't keen on stirring up old memories. Magnus was reading her expression, something he was good at.

'It's OK. We can go to a restaurant.'

Rhona decided to banish her fears. 'No. If you've got food, I'll eat it.'

The flat was just as Rhona remembered; a chess game in play on a low table, large leather armchairs, double doors to the balcony that looked over the river. They had drunk whisky here and played mind games. Magnus had been more confident and assured then, arrogant even. It was the Henderson case and his part in it which had changed him. That role had almost ended his professional career. In the end the authorities hadn't held Magnus culpable, even though Rhona suspected he continued to blame himself.

While Magnus busied himself in the kitchen, Rhona called the police station to be told that neither DS McNab nor DI Wilson was available, so she asked to speak to DC Clark instead. A few minutes later Janice came on the line. Her voice sounded choked, as though she'd been crying.

'What's wrong?'

'The Procurator Fiscal's decided there's enough evidence to proceed against the DI. He's been suspended until the case comes to court.'

'My God.' Rhona's heart plummeted. 'And McNab?'

'He got off with a warning.'

'Is Bill there?'

'They sent him home.'

Once Bill had been charged, the Fiscal would have wanted to remove any possibility of access to case papers and witnesses. Bill would have been told to leave immediately. Rhona could imagine the scene and the reaction of his colleagues. Anger welled up in her. The whole thing was hideous. She contemplated calling Bill at home, then decided to leave it for now. He needed to be with his wife and family. Margaret was his strength. He would need her more than ever now.

'Is McNab there?'

'He went out after the announcement. I don't know where to. You could try his mobile.'

'He's not answering. If he calls in will you get him to phone me?'

'I'll try,' Janice promised.

Rhona snapped her mobile shut and threw it into her bag. She'd been thinking about Magnus's career and all the time Bill's was coming to an end. A conviction for assaulting a prisoner in custody could see him at worst dismissed, at the least dropping a rank and being moved out of CID altogether.

She glanced at her watch. It was after six. McNab could be anywhere and was more than likely drowning his sorrows. She'd smelled whisky on his breath yesterday in the café. He'd been alert and definitely not drunk, but she suspected he was using alcohol to get him through the day.

Magnus came in, carrying cutlery. 'What's happened?' he said when he saw her face.

'They've charged Bill with assault and suspended him.'

He swore under his breath. 'Is there anything we can do?'

'Nothing.'

'But there were mitigating circumstances.'

'They know all about those,' Rhona said bitterly.

'What about McNab?'

There was no love lost between the two men, but you wouldn't have known from Magnus's concerned expression.

'He got off with a warning.'

'What do you want to do?'

Rhona had already accepted there was little she could do. 'I'll keep trying McNab's number. Meanwhile, we eat, if that's OK, then talk about Emma.'

The microwave pinged in the kitchen.

'Not home-made, I'm afraid,' said Magnus ruefully.

Rhona didn't care. She suspected the food would stick in her throat anyway.

They sat together at the table and he produced a bottle of red wine to go with the casserole. 'You can always leave your car here and take a taxi back.'

Suddenly Rhona didn't want to spend the evening alone worrying about Bill and McNab. 'I'll do that.' She gestured to Magnus to fill her glass.

Magnus didn't talk as Rhona made an attempt at the food. It was tastier than she'd anticipated and

139

better than the meals she had in her own freezer.

'Local Italian restaurant,' he told her. 'I ask them to freeze some for me.'

'Beats my supermarket buys.'

Magnus refilled her glass.

'Wine's good too. Let me guess. Italian?' Rhona glanced at the label.

When she'd cleared her plate, Magnus put on coffee and brought through a plate of biscuits and cheese. All very civilised, she thought, realising how much she had missed sitting down to a meal with another human being instead of the cat.

They'd finished the wine, so Magnus brought a bottle of Highland Park and two glasses to the coffee table. Rhona checked her phone one more time before she settled into the armchair. The alcohol had taken the edge off her horror at the news of Bill's suspension. Her usual reaction when something bad happened was to find a way to fight back, and throughout the meal her brain had been doing just that, running endless scenarios where she might yet intervene to help Bill. At the same time she knew that as soon as Bill decided to go down this route there was nothing anyone could do. McNab had made it plain enough that he'd been the one responsible for the assault, and even that hadn't helped.

'Hey.'

Magnus's voice broke into her reverie.

'I'm sorry,' she said.

'There's nothing to be sorry about. Bill's your friend.'

'Yes, he is.'

'What happens now?'

'They'll bring in someone to take over his

140

caseload, including this one.'

'Do you know who?'

'I've got a pretty good idea.'

Detective Inspector Geoffrey Slater had been parachuted in once before. He hadn't endeared himself to DS McNab or the rest of the team then, and was unlikely to do so now, especially in view of McNab's state of mind.

'And I'm not sure he'll be interested in Emma's stories about other bodies.'

'So a replacement DI might not sanction a search of the loch?'

'Time and money on the whim of a kid?'

Magnus looked worried. 'I didn't want to say anything at the time, in front of Emma or her mother, but I got the feeling we weren't the only ones in that part of the wood.'

'I never saw anyone.'

'Neither did I.'

'So?'

'I caught a scent that seemed out of place.'

Magnus's highly developed sense of smell had become legendary during the Henderson case, proving to be both a blessing and a curse.

'It's amenity woodland,' Rhona reminded him. 'It's open to the public.'

'I know.'

'Which means anyone can walk there.'

'But why trail us?'

'You actually think someone was following us?'

'I'm not sure. I think it's a possibility.'

She tried to recall whether she'd had any sense of this. Emma and Magnus had been in the lead, she at the back. Surely if someone had been following them, she would have noticed?

141

'There weren't any cars parked when we came out, or when we arrived,' she said. 'I suppose someone could have entered the woods elsewhere, seen us and followed out of curiosity.'

Magnus didn't look convinced.

'How come we never heard anything?' Rhona asked.

'If they moved when we moved, we wouldn't have heard them.'

They'd made plenty of noise as they walked, plus Magnus and Emma had kept up a running conversation. Rhona herself had been preoccupied with both the video recording and her thoughts.

'I took a video en route,' she said. 'I can check, see if it picked up anything.'

'Yes, do that.'

Rhona, unconvinced, changed the subject. 'What else did you learn from Emma?'

'She told me her father died when she was small. They used to live in Glasgow, but her mum wanted to move to the country.'

'Did she say why?'

'She said her mum feels safe there.'

'Safe from what?'

'That's what she didn't want to tell me. She didn't want to talk about Nick either.'

'Did Emma really remember the loch or did she just come on it by chance?'

'I thought she was just wandering about at first, then she suddenly said she remembered hearing running water.'

'She never told McNab she'd been near water,' mused Rhona.

'She was frightened and probably concussed that night. I don't think she remembered until she began to retrace her steps.'

'Or she made it up when she saw the place.'

'She talked about it before we found it,' said Magnus firmly.

'Did it ever occur to you that Emma visited those woods before the crash?'

'She says she hasn't. They haven't lived in the cottage for very long.'

'This still doesn't explain the drawing.'

'No, it doesn't,' he agreed. 'And I don't think Claire will be keen for us to question Emma again.'

*   *   *

Claire sat alone in the sitting room, staring into the fire. Emma was no longer moving about upstairs. She imagined her daughter sitting on the bed, staring into the darkness. Claire didn't dare go up the stairs. She didn't want to hear that humming noise again. She didn't want to open the bedroom door and find the child like that.

She took refuge in the kitchen, switching on the radio to fill the void of silence. The constant stream of news that dominated the airways between four and six o'clock didn't distract her. She'd hoped that the excursion through the woods would prove to the police that this was all a product of Emma's imagination. Instead the opposite had happened.

She took a pizza out of the freezer and began to unwrap the cellophane, her hands shaking. This had gone far enough, she decided. She would not let her daughter be interviewed again. But what if there was something in that loch in the woods?

143

What if they did find another body?

She slid on to a chair, the partly unwrapped pizza discarded on the table. The crushing pain was back, weighing so heavily on her chest she could barely draw air into her lungs. She fisted her hands, pressing the nails deep into the palms, concentrating solely on the discomfort that brought. The knife she'd used to pierce the cellophane lay discarded on the table near by. She stared at it, willing herself not to reach out. She tried to move her mind to a good place. A place where she'd been happy. She conjured up Emma's tiny face, hours old. The feeling she'd had nursing her child, Dougie, the proud father, by her side. The image brought calm for a few moments.

She rose and walked to the sink. The nail marks on her palms showed up as four crescent moons. She turned on the tap and carefully washed her hands, soaping them well before rinsing. In the background, the forecast promised that the bad weather would return, with blizzards expected over the Christmas period. As if on cue, flakes of wet snow began to hit the darkness of the windowpane, dissolving immediately to trickle their way down the glass.

The police would not disturb them over Christmas, whatever they found in that wood. She turned her attention to the window in her mother's house. Maybe she'd overreacted, fuelled by her underlying fear and her daughter's vivid imagination. Perhaps her mother had had the window replaced without telling her? There had been nothing else in the house to suggest an intruder, she reminded herself. Nothing except Emma's story about the writing on the window,

144

and that didn't prove anything. Even if Nick had gained entry to the bungalow, there was nothing there to point him here, to Fern Cottage. She needed to remain strong and calm for Emma's sake.

Claire dried her hands and drew the curtains.

25

He took refuge in his workshop. He was too agitated for the garden, or the greenhouse. Plants reacted to his anger. It was better to be among inanimate objects.

He closed the workshop door behind him and switched on the light. In here the splintered gleam of broken glass reflected his mood.

He'd been working on a new stained-glass window for the local church. An American benefactor, one of the great diaspora, had offered the money to replace the current painted window, whose picture was fading. It was not the only project on the long two-and-a-half-by-three-metre work table. There was another, but it was his alone. For the paid job he'd merely to follow the design pattern dictated by the benefactor.

He bypassed the American job and went immediately to his newest project—the memorial to the child. He had long since learned how to disguise an image among abstract swirls and contours of coloured glass. It would take an eye as keen as his to discern the flow of white-gold hair, the rosy flush of a child's cheek.

Above the table, wall racks held his store of

twenty-by-twenty-centimetre art glass. In a variety of colours and textures, it had been created by the careful addition of metals and salts; cobalt oxide for blue, green created by chromium oxide, red made ruby by the addition of twenty-two-carat gold, cadmium yellow, sulphurous amber, white arsenic and finally the purple stain of manganese. He loved to think about the essence of the glass before he chose his colour and texture. Even within each sheet the refraction of the glass differed, because of the density of colour.

He gazed lovingly at the work in progress. He had chosen opalescent glass for the girl's hair. The result, he decided, resembled oil flowing on water. It seemed appropriate somehow.

*   *   *

He'd known as soon as he saw the child that he had chosen well. Her hair was just as he'd imagined when he found the hairbrush in her bedroom.

It had been easy to mingle with the funeral party that followed the old woman's ceremony. A disparate group of people from various eras of the deceased's life, they barely knew one another.

He'd hung around the entrance as the group filed in for the service, easily identifying the child, watching her get into a car with a man and a woman. The woman he'd presumed to be her mother, the tall man perhaps the mother's current partner. The male presence had concerned him. Alone, the girl and her mother were vulnerable, but with a man to protect them . . .

He'd followed the car, expecting them to attend

a funeral lunch before going home, but they'd surprised him by driving to the wood.

Why go back there?

He'd learned the truth near the pool. It had been the child who'd desecrated the grave, and she was looking for another.

The knowledge had shocked him more than the memory of that night when the car had hurtled towards him, shattering his peace of mind for ever. It was no longer only the woman he had to fear. The greatest threat now came from her daughter.

Had the man not been with them, he would have finished it there, beside the deep, dark pool.

*   *   *

He selected a piece of ruby-red glass and used the diamond wheel to score it, releasing the rigid surface tension and showering his hands and the surrounding surface with a myriad of invisible fragments.

He fetched some copper foil, stripped off the adhesive backing and wrapped it round the edge of the three small pieces he'd cut. The red droplets would be tricky to solder into place, but he was excited by the prospect.

He brushed the workbench, feeling the sting where minute shards had punctured the skin. He went to the sink and turned on the tap, placing his hands in the flow and watching as the stream of water turned pink with his blood.

The work had calmed him. He could concentrate now on what had to be done. Now that he knew where they lived, it would only be a matter of time before he cleared up the mess.

26

McNab was drunk. Not mean drunk, nor swaying or slurring drunk. The alcohol he'd consumed had made him as brittle as glass, his despair almost tangible.

He had finally returned her call shortly before midnight. Rhona was sitting by the fire in semi-darkness, watching the flickering screen of the television with no desire to go to bed and lie awake.

She had suggested he come round, preferring to know where he was tonight. In his state of mind she feared what might happen, and at least here he could sober up before he had to face his colleagues tomorrow.

When she opened the door, her first instinct was to embrace him. Only then did Rhona acknowledge how truly worried she had been.

'Dr MacLeod. You haven't done that for a long time.'

She drew back to find him observing her with just a hint of the old cynicism.

'You're drunk.'

'No, but I plan to be very soon.'

She led him into the sitting room. He sat down on the sofa and pulled out a half-bottle. When Rhona attempted to suggest he'd had enough, McNab held up his hand to silence her.

'Michael,' she said gently.

He looked surprised, then smiled a slow smile. 'I like it when you call me that.'

Rhona held her tongue.

He took a deep swallow. 'They've suspended him. I got a fucking warning and they suspended my boss. And there's fuck all I can do about it.'

'You can give evidence in court. They'll call you as a witness. You can tell them what really happened.'

McNab wasn't listening. 'I phoned *Ms* Morris. Stupid bitch told me to leave it to the disciplinary inquiry.'

'She was only doing her job.'

'Only *doing* her job! If Henderson got half a chance he would do Ms Morris like he *did* the others. And she's defending the bastard.'

'Not defending, representing.'

'Would you defend him, after the way he assaulted you?' McNab's look seemed to go right through Rhona. He was no fool. He knew what had happened to her didn't come without repercussions.

'I'm fine,' she lied.

He gave her a twisted smile, his expression one of disbelief. 'Like hell you are.'

He rose and faced her square-on. His green eyes were glittering in anger, his skin pale behind the auburn stubble. He smelt of adrenalin and whisky and male sweat. He searched her face.

'Let me guess. You can still smell the bastard. I bet you shower all the time just to get rid of his stink.'

Rhona felt the blood drain from her face.

McNab wasn't finished. 'You haven't been with a man since he got to you, right? That's why you and the Irishman are over?'

Rhona's anger rose to meet his. How dare he come here and tell her what she felt? How dare he remind her how dirty and violated and frightened she still was?

'That's none of your business.' If her hands hadn't been so tightly clenched she would have hit him.

Suddenly he registered her distress, and lifted his hand as though to touch her face. When she flinched, his own face creased in pain. 'I'm sorry. I should never have left you that day. I should have known.'

'So what happened was *your* fault?' she railed. 'Lisa was *your* fault. Bill was *your* fault. What about Magnus? Was what happened to Magnus *your* fault too?'

'Fuck, no! That was all his own fault!'

There was a moment's silence as they both digested his reply. He placed his hand on her arm, tentative and reassuring. Rhona didn't step away this time.

'I'm sorry for what happened between us. I wanted to control you. It was wrong.'

She said nothing.

'I hope you'll forgive me.'

'I already have.'

McNab lightly touched the top of her head with his lips and made to move away. She stopped him.

'You were right. I do smell him.'

He pulled her against him, wrapping his arms tightly about her. It was something Sean had never done. He had never asked her what had happened. He had never listened to her fear. His first thought had been revenge. Sean had barely been able to bring himself to look at her, so desperate was he to find someone to blame. McNab was a cynical bastard, but he understood that night and what it

150

had truly meant to her.

They stood like that for several minutes. Rhona knew he would let her go as soon as she attempted to draw away, but she didn't want to. She wanted to be held like this. She wanted to feel safe, if only for a few moments.

It was she who raised her face and kissed him. It felt natural. A way of laying ghosts to rest. A way to survive the night. McNab looked perturbed.

'You're sure about this?'

'We both need company tonight.' It was the understatement of the century.

He examined her closely. For a moment she thought he would turn her down.

Later, she would remember his touch as both familiar and new. In the past their coupling had been a competitive game, where both strove to win. Tonight was different. McNab knew what she feared most, and he did his best to replace those memories with something better.

When Rhona woke early next morning, he was gone. She reached out and touched the warm place where he'd lain and knew it hadn't been a dream.

27

Chrissy separated the three pieces of paper and laid them out on the table.

'You're sure they're significant?'

'Come on,' said McNab. 'A Glasgow gang boss calls me to his gambling club and hands me a licence in full view of his Russian bodyguard and it's not significant? Call mc dumb. Call me George Double-Ya Bush. But I think he was trying to tell me something.'

'This guy's a poker player?'

'The best. Maybe even better than his father, *the* Poker Billy.'

Chrissy regarded McNab blankly.

'Paddy Brogan is good,' he said. 'Maybe even better than his father.'

'Mmmm.' She studied the papers again. 'I can't see anything unusual.'

'There's got to be something,' he insisted.

'OK. There are a few italicised and emboldened words, but they look OK in context. I thought there might be a poker pattern in there somewhere, but I can't see any. Does Paddy Brogan cheat?'

McNab gave her a look that spoke volumes. 'All poker players cheat. You know that.'

Chrissy stared at him thoughtfully for a moment. He could almost hear the wheels turning.

'I've got an idea,' she said.

'What?'

She produced a small forensic torch and began running the powerful beam along the back of the first sheet of paper.

Her face lit up. 'Bingo.' She motioned McNab across.

At first he saw nothing, then he gradually became aware that a selection of words appeared marginally brighter than the others.

'The paper's been pierced in places with a pin, similar to the marked cards we found in the skip,' said Chrissy. 'The puncture holes are invisible to the naked eye. Mr Brogan must have known you

152

were a cheat.'

McNab was impressed. 'Well done.'

She wrote down the marked words in the order they appeared.

Such opening licence opening need keep inside lower late exact reason

'They don't make any sense,' he said, disappointed.

'Maybe there's a pattern in the letters?' she suggested. 'Like a flush or four of a kind?'

McNab regarded her with male-poker-player superiority.

'Don't look at me like that. You brought this stuff to me, remember?' Chrissy pondered for a moment. 'Maybe we need to extract letters from the words to fit one of the patterns?' She studied the word list again. 'Let's start simple and just take the first letter of each of the punctured words.'

She presented McNab with the result.

He misread it at first. 'Salon Killer? Somebody's murdering hairdressers?'

'How come you're so cheery?' She gave him a searching look, which he avoided. She corrected him. 'It says *solonkiller*.'

'Solonkiller?' McNab was mystified. He tried pronouncing the word in a variety of ways, then whistled through his teeth as it dawned on him. 'Brogan's minder was called Solonik.'

'Was he, now?'

If the Russians were muscling in on Glasgow gambling, the Poker Club would be high on their list. McNab had gained the distinct impression that Brogan didn't like having the Russian around. Maybe he had good reason.

'The guy in the skip ate a Russian meal before he

153

died,' Chrissy reminded him. '*And* he had a deck of cards marked like this in his pocket.'

'You think Brogan's trying to set up Solonik for the skip murder?' McNab remembered the Russian's huge hands, easily powerful enough to snap a man's neck.

'Maybe Brogan just wants him off his back?'

'Anything in the skip that might link Solonik to the fire?'

'Apart from skull fragments and bits of brain, you mean?'

McNab grimaced. 'God, I couldn't do your job.'

'No, you couldn't,' agreed Chrissy.

He decided they had gone as far as they could on this subject. 'Your boss about?' He used what he hoped was a neutral tone. If he could fool Chrissy, he could fool anyone.

'She's in the back lab working on the brushwood from the deposition site.'

'I wondered how she'd got on with the kid?' When lying you should use as much of the truth as possible, an established rule for policeman and criminal alike. It seemed to work.

'She wants to talk to you about that. Seems like the girl identified a possible second location.'

McNab frowned. Rhona hadn't mentioned that last night. True, there had been little opportunity, between arguing and . . . other things.

Chrissy was grinning at him and for a brief moment he thought Rhona might have told her what had happened, then it dawned that Chrissy just liked to be seen to know more than him.

'*And,*' she continued in a dramatic tone, 'Magnus thought they were being followed when they were in the woods.'

154

'He saw someone?'

She tapped her nose with her index finger. 'Apparently he could smell them.'

McNab's heart sank. He didn't want to be reminded of Magnus or his legendary sense of smell. He forbore saying what he was thinking, that the Orcadian professor of psychology was a nutter.

'If you're going in, you'll have to kit up,' Chrissy told him.

*   *   *

Rhona was encased in white, a pale blue mask covering her lower face. She didn't hear his entrance, so absorbed was she in what she was doing. McNab stood silently for a moment, just enjoying watching her work.

He had never imagined for a moment that he would be invited back into Rhona MacLeod's bed. What had happened last night was little short of a miracle, a one-off that would never recur if he messed up in the next few moments. McNab thanked God for the anonymity of the forensic suit.

Rhona looked up and registered his presence. Their eyes met briefly. McNab smiled behind the mask and wondered whether it was visible.

'Hey,' he mumbled, for want of something better.

'Chrissy told you about Emma?'

'She said the girl identified another location.'

McNab was trying to read the expression in Rhona's eyes without appearing to do so. He suspected if Magnus had been in the room, he would have known the truth about them in seconds.

'It never happened,' she said calmly.

'Whatever you want.'

He thought she looked surprised, but she talked on as though the interchange had never occurred.

'Emma led us to a small loch in the north-west corner of the woods, almost parallel to the road. I think we should take a look at it.'

'You mean send in divers?'

She nodded. 'Also, Magnus thought someone followed us there. I saw and heard nothing, but he believes he could smell them.'

McNab concentrated on keeping his eyebrows horizontal.

'He called me a short while ago to say he'd checked his recall against a number of substances and thinks he knows what it was he picked up. Linseed oil is used in cementing stained-glass windows. The wet part of the mix is fifty per cent boiled linseed oil and fifty per cent raw linseed oil. Apparently the smell lingers for hours even after you wash your hands.' She then answered McNab's question before he could pose it. 'Magnus knows nothing about the glass fragments I unearthed at the deposition site.'

McNab didn't want Magnus Pirie to be part of this investigation. In fact he rued the day he'd suggested using a psychologist in the strategy meeting.

Rhona was studying his reaction, well aware of his antagonism towards Pirie. 'Claire says she swerved to avoid a man on the road that night. You said yourself you thought he must have been looking back at the site. Why would he do that?'

It was the question he had asked himself when he reviewed the R2S recording. He had no answer then and he didn't have one now. He had planned to run the whole scenario past the boss. If the DI had given credence to the man's existence and the possibility he was linked with the crime, then the case would no longer be cold but current, which upped the manpower and time.

Rhona appeared to be reading his mind. 'Any word who's taking over from Bill?'

'I left before the news broke.'

'Maybe you'd better find out.'

*   *   *

Rhona watched McNab leave the lab to make the call. It was OK, she told herself. It would never happen again and they would never mention it. But that didn't mean it hadn't been the right thing to do in the circumstances. She tried to ignore the nagging thought that McNab would not give up. She didn't want to return to the bad times when he'd refused to acknowledge the end of their relationship, thinking it deeper than it was. Bill had been the one to recognise the problem between them and had solved it by removing McNab from the scene until he saw things more clearly. Rhona didn't like to think what Bill would have made of her actions last night.

She dismissed McNab from her mind and returned to studying the debris from the wood. She could never be wholly certain, but by now she could make an estimate of how long the material had lain over the corpse. The management of woodland didn't require tree thinning every year, but she knew when the work had begun. Coupled with her botanical results, this suggested that the vegetation cover had been built up over a period of six to eight years.

Rhona took another look at the preliminary report from forensic anthropology. Digital facial construction had provided an image of a pretty child with delicate features, not obviously male or female. A study of the skeletised remains had come up with an approximate height. Taken together with the mix of baby and adult teeth and the relative fusion of the epiphyses, an age range of between five and ten years had been estimated.

'I've called her Samantha . . .' said Professor Esther Bowman's notes, 'although I haven't yet proven conclusively that she is a girl. I suppose we could always change it to Samuel, if I'm wrong.'

By putting flesh on the bones and giving her a name, the anthropologist had brought Samantha to life. Rhona's work had established when the child had died. Now they had to discover how she died and by whose hand.

28

'You messed up, Sergeant. That's why I'm here.'

DI Geoffrey Slater swivelled round on the leather chair until he and McNab were eye to eye. Slater hadn't changed much. He was still overweight and still a piss artist. Neither of these attributes irritated McNab half as much as seeing Slater commandeer the boss's beloved chair.

'Assaulting a suspect. Who would have thought

that of Wilson.' Slater shook his head.

'The DI didn't assault Henderson, *sir*, I did.'

'Not how the Fiscal sees it.'

'The Fiscal's wrong, *sir*.'

'Are you saying that DI Wilson is planning to commit perjury, *Sergeant*?'

McNab bit back a retort.

The replacement DI regarded him for a few moments.

'Until such time as DI Wilson is proved guilty or not guilty, I'm in charge. I suggest you call the team together so we can all get better acquainted.'

'Yes, sir.' McNab didn't emphasise the *sir* this time. They were done playing that game.

McNab left the room, his jawbone so tight he thought he heard it crack. Of all the DIs they might have had foisted upon them, it had to be Slater.

Janice looked up as he emerged from the office. The tension in the incident room was palpable. Those who knew Slater knew why; the others were just soaking up the atmosphere.

McNab and Slater had been partners at detective constable level, although Slater didn't believe in teamwork. He believed in always taking the credit, deservedly or otherwise, and in getting results whatever it took. If someone had to be the fall guy to achieve that, so be it. More than once McNab had been that fall guy. That's why he was a detective sergeant and Slater was an inspector.

*　　　*　　　*

'OK, I want to concentrate our resources on the skip murder. We know the Russian mafia has

Glasgow on its list. Gambling, prostitution using eastern European women, racketeering and, more recently, gun smuggling. I understand forensic reports suggest the victim probably ate in the Russian Restaurant prior to his death. Who's following that up?'

A few heads turned towards McNab.

'Sergeant?'

'I was on my way there when I got a call . . .' He didn't get a chance to explain before Slater cut him off.

'Get back there. Find out who the dead guy was.'

McNab smothered a reply. That was DI Slater's way. Don't listen, just give orders.

Slater continued. 'Until recently Prokhorov, who we believe runs the British arm of vory v zakone, the Russian equivalent of the Mafia, was London based. But now he appears to have developed a liking for the Dear Green Place. I think he's moving in and your skip death is linked to the takeover. Similar incidents have been reported in Birmingham, Manchester and Nottingham.'

He brought up a photo on the overhead screen of a dark-haired, handsome man who looked to be in his thirties, dressed in a suit and a smart dark overcoat. 'We don't have a picture of Prokhorov, man of mystery, but we think this is his deputy, Nikolai Kalinin. Kalinin's father is Russian, his mother English. We're pretty sure he's been on Scottish soil for some time, having been sent as Prokhorov's advance guard. If we can link our skip murder to either of these two men, our London colleagues will be *very* happy. OK, let's get on with it.'

'What about the woods case?' McNab called out,

halting the mass exodus.

Slater shot him a look. 'What about it?'

McNab cleared his throat. He would rather have discussed this in a proper strategy meeting, but it didn't look as though there was going to be one.

'Dr MacLeod . . .' he began.

'Who?'

'Forensic Services.'

Slater nodded.

'Dr MacLeod took the girl who discovered the skull, Emma Watson, back to the wood.'

'Why?'

McNab knew Slater was trying to make him look foolish. He also realised that what he was about to say could only reinforce that impression. He said it anyway.

'The girl thinks there's another body near by.'

The DI looked bemused. 'Is she *forensic* too?'

'No . . . she's psychic.'

McNab could have drowned in the ensuing silence as his colleagues tried to work out what the hell he was up to. They were all aware of the search for the kid after the crash, and some of them had been in the woods when she was discovered sitting under the tree, nursing the skull. But no one knew about the drawing she'd sent to McNab, bar Rhona and Magnus. He suspected most of his colleagues would dismiss the drawing out of hand as the work of a kid's vivid imagination and desire to be the centre of attention, and he would have preferred to do the same. But here he was, about to defend the girl's fanciful ideas.

'You're not serious, Sergeant?'

McNab took a deep breath and dug his grave deeper. 'Emma told me that the skull called to her

161

and that's how she found it. She also insisted she'd heard a second voice and thought there was another body.' He rushed on before a bemused Slater could intervene. 'DI Wilson agreed to have a psychologist talk to Emma, so Professor Magnus Pirie accompanied Dr MacLeod on her trip to the deposition site. Emma indicated a small loch as being the source of the second voice. I suggest we get a couple of divers to take a look.'

Slater was trying to keep a straight face.

'You want me to send in divers?'

'I think we should check out the loch.'

'Have the original remains been identified?'

'Not yet.'

'Then let's concentrate on doing that before we spend manpower and resources on a disturbed kid's ramblings.'

McNab wasn't ready to give up. As well as digging his own grave, he seemed intent on suicide. 'There's something else, sir.'

Less amused now, Slater was waiting in simmering silence for McNab to continue.

'Professor Pirie believes they were followed when in the woods.' McNab couldn't believe he was about to champion Magnus.

'This professor saw someone?'

'Professor Pirie has a powerful sense of smell. He says he could smell him.'

The silence in the room was now as heavy as the soil about to be heaped on McNab's grave.

Slater's voice dripped ice. 'That's enough, Sergeant.'

'Sir . . .'

'I said that is enough.'

Slater turned on his heel and walked out. McNab

stood alone as the rest of the team shuffled past. None of them could meet his eye. Only Janice hung back. She waited until the room emptied before she spoke.

'Is what you said about the girl true?'

McNab gave her a wry smile. He and Janice had had a brief relationship a year before. He liked her and would have stayed around longer if she'd let him, but she'd seen the light. Fortunately neither of them held a grudge.

'Have you ever known me to lie?'

'You weren't just winding Slater up?'

'You know he's ditching the woods case so he can look good chasing the Russian mafia. The boss thought the girl's story might be important, so I followed it up.'

'And is it?'

McNab produced a copy of Emma's drawing, and was reminded of its power by Janice's reaction.

'This is what she thinks is in the wood?'

'That's why Rhona went back there with her, in case Emma had seen something when she was lost that's bothering her now. That's when the professor thinks they were followed.'

'It's open to the public, isn't it?'

'Yes, it is.' McNab was fed up hearing that mantra. He'd used it himself. 'Pirie says he smelt linseed oil. A bit like the smell of putty, only stronger.' He explained about the stained-glass fragment in the grave soil and its connection with linseed. 'Slater didn't give me a chance to tell him that.'

'You could have started with that rather than the psychic bit,' she suggested.

163

McNab ignored the well-deserved reprimand. 'On the night of the crash, if the man on the road was standing as Claire Watson described, he was facing the woods in an almost direct line of sight to the locus of crime.'

Putting it all into words for Janice gave it more credence somehow. That was what he had wanted to do with the boss: run it past him, warts and all. DI Wilson would not have interrupted or been sarcastic, he would have listened and weighed it up as a detective inspector should.

'What d'you think?' he said.

'I think DI Wilson would have sent in a couple of divers.'

'So do I.'

Janice gave him a searching look. 'What do you plan to do?'

'I'm going to do the same.'

29

Emma was asleep, her breathing hushed. The album lay open on the bed. Claire lifted it and went to shut the curtains. A light fall of snow had dressed the fields in a pearly-white sheen under a three-quarters moon. She stood for a moment, breathing in the peace of the place. This was why she'd come here, and despite everything that had happened in the past week she didn't regret the move.

Claire wished she could save this moment for ever, bring it back in all its intensity when she needed it most. She closed her eyes and focused on remembering all aspects of it; moonlight on snow, the inky blue of the sky, the soft delicate light in the room, the sound of Emma's quiet, untroubled breath and the scent of warm-washed child, hair still damp from the bath.

She shut the door quietly behind her and went downstairs, taking the album with her. In the sitting room the fire had settled to a steady glow. This was the time Claire liked best, when the day had drawn to a close and she could sit alone, knowing Emma was safely asleep upstairs. Knowing she would not spend the evening listening for a car, for the sound of Nick's key turning in the lock. She no longer had to dread that look on his face.

She sat beside the fire and opened the album. The inscription on the front page read, *To Emma, darling grandchild, from Granny. Here is your story.*

The album was divided into three parts. Three generations of women told in pictures and words. Claire leafed through the section devoted to Emma first. It was a strange thing to experience your daughter's life through your own mother's eyes. Claire was both moved and surprised, as she discovered little references and comments her mother and Emma had obviously shared which she hadn't been party to. Claire thought back to that night in the car when Emma had asked whether Granny would die and she, caught up in her own worries, had answered sharply. Tears pricked at her eyes.

Claire flipped forward a few pages to find a photograph of herself held in her mother's arms. Beneath was the inscription *Claire 6 months*. She registered the strong resemblance between the

165

baby she had been and her own daughter at the same age. A later photo showed her sitting on a bed, totally absorbed in a book, a pile of others beside her, much like Emma. It was the words written below which startled Claire. *Your mum would hum to herself, especially if she was concentrating hard or worrying about something.*

Claire had no recollection of doing that, yet there it was in black and white. It comforted her somehow. How she'd hated hearing that sound coming from Emma's room, seeing her blank-eyed absorption. Yet apparently she had done the same herself.

Claire skimmed through a few more pages, seeing herself grow taller, more gangly, awkward and shy. Then a photograph with Dougie when her pregnancy was just showing. If Dougie had lived, how different things would have been. *If.* How often had she played that game, imagining scenes from their life together, playing them endlessly in her head. The *what if* scenario had ceased when she'd met Nick, for a short while at least.

Claire went through the remaining pages dedicated to her. There was nothing there about Nick. No photographs, no comments. Well, there wouldn't be, would there? She'd kept the relationship from her mother, using a babysitter rather than ask her to look after Emma. It had started so well. Nick had been attentive and kind, had not seemed remotely put off by the existence of a young daughter. When they did meet, Emma had taken to him right away, and there had even been times when Claire resented the camaraderie between her daughter and her lover. That was what had made it so difficult when Claire began to

166

realise who and what Nick really was.

As her mind moved among those painful memories, Claire registered the familiar trembling of her left hand. She released the pressure of her thumb against the paper. When that didn't help, she laid down the album and clasped her hands together to steady them.

She was seated like this when she first heard it. The muffled crunch of a footfall on freshly fallen snow. She sat perfectly still, her ears straining to listen, hoping it had only been her imagination. The fire shifted, breaking the silence as a half-consumed log dropped into its bed of ash. On the mantelpiece the clock ticked on, its steady sound suddenly deafening in her self-imposed quiet.

Then she heard it again.

Claire rose with a strangled cry, her hand moving quickly to cover her mouth. She must not scream and wake Emma. It would be a roe deer foraging in the garden. She had spotted one only days before watching the house from a nearby cluster of trees. The farmer had warned her that the garden and its plants were regarded as free grazing for deer and rabbits alike. It must be a deer.

Claire knew she had to look out, if only to set her mind at ease. She made her way to the window and abruptly pulled back one curtain. She could see nothing at first, fear blinding her, then the smooth whiteness of the snowy garden came into focus, the distant shadow of the familiar grove of trees, the dark ribbon of the drive weaving away from the house. There were no lights, near by or distant. There was no one there.

She took a deep breath and allowed the curtain to fall back into place. This is what happened when you were used to the constant noise of a city. Every small sound set your nerves on edge. She returned to her seat by the fire. She would turn on the television to fill the emptiness and prevent her from listening too hard.

As she reached for the remote, her mobile rang, playing some bright musical tone that Emma had downloaded for her. When Claire glanced at the screen, the number and identity had been withheld. She hesitated then answered.

'Hello?'

The connection crackled, distorting the voice. 'Claire?'

'Who is this?' The irritating sound shut off abruptly as the line went dead. She closed the phone and set it down on a nearby table. She sat for a moment trying to marshal her thoughts. She didn't recognise the voice, but whoever it was knew her name. Could it have been Nick? But how could he have found out her new number?

For a moment Claire was gripped by terror. Nick had tracked her down. His voice was so loud in her head that she turned, expecting to see him already in the room. She was paralysed with fear, just as she had been many times before. Then, his violent words had grown honeyed and persuasive, the strength in his arms manipulating her into whatever position he desired.

She bent her head to her knees, covering it with her arms, and blanked her mind. Eventually the sounds in the room reasserted themselves; the comforting murmur of the fire, the ticking clock. When the mobile rang again she checked the screen and recognised DS McNab's number. She answered immediately.

'Claire?'

'Yes.'

'It's Detective Sergeant McNab. Are you OK?'

Claire attempted to lift her tone. 'I'm fine.' Her pleasure at hearing his voice was now tempered with worry about what the call might mean. 'What's wrong?'

He took a moment to answer. 'I wondered if it would be OK to come down and visit you and Emma tomorrow.'

'If it's about the loch . . .'

'It isn't. I just wanted to drop off a small Christmas present for Emma.'

Claire found herself at a loss for words.

'If it's not convenient I understand.'

She felt ashamed of her reaction. DS McNab had been kind to them, especially to Emma. It wasn't his fault that her daughter made up stories to get attention.

'I'm sorry. Of course you can come.' She hesitated for a moment. 'But I don't want you to ask Emma any more questions.'

'I won't. What time would suit you best?'

'About two?' she suggested.

'Two o'clock it is.'

Claire stopped him before he rang off. 'What's going to happen about the loch?'

'We're going to send a couple of divers to take a look.'

'Are you going to tell Emma that?'

'Not if you don't want me to.'

'I don't, but, knowing Emma, she'll ask. Only tell her if you have to.'

'That's probably the best way.'

He sounded relieved.

Claire got the impression he didn't want to lie to the girl and she respected him for that. She went through to the kitchen. Her adrenalin rush had dissipated, leaving her weak and tired. She began making tea, resisting the desire to have a glass of wine instead. Alcohol only made sleep more difficult and the thoughts she could bear in the waking day she couldn't survive in the long dark hours of the night.

The snow was now on in earnest, big flakes fluttering past the window to settle on the earlier fall. Emma would love this when she woke up in the morning. They had discovered a sledge in the shed, left behind by a previous occupant. It might be deep enough for sledging tomorrow.

Through the open door to the sitting room Claire caught sight of the twinkling lights of the Christmas tree. At the top was an angel Emma had made from cardboard and a paper doily she'd found in a kitchen drawer. The wings were painted gold, a piece of golden tinsel round its head as a halo. Emma had drawn a big smile on the angel's face with a red crayon. Claire smiled back at her daughter's handiwork. Suddenly DS McNab's visit didn't seem so worrying. Maybe they could spend the time together outside in the snow.

She took her tea to bed with her, checking front and back doors were locked before she climbed the stairs.

30

'Mollie Curtis, a ten-year-old from Manchester, came to stay with her gran in Glasgow in the summer of 2000,' Rhona told McNab. 'She disappeared on fifth August from outside the woman's front door. The next-door neighbour was called Colin McCarthy, and a search of his home discovered Mollie's signet ring. His jeans, stuffed in the washing machine but not yet washed, had traces of Mollie's blood and his semen. Under questioning he admitted to killing the girl but couldn't—or wouldn't—say where he'd concealed the body. McCarthy's IQ is very low; he had behavioural difficulties as a child and the psychologist reported him as "easily led". He began denying the murder by the time it reached court, but the circumstantial evidence plus the original confession stood and he was convicted of manslaughter. There was some talk of mental illness but in the end he was sent to prison and not a psychiatric hospital.'

'And you think the remains in the wood might be Mollie's?' he replied.

'I do.'

She showed him the facial reconstruction on the computer screen next to a photograph of the missing girl. There was a strong similarity.

'According to the database entry Mollie's hair was short like this when she disappeared.'

'She looks a bit boyish,' observed McNab.

'At that age the skeleton's pretty much the same.'

'What about the teeth?'

'That's where it gets really interesting.'

Rhona produced a plastic evidence bag. Inside was a thin, curved metal wire. 'Worm action had filtered this deeper into the soil. Mollie wore a brace on her teeth, just like this one.'

'So it could be her, but you're not sure?'

'Mitochondrial DNA testing won't tell us it's definitely Mollie, but it would establish matrilineage.'

'So we need to locate the DNA of the mother or grandmother of Mollie Curtis?'

'Yes.'

'I'll take a look at the case file and set up a visit with McCarthy. See what he has to say,' said McNab.

'Find out if he's had any connection with stained glass.'

Now that the immediate shop talk was over they lapsed into silence. Rhona filled it with an enquiry about Bill. 'I tried calling the house but there's no answer.'

'He took Margaret and the kids away for Christmas. Orkney, Janice said.' At the mention of his boss's name, McNab looked gloomy again.

Bill had spoken about his holidays in Stromness when they'd first met Magnus. 'It'll be good for him to get away,' Rhona said.

McNab scowled. Rhona wished she hadn't brought up the subject, but he had seemed the obvious one to ask where Bill was.

'What about the loch?'

'Slater's not interested. Orders were to find out who the victim was first.'

She had already heard the story of McNab's 'psychic' performance in front of Slater. News like that travelled fast, especially with Chrissy as resident bush telegraph.

'I heard you were planning to send in an underwater team anyway?'

He shot her a look.

'Janice told Chrissy.'

He shrugged.

'I'm headed there now. I'm planning to call on Emma once the team's in place.'

'Is that wise?'

'I've got her a Christmas present.'

'Really?'

'If we find something, we'll need to go back to the kid. Better to keep the mother sweet.'

'A talent of yours, keeping women sweet.' The retort was delivered with more sarcasm than Rhona intended.

McNab turned abruptly away.

'Sorry, that was unnecessary,' she said.

'Forget it.'

Rhona quickly changed tack.

'Any luck with identifying the skip victim?'

'I'm working on it.'

'Have you spoken to Misha?'

'I was sidetracked by a visit to the Poker Club.'

Rhona realised he was being particularly obtuse to get back at her, which she probably deserved.

'Are you going to tell me why?'

'No, Chrissy's dealing with it.'

'She's not here.'

'Then I'll come back tomorrow.'

There was a moment's stand-off, then Rhona said, 'We can't do this.'

'Do what?'

'Act this way.'

'You started it.'

It was true, she had. 'I said I was sorry.'

'And I said forget it.'

Rhona caught the scent of whisky on his breath. This thing with Bill was really eating at him. He didn't need her on his back as well. McNab had responded when she needed him and she owed him.

'Last night—it helped.'

The cloud lifted from McNab's face.

'That's good to know.'

31

He visited McCarthy as normal on Saturday morning. The weather was sharp and cold, the northern sky threatening more snow. The prison, although fairly new, looked as bleak and forbidding as its Victorian predecessor—a construction of small windows, small cells and suffocated lives.

Each visit there had reinforced his belief that only the stupid and ignorant got caught and put away. McCarthy was a perfect example. Ignorant, worse than stupid. The man had an IQ of a child and should have been in a mental asylum, not a prison.

He went through the rigmarole at the entrance. His mobile taken away, the body search, filling in forms. He passed the time reminding himself that he would never be in here other than by choice, and observing the officers with carefully disguised contempt.

On other occasions, when the searches had been heavier than usual, he'd delighted in slicing the thick neck of a prison officer with broken glass. All in his imagination of course, yet sweetly erotic all the same. There was only one prison officer, quite new, quite nervous and ridiculously youthful, that he did look forward to seeing on his visits.

He was the one to show McCarthy into the small visiting room with its half-dozen tables. They were the only ones present. As a trusted prison visitor who was seen to placate McCarthy, thus making him easier to deal with, he was often rewarded with privacy.

McCarthy's face was a pasty yellow. Like putty, he thought, and smiled. McCarthy wasn't used to smiles and reacted with involuntary mimicry, revealing plaque-rimmed teeth and reddened gums.

They made the usual small talk. McCarthy told him that he'd been sexually assaulted in the showers but had managed to avoid all-out rape. It was a story he'd told before. Then he talked about a recent posting to kitchen duty. That this man should handle food turned the visitor's stomach. He thought once again how much kinder it would have been to hang McCarthy. It would have spared them both a lot of grief. He murmured half-heartedly, giving the impression that he actually cared, until McCarthy's final announcement sent his nerves jangling.

The prisoner leaned towards him, his mean little eyes shining self-importantly. 'The police want to question me.'

He kept a hold on his emotions and asked why.

'They found a kid's body in a wood.' The idiot

beamcd as though he'd announced a lottery win.

He gripped his hands tightly below the table, his brain full of the sound of shattering glass.

'They think it's the one they said I killed.'

'And is it?' he heard himself say.

McCarthy's face resembled a broken doll's. For a moment it seemed he might cry. 'I never killed no one. You know that.'

The visitor nodded reassuringly.

'Maybe they know that, now that they've found her,' McCarthy offered.

'What do you mean?'

A dribble of saliva ran from the corner of the prisoner's mouth. 'Evidence,' he said. 'Trace evidence. Like in those TV programmes.' He said it as though he knew what he was talking about.

The man gave McCarthy an encouraging smile. 'That would be a turn-up for the books.'

'They'll find the real killer and I'll be freed. I can come and visit you.' McCarthy's teeth were on show again, plaque and all.

He glanced at his watch, signalling his time was almost up. McCarthy looked disappointed, obviously wanting to talk more about his early release.

'What about the other one?'

'What other one?' McCarthy's eyes narrowed.

'The one you told me about.'

McCarthy's face crumpled again, his mouth a cartoonist's jagged line.

'I never did.'

He shook his head lightly, smiling as though McCarthy had just indulged in a white lie. He leaned slightly forward and looked directly into his face. 'I remember. A little boy, wasn't it? You

176

picked him up in Sunderland. He was playing on the pavement outside his house.'

McCarthy's face flushed red. 'I never said that.'

He smiled a slow, sad smile. 'I think you did.'

McCarthy looked puzzled. 'You won't tell them, will you?'

'Of course not.'

They offered him a cup of tea afterwards. He would have preferred something stronger after McCarthy's revelations, but accepted anyway. The young guard he'd fantasised about arrived carrying a mug and a plate with a chocolate biscuit on it.

'McCarthy told you about the proposed visit from CID?'

He merely nodded.

'He doesn't seem like the type to murder kids.'

'People are rarely what they seem.'

'That's true.'

The young guy gave him a look that could be read as flirtatious.

'I understand you work in stained glass?'

He nodded again.

'I studied art at college, dropped out and ended up here.' The guard rolled his eyes as though he couldn't believe his bad luck and smiled conspiratorially.

He raised the mug to his lips and caught the faint scent of linseed oil on his hands. He'd been working on the window first thing, setting in the ruby droplets.

'Are you interested in glass work?'

'I did a little at college. I didn't like cutting the glass, but I liked the creative aspect.'

He examined the boy's face with its smooth, childlike skin. The young guy hardly looked old

177

enough to shave but he was too old for his liking. Nevertheless, he fetched out his card. 'Give me a call if you'd like a look at my workshop.'

Outside, the large gate clanging shut behind him, he questioned his actions. Now was not the time. Yet . . . why not? The mess would soon be cleared up, and he liked the idea of having a disciple to admire his work.

32

McNab was almost an hour late arriving at the cottage.

It had taken longer than he'd expected to organise the divers at the loch. He'd found the location using Rhona's GPS reading and had had a look round while the team got kitted up, then left DC Clark in charge. He and Janice had made a joint decision to pursue this line of enquiry together, using Rhona's identification of the remains as an excuse.

In the wood, a couple of inches of overnight snow had weighed down the branches of the pines. Underfoot the snow had been crisp and white, in contrast to the grey slush of Glasgow. The loch itself had been covered by a thin coating of ice, but not enough to worry the divers. McNab had left them to it, promising to be back within a couple of hours. Janice knew where he was heading. He got the impression she would have liked to meet the kid who was the cause of all of this.

He found his way to Fern Cottage without getting lost this time. The track to the front door was tricky to negotiate without four-wheel drive, and he swerved and slithered on the frozen snow before pulling up outside. No one was at the door to greet him.

McNab decided to turn the car while he still had momentum in the snow. He also wanted a bit of extra time to compose himself. He was slightly nervous about the meeting, mostly because of his present. He had no idea what you should buy for a nine-year-old girl. It was at times like these he wished he had a married brother or sister with kids so he could have someone to advise him. The thought of asking Rhona had never occurred. She didn't seem the type to know, and as far as he was aware she didn't have brothers or sisters either. Chrissy had plenty of family, that he did know, having encountered two of her wayward brothers in the past.

McNab reached into the back seat and grabbed the box the assistant had carefully wrapped for him. He had the horrible feeling his coming here might be construed by Emma as a thinly disguised courtship visit to her mother. In a way, it was; he had to keep Claire onside until the case was over.

It wasn't until he exited the car that he noticed there was no smoke coming from the chimney. When he'd knocked a couple of times he stepped back and looked up at Emma's bedroom window. The house, he decided, had an empty look to it. Perhaps Claire had decided he wasn't coming after all and she and Emma had gone for a walk.

McNab castigated himself for not calling to say he'd be late. He shaded his eyes from the sun's reflection on the snow and scanned the horizon. There was nothing in the surrounding fields but the usual sheep.

When the front door proved locked, he decided to take a look round the back. There was no car out front and there wasn't one parked at the side either. He tried to remember what Claire had said about the replacement car the insurance company had supplied after the crash. How long did that arrangement last for? As he cornered the building he heard what sounded like the crunch of footsteps. 'Hello?' he called.

A roe deer, her coat a deep russet against the glistening snow, stood in the middle of the back garden, ears pricked up. When she registered McNab she froze for a moment then bounded off towards the safety of the nearby trees.

The deer hadn't been the only creature wandering about the garden. The snow was criss-crossed by numerous tracks, including what looked like a whole family of rabbits come to scavenge the remains of a summer vegetable patch.

He turned the back-door handle and struck lucky this time. As the door swung open he called out Claire's name. When there was no answer he stepped into the kitchen and called again. His suspicion that the place was empty was reinforced by the temperature. Last time he'd visited the cottage had been gloriously warm, but now his breath blew white in the icy air.

There was a teapot and a milk carton on the kitchen table. McNab touched the metal. It too was stone cold. He headed for the sitting room. The tree lights had been switched off and the fire in the grate was long dead.

His sense of unease deepening, he took the stairs two at a time and stood poised on the upper

180

landing. Both bedroom doors were partially open. He hesitated, conscious that if this turned into a crime scene, then he was trampling all over it. He chose the door on the right. It swung open and he caught a glimpse of a single bed, a brightly coloured duvet on the floor. Nothing wrong yet, so why was his heart hammering in his chest? McNab stepped into the room and looked around.

His gaze registered soft toys and piles of books, a doll's house in the corner, an open wardrobe with clothes pulled from hangers and scattered about. Just an untidy bedroom? His heart still jammering, he felt the crunch of broken glass beneath his feet. He stepped back. A smashed tumbler littered the carpet, a stain around it. Something had happened here.

McNab retreated into the hall and turned left, his senses on full alert. As he approached the second door he spotted a reddish-brown spray pattern on the cream paint of the frame and the neighbouring wall. He knew immediately what it was. He'd seen it often enough. Impact spattering was the most common type of blood pattern encountered at a crime scene, caused by kicking, stamping, beating, punching or shooting your victim.

He was already picturing Claire running up the stairs, being caught here on the landing just outside her bedroom door. When she'd struggled her attacker had responded by slamming her head against the wooden frame. Judging by the mess, he'd done it not once but many times. McNab felt sick. He stood for a moment before opening the door. The horrific memory of a crime scene he'd once attended reappeared in his head: a woman and child lying entwined on a blood-drenched bed, after the frenzied knife attack of the mother's deranged partner.

When he found the courage to push open the door, the first thing that hit him was the sickly odour of stale vomit. Long orange-brown strands stained the bedcover. A trail of blood from the doorway marked a path to the bed and the bundled mound of the duvet. McNab pictured Claire's body hunched beneath. He forced himself forward, reached for the duvet and jerked it back.

The bed was empty.

He sucked in air like a dying man, only now realising how long he'd held his breath. Neither the girl nor her mother was in the house, but one of them was badly hurt and it looked as if it was Claire.

He retraced his steps and stood for a moment in the doorway, waiting for his heart to slow. He was a crime scene manager. He had to distance himself, get a proper perspective on this. Forget that he knew the woman and child who lived in this house. Read the signs properly and without emotion.

He examined the area of wall next to the door frame. As well as the spattering, he could make out a set of bloodied fingerprints and a long light-brown hair. He examined the patterned carpet, cursing himself for entering the room without first checking for other footprints.

McNab retreated downstairs. If Claire and Emma were no longer in the house, where the hell were they? He pulled out his mobile and brought up Claire's number. When it rang he heard a corresponding musical ringtone and followed it through to the sitting room. He located Claire's mobile on the sofa, tucked beneath a photo album. On the floor beside the sofa was her handbag. Claire and Emma had not left the house voluntarily.

He called Rhona on her direct line, and she answered almost immediately.

'Can you get down here right away?'

'What's wrong?'

'Something's happened to Claire and Emma.'

33

A couple of police vehicles stood by the side of the road near the crash site, and Rhona gave them a cursory glance as she drove past. The underwater team would call it a day soon. She wondered whether they'd discovered anything. McNab had said nothing about the search of the loch when he'd called her. He'd sounded too agitated about what he'd found at Fern Cottage.

The light was almost gone by the time she reached the access road. Weaving tyre tracks were visible in the snow, evidence of how slippery it had been earlier. It had melted a little during the day, turning to slush in the wetter sections, making her own approach easier. Rhona was beginning to question whether she had in fact taken the right road when she crested a hill and finally saw the lights below.

McNab was waiting at the front door.

'There was an intruder. I've found his point of entry. I didn't notice at first, but the window glass in the toilet next to the kitchen has been cut. The cottage was Baltic when I went in. I assumed it was because the heating had been switched off.'

Rhona got kitted up and handed McNab a set of overalls before he led her round the back. The open window to the right of the back door had a clean circular hole cut in it, big enough for a hand.

'He must have suctioned it free. There's no broken glass inside or out, as far as I can see. When I drove up, the snow was undisturbed. So the break-in must have occurred some time before midnight when the snow came on in earnest.' He looked exhausted, as though he'd been running it over again and again in his head. 'I tried calling Claire's mobile and found it lying in the sitting room along with her handbag, purse, credit and debit cards.'

'Hospitals?'

'Tried all A & E departments within range while I was waiting for you. I also rang the local doctor's surgery.' He shook his head. 'Nobody fitting Claire's description turned up at any of them.'

'What about the farm?'

'The farmer's name is Jenkins. He says he hasn't seen Claire for the past three days. He got the impression she wanted to be left alone.'

'Have you told Slater about this?'

McNab's jaw hardened. 'Slater's orders were to forget the kid.'

'That was before this happened. Have you heard from the divers?'

'They didn't find anything.'

'So Emma was making it up?'

'Looks like it.'

Rhona told him about the feeling both she and

184

Magnus had had, that Claire was frightened of something not necessarily connected to Emma's discovery of the skull.

'There were only three numbers stored on Claire's phone,' he told her. 'The hospice, her mother's number and the farmhouse.'

'Nobody has three numbers on their mobile.'

'I know,' he agreed. 'I checked the log. Just my call and one other, number withheld. I'm beginning to get the feeling Claire came here to hide from something.'

'She must have friends back in Glasgow,' said Rhona, puzzled. 'What about her work?'

'She never mentioned what she did and I never asked.'

'Emma's school?'

'She told me she was going to the local primary after the holidays. Maybe they'll know the name of her previous school. I'll get on to the station while you take a look inside.'

Rhona entered the cottage by the back door. McNab was right, it was very cold in here. Nothing like the day she'd sat by the fire with Magnus. She went to the supposed point of entry first, taking video footage on the way.

The small back room housed a toilet and handbasin. The window above the sink had a deep ledge, indicating the thickness of the old stone walls. It had a brass catch at the bottom and a metal lock that swung between upper and lower sections. A circle of glass in the upper section had been removed, allowing a hand to reach in and free the lock. Pulling up the lower section had provided easy entry.

Rhona took a look at the kitchen next. There

185

werc no obvious signs of a struggle and no immediate evidence of blood, although anyone exiting the cottage with a head wound would probably have dripped blood somewhere along the way.

The sitting room was as McNab had described. Rhona couldn't imagine Claire going off in a car without her mobile and handbag, although it wasn't unheard of for people to rush to hospital after an accident forgetting such things. But if Claire had been as badly hurt as McNab feared, would she have been able to drive?

After she'd recorded the sitting room, she headed upstairs. The upper landing was narrow, with two doors leading off. Rhona went into Emma's room first. The cupboard was open, clothes and shoes scattered about. The smashed tumbler lay on a damp patch on the carpet. She picked up a piece of glass and sniffed it, catching a sweet syrupy scent. A pile of jotters, a pencil case and a textbook lay in a heap next to the bed, as though they'd been tipped from a bag. Wondering whether this was evidence of a sudden and rapid packing session, Rhona checked the wardrobe for a backpack or holdall, but couldn't find one.

McNab joined her outside Claire's room as she recorded the bloodstains.

'It looks bad, doesn't it?' he said.

'Head wounds always bleed a lot.' What she said was true but he still looked worried.

'I called the lab,' he said, 'asked for someone to help you process the scene.'

She nodded. On her own it would take time, and she didn't want to spend her entire Christmas Eve down here. 'What about Claire's car?'

'The insurance company says she returned the hire car. Apparently she bought a replacement to be delivered after Christmas.'

'So she had no transport?'

'Mr Jenkins said he offered her the use of a farm van. Claire told him she planned a quiet Christmas at home with Emma and wouldn't need it.'

So any hope that Claire had driven away from the scene with Emma was gone.

'Someone's taken them,' said McNab.

'Or they ran away from the intruder and are lying low.'

'They would have made for the farm.'

Rhona suspected he was right. If Claire and Emma had been frightened by an intruder, they would have made for the nearest house. She went to the window. The snow was on again, thick flakes drifting down to form a second layer. What if mother and daughter were out in the open with night coming on?

'The intruder must have come and gone by car,' she said. McNab had driven down the unsurfaced road. So had she. There was no other route to the cottage.

McNab was reading her mind. 'Jenkins says he brought fodder to the sheep by tractor early this morning. The gate into the field is about half a mile up from the main road.'

So the drive had been well churned up after the intruder left. With that and a further fall of snow, they had little chance of identifying his tracks.

'What if Claire came here to hide from a former partner who was . . .'

'Harassing her?' McNab said stiffly.

There was a moment's uncomfortable silence.

187

'You didn't harass me.'

'Texts, emails, phone calls.' He shook his head. 'No wonder you hated me.'

'I never hated you.'

They fell silent, both wanting to change the subject.

'Did Emma sound afraid of Nick?' said Rhona, eventually.

McNab thought for a moment, then shook his head. 'On the contrary, I got the impression she liked him.'

*   *   *

The extra forensic help consisted of Chrissy. Rhona was over the moon to see her auburn head emerge from the van half an hour after McNab's departure.

'Wondered where you'd disappeared off to,' scolded Chrissy.

'You weren't at the lab to tell,' Rhona replied.

Her assistant patted her bulge. 'Antenatal appointment.'

'This wouldn't be a good place to go into labour.'

'Stop worrying, I've got three weeks yet. I predict the ninth of January. D'you want to place a bet?'

'With a known cheat? No way.'

They began upstairs in Claire's room. Rhona and McNab had laid treads when they first entered. They were set a little wide apart for Chrissy, who was making a meal of negotiating them. She finally settled to spraying the carpet with luminol, trying to pick up footprints in the blood.

'Apparently when Slater found out about the underwater search team he went ballistic. I hope for McNab's sake they found something in that loch.' She threw Rhona a look, her eyebrows perfectly poised above the mask.

Rhona shook her head.

'The kid was playing you along?'

'Looks like it.'

'God, I hope I don't have one like that. Or one like any of my brothers.' Chrissy looked worried.

'Don't be daft. You'll have a boy and he'll be like Sam.'

'Sam's back in Nigeria. Lagos.'

'How do you know?'

'He phoned me. I'm going to visit him there after the baby's born.'

'That's good.' Rhona knew all about the Suleimans and their vendetta against Sam. Since Sam had been instrumental in the African case last year, rescuing a child the Suleiman family had abducted, he had been in hiding from their henchmen and the police force here. Sean had gone with Sam to London. She didn't ask about Sean, but Chrissy told her anyway.

'Sean's back in Glasgow.'

Rhona said nothing, but she could feel her heart begin to race. It had to happen some time. Sean's life and work were in Glasgow. She knew he wouldn't stay in London for ever.

'He's been sleeping at the Jazz Club the last couple of nights. He didn't think he'd be welcome at the flat.'

'He's right.'

'Rhona . . .'

'Leave it, Chrissy.'

Chrissy turned away. Rhona was sorry for her harsh words. The mess between herself and Sean wasn't Chrissy's fault. She might have an idea what had prompted the break-up, but Rhona had never discussed it with her. The nearest she'd come to talking to anyone about it was with McNab, and she regretted even that now. Talking about bad things only made you remember them more. She would have to face Sean some time, just not yet.

*   *   *

Despite the weather and the hastening darkness, McNab had made a brief attempt at searching for tracks around the cottage before heading back to the city. He'd found nothing except the criss-crossing of animals, mostly sheep. They would have to take a closer look in daylight.

Rhona checked the snowfall from the window. If the wind got up they might have a problem getting out. She decided to call it a day. Their extensive search of the cottage had revealed little more than they'd gleaned in the first instance—a few spots of blood in the kitchen, a partial imprint in blood in Claire's room. Chrissy had picked up lots of prints, but none round the access window. They'd bagged everything they could take away that might provide trace evidence of the intruder.

'A cup of something hot before we set out?'

Chrissy read that as a peace offering. 'I'm starving.'

'You're always starving. You should bring sandwiches.'

'We could try for a chippy on the way back?'

'Don't we always?'

Rhona boiled the kettle and made a pot of tea. The cottage was freezing. A thermometer hanging

190

on the wall near the back door hovered just above zero. If it was that cold in here, God knows what it was like outside. Rhona heard the toilet flush again. Chrissy hadn't been able to go until they'd processed the room. Now she was making the most of it.

Rhona poured two mugs and checked the fridge for milk. The shelves were well stocked. Now that the groundwork was over, Rhona reminded herself of the real reason they were here. Something bad had happened, by accident or intent. She remembered Emma's intense little face, her conviction that there was another body. It wasn't unknown for a young child to hallucinate when dealing with intense stress. Abducted children often imagined scenarios to deal with the situation, often so powerfully that they came to believe them to be real. Perhaps Emma really needed psychological help.

Magnus! She should call Magnus and tell him what had happened. Maybe Emma had revealed something to him that might throw a light on her disappearance.

'Any sugar?' Chrissy was back from the toilet.

'Try the cupboard.'

Chrissy fished about and emerged with a packet of icing sugar.

'You're not putting that in your tea?'

'It's the same stuff, just ground down a bit.' She helped herself to two large spoonfuls.

'We'd better make this quick or we might get snowed in,' Rhona said.

'I saw myself with my feet up in front of the telly on Christmas Eve, not stuck in a cottage miles from anywhere.'

191

'You could come back with me, make a night of it.'

'And watch you getting pissed on glasses of fine wine, while I drink orange juice?'

'Sounds about right.'

'OK, but don't expect me to produce a present for you tomorrow morning.'

'Hey, I've got one for you.'

'Bloody hell.'

'Only joking, but I have bought something for the baby.'

'You have?' Chrissy's eyes lit up. 'What is it?'

'I'm not telling you.'

'Go on.'

Rhona wished she'd never mentioned it. 'If you torment me, you won't get it,' she warned.

'You'd deprive my poor baby because I'm a pain in the neck?'

There was no answer to that one.

They drew the bolt on the front door and exited by the back. There was no back-door key but Rhona hoped that the police tape across both doors would dissuade any casual visitors.

The wind had picked up, whipping the snow in their faces. It would be difficult driving in this.

'You lead, I'll follow,' Chrissy said sweetly.

'Thanks very much.'

34

Rhona turned the heater on full blast. It was the first time she'd felt warm since she'd climbed out of the car at the cottage. She'd tried to act blasé when Chrissy had voiced some concern about getting stuck down here. The truth was she'd had the same thought. If they managed to negotiate the track and reach the main road then all would be well. But if not . . . ?

She considered the alternatives; a trek to the farmhouse or holing up in the cottage. To be truthful, she wasn't sure in which direction the main farm lay. No doubt there was a sign somewhere on the road.

She switched the wipers to a higher setting. Chrissy had dipped her headlights but each time they went over a bump Rhona was still blinded by their reflection in her rear-view mirror. That, coupled with the whirling snow, meant she was having real difficulty seeing where she was going.

She slowed down even further, causing Chrissy to sound the horn in alarm. Rhona peered out through the windscreen. Snow blown from the right-hand field had built up against the opposite bank, creating a mini-drift. She put her foot down and heard the wheels attempt to get a grip on the powdery surface. The car moved forward three feet then stopped. She revved the engine and re-engaged, this time in first gear. The wheels whirred but got no traction, so she pulled on the brake and climbed out to take a look.

The drift was higher and deeper than she'd first

thought. She went back to the car and opened the boot, and Chrissy came to join her.

'I've got a couple of trowels. We can try and dig our way through with them.' Rhona had to raise her voice against the wind.

'We need a shovel.'

'Well, we haven't got one.'

'Says who?'

Chrissy headed back to her car and appeared carrying a shovel. 'Part of my emergency getting-to-hospital-in-a-snowstorm pack.'

Rhona could have kissed her. 'What else do you have in the boot?'

'My overnight bag in case I get caught short, and stuff for the baby.'

'You're amazing.'

'I know.'

Chrissy looked frozen. 'Get back in the car,' said Rhona. 'I'll sound the horn when I'm ready to move off.'

She began clearing the road. The snow was soft and light, which explained why it was travelling so well on the wind. Five minutes later she had cleared a way through.

She sounded the horn and Chrissy flashed her lights in response. The next section of track had little snow covering, protected as it was between two high banks. She was beginning to think they might make the main road after all when she turned a corner and ran straight into another drift.

Her abrupt halt brought Chrissy to within inches of her. If this kept happening it would take for ever to reach the turn-off. She could dig a way through and try to keep going, but there was no guarantee they would make the road in the worsening weather. The farther they got away from the safety of the cottage, the harder it would be to make their way back there.

The cottage had food and water, and heating if they lit the fire. She could call McNab and let him know what had happened. It wouldn't be the first time they'd spent the entire night at a crime scene, and at least on this occasion they wouldn't be working. Rhona headed for Chrissy's car to give her the good news.

'I think we should go back. The weather's getting worse and we'd be safer at the cottage.'

'Walking?'

'There's no way we'll get turned.'

'OK, but I want to take my overnight bag.'

'All right, but I'll carry it.'

Rhona suggested they don forensic suits and boots over their clothes to keep them dry. God knew what they looked like, Rhona carrying Chrissy's bag, the small intense beams of two forensic torches shining the way.

Battling against the wind with the snow swirling in their faces, they could hardly see a foot in front of them. Had it not been for the fence wire on either side, they might easily have ended up in a field. The cold was working its way through Rhona's forensic suit and all subsequent layers. If they were out in this for much longer there was a real danger of hypothermia.

Chrissy had said nothing for the last half-hour, except for uttering the occasional curse when she'd slipped or had to fight doubly hard against the wind. Rhona was beginning to doubt whether leaving the car had been the right decision after all. They could have bundled up together, kept each other warm and sat out the worst of the storm.

Chrissy had resisted any attempts to help her by taking her arm. She must be tired by now. Rhona shot her a worried look, but could make out only the shadowy form of the suit and the curve of her cheek in the thickly falling snow.

'Not far now,' she heard herself say, although she had no idea how true that was.

'I'm definitely going to Lagos after this.'

They were nearly on the cottage before they saw it.

'My God!' exclaimed Chrissy. Drifting snow had piled up against the walls, almost to the windows in some places.

'Come on.'

The fought their way round the back. Rhona's frozen fingers struggled to turn the handle, then they were tumbling in, desperate to get out of the wind. She closed the door and slid the bolt. The sudden silence left them shouting at one another.

'Jesus, Mary and Joseph!' Chrissy always favoured religious curses when things got really bad.

'That's what Bill would have said.'

'Good Catholics know how to blaspheme. What would a Protestant like yourself say in such circumstances?'

'Bloody hell?'

Chrissy shook the snow from her body. 'Not in the same league. You light the fire,' she ordered. 'I'm going to find food.'

There was kindling in a basket and a small supply of cut logs. There would be more in the woodshed, but that would mean going outside

196

again. Rhona decided it was better to do it now before she took off her suit.

Thankfully the shed was only yards away, otherwise she would have been crawling there. She filled a basket and unloaded it just inside the back door, then went for a second load, determined to make sure there was enough to last them through the night.

She set and lit the fire, stacking the remaining logs near by. They would sleep here in the sitting room. There were a couple of small couches, a bit cramped but better than the back seat of a car. They just needed something to cover them. She eventually found a couple of blankets in a linen cupboard under the stairs. When she returned to the sitting room the fire had caught and was burning well. Already the air temperature had risen. Rhona went in search of Chrissy and found her putting a casserole dish in the microwave.

'There's loads of cooked stuff in the freezer, so we won't starve.' Chrissy nodded at the range. 'I don't understand why that's not on. Any idea where the oil tank is?'

'Near the back door.'

'I'll take a look.'

'Chrissy,' Rhona warned, but Chrissy was already pulling on a coat she'd found somewhere. She was gone only minutes.

'There's plenty of oil. Probably the wind blew out the pilot light.'

She reached for a nearby box of matches, knelt down and opened the left-hand door.

'Are you sure you should be on your knees like that?'

There was a grunting sound then Rhona heard a

pop followed by a small roar.

Chrissy pulled herself groaning to her feet just as the microwave pinged behind her. 'Right, a quick stir then in again for a further five minutes and dinner is served.'

They carried their plates through to the sitting room.

'I hope Claire doesn't mind us eating her food.' Chrissy's remark brought them both up short.

'I think they both left this place alive,' said Rhona. 'We've done enough to know that.'

There hadn't been sufficient blood to suggest a fatal wound, and no evidence that Emma had been hurt. Until it was proved otherwise, they had to believe that Claire and her daughter were alive.

'You need a stiff drink,' Chrissy declared. 'There's a couple of bottles of red in the cupboard. I'll have to make do with tea.' She gave a long-suffering sigh and headed for the kitchen to fetch the wine.

After consuming two large plates of food, Chrissy stretched out and fell fast asleep on the sofa. Rhona was relieved to see that her white, strained look was gone, replaced by two round rosy cheeks. She took the plates through to the kitchen then tried her phone again. There was still no signal. The phone in the hall gave her a dead tone, so it looked as if the wind had brought a line down somewhere. There would be no contact with McNab or anyone else tonight. She would just have to make herself comfortable until the storm blew itself out and she could walk to the farm.

She fed the fire and lay down herself. Now that they were enclosed within the thick walls, the howling of the wind had become a distant murmur.

Rhona closed her eyes, allowing the steady tick of the clock and the hiss and crackle of the fire to lull her into sleep.

35

McNab pulled up in front of the Russian Restaurant. He was on a double yellow line, though you couldn't see it for grey slush. He glanced at his watch. There would be no parking attendants around at this time, especially on Christmas Eve.

He glanced in at the steamed-up windows, feeling like Tiny Tim in *A Christmas Carol*. The place was packed with what looked like office parties. Boozy faces under paper hats. McNab wished he was one of them. He could do with getting drunk and disorderly. The way things were going he would finish late, pick up a chippie or a pizza and drown his sorrows at home. Merry Christmas.

Slater had left him in no doubt that he would be going the way of his DI if he fucked up again. McNab had had no business ordering an underwater team out on Christmas Eve, or swanning off to the middle of nowhere when he had been given a very precise order to visit the Russian Restaurant and find out who the hell the dead guy in the skip was. The job was his because it was a crap one and it was Christmas Eve and he had pissed off his new boss with some fancy fairy tale about voices in a wee girl's head.

McNab pushed open the door and the fug hit

him. No cigarette smoke now, just heat, a babble of voices and a multitude of food aromas. A young woman with jet-black hair and eyes like blackened saucers shook her head, rattling her long red earrings at him.

'I'm sorry. We're fully booked.'

McNab flashed his photo ID at her. 'Police. Is the boss in?'

She looked perturbed. 'He's in the kitchen.'

'Well, can you call him out here please. I would like to speak to him.'

'We're really busy . . .'

A shriek of laughter erupted at a nearby table.

'Just get him.'

Black-eyes went in search of her boss. McNab waved to another girl behind the bar and asked for a Famous Grouse.

'Can I tempt you to a vodka instead? We do all kinds.'

He cut her short. 'Whisky'll do fine.'

A tall, slim, broad-shouldered guy emerged from behind swing-doors and walked purposefully towards him.

'DS McNab,' he said, flashing his badge once more.

'Ah, Rhona said to expect a visit from the police, but not on Christmas Eve. I am Mikhail Grigorovitch.'

There was something in the way the guy used Rhona's name, as if he actually knew her.

The shrieking woman behind him let rip again.

'Is there somewhere quiet we can talk?'

'We're really busy. You couldn't . . .'

'No.' McNab wasn't in the mood for compromise.

'OK.' Grigorovitch was picking up on his ill temper and seemed about to match it with a tantrum of his own.

He turned on his heel and walked towards the back of the dining room. They passed a small stage where three musicians were preparing to play. Back here the party people were slightly more subdued, or maybe they hadn't drunk enough vodka yet.

The Russian swept through a beaded curtain, letting the strings of beads rattle back on McNab. On the other side things were much quieter. The man took a swift right into a small office, just short of a stairway heading upwards, and shut the door firmly behind them.

'I only have a few moments or my clientele will riot. I let one of the chefs have the night off, so I'm taking his place.'

'The guy who ate here before he died—' McNab began.

'We are not the only place to serve Russian food.'

'Dr MacLeod thinks he ate here.' McNab deliberately avoided calling her Rhona.

'Many young men eat here who would fit Rhona's description.'

Now Grigorovitch was really pissing McNab off.

'You have receipts for that night, credit and debit card records?'

The man looked mildly uncomfortable. 'Yes, of course, but some pay in cash.'

'Which doesn't go in the till?'

He'd hit a raw nerve.

'There are many people who live hand to mouth in Glasgow, especially migrants from eastern

Europe. I feed them, they pay cash.'

'And no one knows the difference?'

Grigorovitch didn't answer.

'You like to gamble?'

McNab's change of tack caught him by surprise.

He considered before answering. 'Coming to live in a foreign country is a gamble.'

'Poker. You play poker?'

The man's handsome face clouded. Clearly he was wondering where this was going.

'Sometimes,' he conceded.

'Your clientele from eastern Europe. They like to gamble too?'

'All Russians like to gamble.' The smile didn't reach his eyes.

'What's upstairs?'

The reply was quick, maybe too quick.

'Nothing, a store.' A shrug.

'Can I take a look?'

He hesitated, then nodded.

McNab followed him out.

They climbed the stairs slowly. Either Grigorovitch had arthritic hips or he was in no hurry to reach the top.

McNab addressed his broad back. 'You don't happen to know a man called Solonik?'

He couldn't see the face, but the Russian's neck and shoulders stiffened.

'I don't think so.'

They had reached the upper landing. There was only one door. Grigorovitch produced a key from a collection hanging below his white apron and slipped it in the lock.

'What about a Mr Nikolai Kalinin?'

A muffled intake of breath.

'You recognise the name?'

They were still outside the door, waiting to go in.

Grigorovitch was choosing his words carefully. 'It is a common Russian name.'

The small landing was a bit too cosy for McNab's liking. He was tall, but Grigorovitch was taller. He wasn't comfortable with that, especially at close quarters. He made a noise in his throat that suggested they move inside. The other man pushed open the door and flicked on a light switch.

It was primarily a storeroom, but a circular table sat centre stage, illuminated by a hanging lamp. Near by stood a fridge and a small well-stocked bar.

McNab took his time looking round. He could feel Grigorovitch's discomfort and was enjoying it.

'Solonik been here to play? Or maybe Kalinin?'

'I only invite friends.'

'I don't believe you,' hissed McNab.

Grigorovitch muttered something guttural. McNab didn't have to understand Russian to know he was being cursed.

'I want the names and contact numbers of the people who use this room.'

The Russian's expression was stoic. He'd known what would unfold, even as he'd climbed the stairs.

The sounds of a ruckus erupted below, and Grigorovitch looked pleadingly at McNab. 'If you would like to have something to eat while you wait, I will sort out the kitchen and then write your list.'

McNab contemplated the idea. He was ravenous and was being offered food. There wasn't much to think about, and there were worse places to spend an hour on Christmas Eve. A list of Russian gamblers resident in Glasgow would be his pay-off to Slater for not visiting any more establishments. He could eat, then go home.

He nodded curtly. The relief on Grigorovitch's face was obvious. If he hadn't been frightened of revealing his gambling den, what had put the fear of God in him?

'I will find a place for you in the back area, if you don't mind listening to Russian music?'

McNab would gladly listen to screeching hyenas as long as they were accompanied by food.

Grigorovitch showed him to a tiny table, tucked in a dark corner next to the small stage. It looked like the place where the musicians sat down for their break. A girl with liquid brown eyes watched from the stage as her employer scooped up a red shawl and pulled out a seat.

McNab wasn't a music buff, but the young woman's hands were moving swiftly and the sound was very nice, so she must be good. She was certainly attractive, in a Gypsy-bohemian way.

'I'll send out some food,' Grigorovitch told him.

McNab wondered what he'd get. Leftovers most probably, scraped from returning plates and with spit. He didn't give a damn. He would eat a scabby hen at this moment and lick his lips afterwards.

The vodka arrived before the food. The Amy Winehouse lookalike plonked a bottle down together with a small shot glass.

'What is it?'

'The best, courtesy of the boss.'

McNab contemplated the walk home in the thickening snow, with no hope of a taxi. Somehow it didn't put him off. He'd done his bit. Now he was off duty and it was Christmas Eve. The waitress stretched her blood-red lips into a smile and poured him a shot. The cold-misted bottle was still a quarter full when she plonked it down on the table. McNab was beginning to enjoy himself.

The ice-cold vodka slid down. McNab was pleasantly surprised. He could have held out, demanded whisky, but hell, when in Rome . . . The alcohol met his unlined stomach and seeped quickly through to his bloodstream. No wonder they called it a shot. It was like a bullet in the belly, with no burning, no pain, just warmth. He sighed. Even if the food was shite, the vodka would go some way to making it taste better.

The food turned out to be delicious, though in the semi-darkness it was tricky to work out what it was he was eating. He made a guess at pork, with some sort of sour sauce. It was delicious. He refilled his glass. The trio of musicians were finishing their set with a flourish and he joined in the applause. What with the food and the vodka, he was beginning to get in the seasonal mood. The dark-eyed girl came for her shawl, which hung over the adjacent chair.

'That was very good,' said McNab.

'You like Russian music?' Her voice was husky and low.

'What I've heard so far.' He smiled.

The young woman glanced swiftly at the almost empty vodka bottle.

'I haven't drunk all that. I'm just naturally friendly.'

She wrapped the shawl round her shoulders.

'Food's good, too.' McNab wanted to keep her there. 'Pity I don't know what I'm eating.'

'Piglet,' she said helpfully. 'Typical Russian Christmas dish, although it's not yet Christmas.'

He glanced at his watch. 'Not long to go now.'

She smiled and shook her head. 'Western Christmas yes, Russian Christmas no. We have to wait until the seventh of January.'

'Really?'

'Really.'

'So can I offer you a Western Christmas drink?'

She thought about it for a moment.

'Since you've stolen our table, yes.'

McNab pushed his cleared plate to one side. 'We'll need another glass.'

She indicated she would fetch one from the bar. He watched the two female heads come together, then she arrived back with a fresh bottle and a second glass.

'Amy Winehouse over there told you I was a cop.'

She nodded. 'But that's not why we served you pig. It is a traditional dish, just as I said.'

'We?'

'I am Mikhail's little sister, Anya.'

'DS Michael McNab. Pleased to meet you. Your brother has promised me a list of his gambling associates as soon as the kitchen cools down.'

She looked perplexed.

'He doesn't gamble, does he?'

'I am not my brother's keeper.' She had already poured two shots. She took hers and swallowed it swiftly.

'You're a good violinist but a poor liar.'

She glanced somewhere over his shoulder, not meeting his eye.

'Who uses the room upstairs?'

She shrugged. 'Men. I don't know who they are.'

'Don't know, or won't say?'

Fear fluttered in her eyes. He leaned in. 'We

found a man in a rubbish skip on the south side of Glasgow. Someone had set fire to him after breaking his neck. We can't explain exactly why, but his head blew up in the heat. The forensic team had to scrape his brains off the walls. Seems he ate your brother's borscht shortly before he died.'

Her face had turned the colour of putty, but McNab kept going.

'He had a pack of marked cards in his back pocket.' McNab described the dead man to her, including the tattoo. She rose abruptly, her face pale with shock. She was going to vomit. McNab followed her to the ladies' loo and held the door open. She made the sink, just. He waited for her to clean up before he spoke.

'You knew the dead guy?'

She mustered herself. 'Maybe.'

'Is "maybe" strong enough to make you sick?'

'It was a terrible thing to tell someone.'

'Especially if they knew who I was talking about.'

Tears ran down her cheeks.

'Come back to the table. You need to sit down.'

She walked as though in a daze. When they re-entered the dining room, Grigorovitch was waiting, his expression a mixture of concern and fury. A volley of Russian ricocheted between them, his voice the dominant one. Eventually she seemed to brighten a little. Grigorovitch ushered her through to the kitchen and turned on McNab, furious.

'You have upset my sister very badly.'

'She just found out someone she knew was murdered.'

'She made a mistake.'

'Really?'

'The man she thought you were referring to is alive.'

'Who did she think I was referring to?'

'A cousin. Vassili Grigorovitch.'

He was lying on several counts. From Anya's reaction, McNab was sure she hadn't been mourning a cousin but a lover, whose name probably wasn't Vassili.

'If you know the identity of the dead man and you are withholding that information from the police . . .' McNab left the threat hanging in the air.

Grigorovitch stared at him impassively.

'Here is the list of my card-playing friends.'

He glanced at the six names, most—for him—unpronounceable.

'I have included their phone numbers.'

McNab wondered how many of the mobiles would function when he rang them.

*　　*　　*

McNab dipped his head against the wind. Glasgow's downtown grid-patterned streets might be a replica of New York, but tonight it was definitely more like Chicago, gusts meeting him on every corner. In the warmth and comfort of the noisy restaurant, he'd had no idea what the weather was doing outside. It looked as though the Russians had brought their winters with them.

He stepped back from the edge of the road as a car swept by too fast for the conditions and he was sprayed with kicked-back snow. He shouted obscenities at the tail-lights. He shielded his eyes, looking for his own car, tempted to drive home despite the vodka. The alternative of sleeping in the car was almost as risky if some keen plod discovered him there and decided to breathalyse. Drunk in charge of car keys with intent to drive. Slater would just love that.

He decided death by exposure was the preferable option and stared up into a galaxy of whirling snow-stars, trying to get his bearings. His brain, buzzing with the vodka, attempted to map out the route to his flat, and failed. One step at a time. First he would get to George Square. He struggled towards the Trongate and took a left into Argyle Street.

The east wind was like a banshee, screeching down the streets on a mission to knock over everything in its path. McNab imagined Rhona at home in her flat by now, curled up nice and cosy in that big bed. Then the thought struck him that Rhona's flat was a lot closer than his own. He stepped into a doorway and pulled out his mobile. He would feed her the story of the Russian Restaurant as his excuse for not getting home. Slater's persecution of him would surely generate some pity and she wouldn't deny him shelter from the storm, not on a night like this.

When the screen informed him Rhona's mobile was unreachable he swore under his breath. He could just take a chance and turn up. Her flat was on his way and if she wasn't there he could keep on going. He tried the number once more and got the same result. An irritating worry began to niggle at him. It had been snowing a bit when he left Fern Cottage, but not enough to cause concern. There'd been plenty of time for her to get out before the real storm hit, which was when he'd been in the restaurant. And she wasn't on her own there.

God, he hoped Chrissy hadn't taken it into her head to go down there. When he'd called the lab, he had made it plain how off the beaten track the cottage was, no place for a pregnant woman. Chrissy had appeared to take that on board, but he'd left before the forensic vehicle arrived so he couldn't be sure.

He tried calling her and got the same result as with Rhona's phone, then he called a couple of other numbers just to make sure the problem wasn't confined to the forensic team. He was relieved to find he was right: it looked like the storm was the cause.

McNab stepped out into the wind. The sooner he got to Rhona's flat the better. The snow was deep underfoot, more like a Canadian midwinter cityscape than Scotland. There were no snowploughs or gritters to be seen. Glasgow had battened down the hatches and was riding out the storm—indoors.

When the black four-by-four appeared from the white-out, he waved it down. If it was going his way, a lift would be very welcome. Maybe he should flash his warrant card, commandeer the vehicle as far as Rhona's.

His luck was in. The car slid to a halt yards in front of him, smoked glass blocking his view of the occupants. The rear side door swung open. McNab felt the heat escape and hit him in the face. So that was what warmth felt like. He'd almost forgotten, even in the short walk from the restaurant.

McNab pulled out his warrant card and asked for a lift. A voice suggested he get in. He happily obeyed, his eyelashes too thick with snow to make out his saviour. He struggled inside, conscious he was showering snow everywhere.

'You're a lifesaver,' he said, wiping his eyes.

The other occupant of the back seat did not reply. McNab stared at Solonik, the blood freezing in his veins.

36

Solonik pressed his thumb hard into McNab's right eyeball. Lights flashed, pain roared in his ears. He would have heard his own scream, if the gag hadn't swallowed it. Tears streamed from his other free eye, coursing down his cheek. Salt leaked into his mouth. He had the sensation of drowning in his own spit.

A shout from behind and the pressure abruptly ended, but not the pain. It was like having a hot coal burn inside your head. McNab knew he was whimpering but couldn't stop himself.

He heard a cultured voice. 'He can put both eyes out simultaneously. It is a party trick of his. That and snapping your neck.'

McNab attempted to focus his mind elsewhere to prevent it conjuring up images of what would happen next. He thought about Rhona, his pleasure when he managed to make her laugh.

There was no laughter in here.

Solonik was standing, still as stone, waiting for the nod to continue his work.

'What d'you want?' McNab attempted to speak past the gag.

'Brogan.' The voice released the word slowly, rolling the 'r'. 'Why did you visit Brogan?'

McNab mumbled through the dirty cloth in his mouth.

Solonik untied the gag.

When his voice finally emerged from his aching throat, it sounded punch drunk. 'I was checking his licence.' When lying, stick as close as possible to the truth. 'He gave me a copy to take away. It was all in order.' True enough, apart from the puncture marks.

'Are you a gambler, Detective Sergeant?'

'Now and again.' That was also true.

Solonik was pointedly taking off his jacket and rolling up his shirtsleeves. His arms were a mass of intricate tattoos that rippled as he flexed his huge hands.

'If he presses a little harder, Solonik will blind you. Or he may choose to scoop out your eyeballs instead. Another party trick of his.'

McNab felt nausea rise in his throat.

'Assaulting a police officer is a serious offence.'

'By the time they find you, Solonik will no longer be in the country.'

As the big Russian resumed his stance in front of him, McNab met the cold empty eyes defiantly. He had no illusions. Solonik would do what he was told, without compunction and with great pleasure.

He was drawing back his hands like a tightening spring. There was nowhere to go and nothing McNab could do, except tell the truth.

'Brogan told me who killed the guy in the skip.'

For a split second he thought he'd left it too late. Solonik's hands had fastened on his skull. It was the second party trick that was on the agenda. McNab's head became a galaxy of stars. Somewhere in the distance the booming of his blood was forcing itself like a red tide into his heart. Strangled begging spewed from his mouth.

He heard a shouted command. It sounded like God's voice from Heaven. The intense pressure round his eyeballs eased and he slumped like a rag doll in the chair.

The questions flew at him like bullets. He answered them all. He owed Paddy Brogan nothing. Brogan was a gangster like his father, however cultured the voice and demeanour. Even as he embellished the conversation he'd had with Paddy, McNab knew he was condemning Glasgow to something much worse than the Brogans.

When he finally stopped for breath, he found his supply abruptly cut off as Solonik's hands moved to his throat. Party trick number three.

*   *   *

The world is a strange place when you return from the dead. Its colours are too bright, its sounds too intrusive after such a deep and profound silence. McNab saw a rainbow with a preponderance of red and violet. It swirled in front of him like an LSD trip. The sound that filled his ears resembled shattering glass, the shards pricking the tender membrane of his eyeball.

Suddenly, vividly, he remembered a street stabbing he'd attended. Blood bubbling from a hidden wound, the eyes of the puzzled youth staring up at him, his spinal cord severed by the blade. McNab imagined his own neck already

213

snapped, these few moments of consciousness all that was left him before oblivion. He was alive in this position, but what if he moved?

As his rigid body approached full consciousness he was aware of a cold so intense it burned. The first part to fully acknowledge returning life was the tips of his fingers. He moved them in wonder, as though they belonged to someone else, then he remembered those other fingers, thick and blunt, grinding into his eyes. Bile rose in his throat and threatened to enter his windpipe if he didn't move. Coughing and choking, he turned his head. Pain stabbed at his neck and shoulder, but no darkness engulfed him. He vomited a red-hot liquid on to what he now recognised as snow, the liquid's acidity burning his swollen throat and lips.

He fell back, air rasping in and out of his lungs. Above him was thick velvety darkness, punctured by swirling snow. He reached out first to the right, then to the left. Both hands touched metal. He was in some sort of container, closed on three sides.

He had only just acknowledged this when he heard the thrum of a machine starting up. A burst of headlights turned the black sky a burnt orange as McNab forced his body into a sitting position. He heard the whine of a winch. Something was being raised up.

A red bucket swung overhead.

McNab harnessed the last of his strength and pulled himself to one side as the bucket opened its giant teeth. Dust and stench clogged his throat as the debris rained down behind him.

Then it was over. The bucket swung away.

He spat dirt from his mouth and wiped his eyes. 'Fuck you!' he shouted in defiance at the empty sky. His relief was short lived, as the grating sound of the bucket refilling broke the momentary silence. The next load was on its way.

McNab flattened his body to the wall as the bucket swung back, whining and grunting, desperate to unload its next cargo. This time the rubbish hit his back, rattling his body against the metal side and bouncing off his head. One more load like this and he would be buried alive.

37

A white shroud lay over the cottage and surrounding land. The wind had died down, and in its place was a silence so intense Rhona could taste it.

In the cold light of dawn she'd risen as quietly as possible, not wanting to disturb Chrissy, whose regular breathing suggested a deep and untroubled sleep. When she'd opened the front door, the snow stood level with her knees. She'd put on a warm padded jacket and a pair of wellington boots from a selection in the back kitchen and a pair of thick gloves.

Stepping out into the crisp deep snow, she was momentarily blinded by the rising sun's reflection on the crystalline surface. The beauty of the scene rendered her speechless. In the city, snow turned to oily grey soup almost immediately. It never looked like this.

The weaving ribbon of track had been obliterated. There was no evidence of the fences that bordered it, apart from an occasional dark spot that might be the top of a post. She could see a cluster of dark red dots on the horizon, which turned out to be a flock of daubed sheep stranded on higher ground.

The thought struck her that the farmer wouldn't leave his sheep without food. He would come to feed them, Christmas morning or not. If Mr Jenkins could help them get a vehicle to the main road, maybe they would get home today after all.

A raven swooped above the stranded sheep, its diamond-shaped tail black against a cobalt sky and its caw sharp in the still air. It circled for a moment, then spotted something more interesting. Rhona hoped it wasn't a sheep trapped in a snowdrift. Then an even worse thought occurred. What if it was Claire or Emma? She set off towards the spot as fast as possible.

She crested a small hill just as the raven came in to land. Rhona ran at the huge bird, flapping her arms frantically. Eventually it rose, crying its displeasure at her interference.

Now Rhona saw what its intended prey had been.

A snow hole had been dug into the hillside, its entrance pointing away from last night's prevailing wind. Near by lay a man, face down. Blood splattered the snow from a gash on the back of his head.

She pulled off her gloves and knelt beside him, feeling for and finding a strong pulse. He stirred under her touch, his eyes flickering open.

'Are you OK?'

'I think so.' He groaned and tried to sit up. Rhona helped him.

'You've got a bad cut on the back of your head.'

216

'A branch came down in the wind, caught me a cracker. I felt really weird when I woke up. I crawled out of the snow hole and must have passed out.'

'I take it you got caught in the blizzard.'

'The car got stuck in a drift. I decided to try and make it home on foot. Not a good idea.'

'I've come from a cottage just over the hill. I could dress the wound and give you something to eat.'

He seemed to be contemplating refusal, then changed his mind and struggled to his feet. 'Thanks, that would be great.'

Rhona offered him her hand. 'Rhona MacLeod.'

He smiled and took it. 'Alan MacNiven.'

Chrissy must have been watching for her return because she opened the door on their approach, darting Rhona a quizzical look.

'Alan here got caught in the blizzard. Dug himself a snow hole and spent the night in it.'

Chrissy looked impressed.

Rhona led him into the kitchen, where he took a seat at the table. She fetched a bowl of hot water, then groaned.

'The first-aid kit's in the car.'

'I have everything you need in my overnight bag,' Chrissy announced. She departed and reappeared with a kit fit for an expedition up the Amazon.

Rhona cleaned the wound, expecting to pick up small pieces of bark on the gauze. There was none. In fact, the more she studied the cut the less she thought it had been inflicted by a blunt branch. From her experience, the wound had been caused by a sharper implement. She taped a dressing in place.

'It could do with a few stitches.'

'Don't worry. It's fine.'

Rhona studied the man's grimy face. Their visitor looked young, maybe early twenties, and badly in need of a shave. He also smelled a bit. Still, lying out all night could account for that.

Chrissy was rummaging in the fridge. 'Anyone for breakfast? Bacon, sausage, eggs, tattie scones?'

'I'd better be going.'

'You should eat first,' urged Rhona. 'You'll need your strength to plough through that snow. Besides, Mr Jenkins should be here soon.'

'Who?' He looked startled.

'Chapel Mains Farm.'

'Oh, aye.'

Alan said nothing as Chrissy prepared the fry-up, but clearly the desire to eat was winning over the desire to leave. When the food was set in front of him, he wolfed it down. It looked as though he hadn't eaten for a week. Even Chrissy, mammoth eater that she was, couldn't compete.

'D'you want me to fry some more?' she offered.

He looked abashed, suddenly realising what he'd done. 'Sorry, I didn't realise I was so hungry.'

'Where did you learn to dig a snow hole?' she asked.

'I've done some climbing in the Cairngorms. Weather can change there pretty quickly.'

Chrissy tried to top up his mug of tea, but he waved her away. 'Thanks, but I'd better be getting home.'

'So where is home?' Rhona asked.

'A couple of miles south from here.'

'I expect you know everyone in the area. Small rural communities are like that.'

He shrugged non-committally.

'What about the woman and her daughter who live here?'

His eyes flicked between Rhona and Chrissy. 'I thought you two lived here.'

'We're from Forensic Services, Strathclyde Police. Claire Watson and her daughter Emma went missing twenty-four hours ago. That's why we're here.'

'You're the police?'

'Not exactly,' said Chrissy pedantically.

He stood up. 'I don't know anything about a missing woman.'

'You didn't see anyone last night when you were trying to get home?' asked Rhona.

He shook his head. 'You couldn't see an inch in front of you in that blizzard.'

'Too right,' Chrissy agreed.

He swiftly took his leave, obviously anxious to be on his way. They watched as he jumped the fence and set off across the field towards the woods. Before he was out of hearing, Chrissy called, 'Good luck.' He turned just long enough for her to capture his image on her mobile.

'What d'you think?' said Chrissy.

'He was nervous, but not about us or the cottage.'

'Until he found out who we were. If he got into a fight last night that could explain the wound.'

'And his reluctance to talk to the police.'

'I'll maybe show this to McNab, just in case,' Chrissy said.

Rhona shielded her eyes and searched the horizon. The sheep were still there, but no sign of a tractor.

219

'I think we should try for the farm.'

'Where is it exactly?'

'No idea. I'm going to head for the hill with the sheep on it for a better view.'

'What about me?'

Rhona glanced down at her assistant's prominent bump. 'You stay here. I won't be long.'

'What if I go into labour while you're away?'

'Do you think that's a possibility?' Rhona said anxiously.

'Don't worry, I've read enough books on childbirth to deliver it myself.'

As she departed Rhona mouthed a silent prayer that that wouldn't be necessary.

38

McNab had lost all feeling from the waist down. Pinned against the wall by the force and weight of the debris, he was grateful that at least his lungs were still operating, but for how much longer? Each breath he drew was like a fire in his chest. If his back wasn't broken, a few of his ribs were.

The digger had been silent long enough now for him to believe that its operator had gone. Facing the metal side of the container, he couldn't see the sky, yet suspected it was getting light. If he could hold out a little longer, maybe someone would hear his cries and come to his rescue.

Blood trickled from his mouth and nose. There was a gash on the back of his head too, and the blood had soaked his collar and run down under his shirt. He licked his swollen lips, wincing as his tongue met an open wound. How the hell had he got into this mess? He shouldn't have provoked Grigorovitch. He should have taken a simple statement and gone home.

Grigorovitch must have contacted Solonik or Kalinin and told them what had transpired at the restaurant. They had simply come and picked him off, like a rabbit in their headlights.

He wondered why Solonik hadn't snapped his neck. *Maybe I have a guardian angel*, he thought. An angel sent to save me on Christmas Eve. A modern version of *It's a Wonderful Life*.

When he heard voices near by he opened his mouth to shout for help, then shut it again when he realised they were speaking a language that might just be Russian.

The voices were low and guttural, accompanied by scraping boots and winter coughs. A few jocular pleasantries were being exchanged. There were gangmasters working areas of Glasgow, and Govanhill was one of them. They collected groups of immigrants, mostly Romanians and other eastern Europeans, and bussed them to casual jobs. McNab surmised it might be one such gang waiting for a van.

He decided to take a chance and call for help.

His first strangled shout went unnoticed. The second resulted in a single call for silence, and the voices dwindled to a halt.

McNab shouted as loudly as he could. His voice bounced round the container and echoed back at him. He let the noise die down and listened for a response. The voices had changed tone. They were worried now, criss-crossing one another. One rose to take charge. McNab had no idea what was said but he knew someone was coming to look for him. He shouted again.

Footsteps came briskly towards the container, then stopped. He heard fence wire being rattled, then somebody was up and over, followed by another. A fist banged on the metal side. McNab banged back in reply. Tears were streaming down his cheeks, the strength that had kept him alive starting to drain away at the possibility of rescue.

There was a scrambling sound on the outside of the container, then a clear voice shouted down at him. He tried in vain to turn his head. Someone landed on the debris and crept slowly towards McNab, then began to move the rubble piece by piece. He heard someone else drop inside the container and soon began to feel the weight against him lessen. His body, released from the wall, started to tremble. He filled his lungs with air and allowed himself to believe that he would get out of this alive.

His excavation was swift now. The men conversed throughout in low voices in a language McNab didn't understand, although it had the sound of eastern Europe. Freed, he was able to turn and observe his rescuers. Two men stared at him in the chilly light of dawn. They were unshaven and bundled up against the cold. High cheekboned and almond eyed, they regarded him with uneasy concern.

McNab repeated the only word he'd gleaned from his visit to the restaurant. '*Spasibo*.'

They looked puzzled, then one smiled as he deciphered McNab's strangled Russian for *thank you*. He reached out a hand and McNab grabbed a hold of it as if it were a lifeline. As his body was pulled free, feeling flooded his lower half, quickly followed by pain. But his legs worked. He crawled across the debris that had formed his prison.

The two men helped him up and over the container wall. In the poor light McNab could make out part of a demolition site. Half a dozen men gaped at him through a mesh fence. His rescuers urged him towards the fence, obviously anxious to be out of the yard before anyone in authority appeared. With their help he climbed over, his drop on the other side met by welcoming hands. A gaggle of voices greeted his rescuers, obviously demanding to know what the hell had happened.

When McNab pulled out his ID card the men drew back, frightened. He smiled, shook his head. He wasn't planning to cause any trouble, even if they were illegals. He repeated *thank you* in any and every language he knew; English, Russian, French and Italian.

When he was out of sight of the yard, he tried to work out exactly where he was by the skyline and decided he wasn't that far from Polmadie, the site of the skip fire. His limbs, driven by adrenalin, suddenly gave out and he slid down a nearby wall to sit trembling at its foot. He guided a shaking hand to his pocket, looking for his mobile. Solonik must have been so confident of his demise that he hadn't bothered to remove it. The screen was scratched and dirty, but the phone appeared operational. McNab rang Rhona's number.

39

The wind scouring the hill had stacked snow in deep drifts around the summit. The last section saw Rhona buried up to her waist. When she finally managed to scramble to the top, she was met by a score of puzzled eyes, but the sheep didn't scatter.

The farm lay due west, tucked in a valley. She could see the smoke curling from its chimney. She could also make out a red tractor and trailer moving laboriously through the snow, distributing hay to other stranded sheep.

Any shouting she did from here would be unlikely to be heard by the driver. She could either wave her arms and hope he spotted her, or else make her way towards him. She decided on the latter.

She took a bearing and set off back down the hill. Trudging through the undisturbed snow was laborious and tricky, a bit like negotiating deep heather. She had no idea how far her foot would descend before it met firm ground, and the ground was pockmarked with rabbit holes.

The tractor had finished its current delivery and was heading for the next cluster of sheep when she entered the field. Rhona's shout was rewarded by the engine spluttering to a halt. A man climbed down and came towards her.

She introduced herself and asked whether he had seen or heard anything of Claire and Emma.

Mr Jenkins shook his head.

'I phoned round everyone I could think of as

soon as your detective sergeant called me. No one's seen them. I wondered why the cat had turned up here when it had taken such a liking to Emma.'

'Is there any mobile reception at the farm, or is your landline working?'

'Afraid not. The radio says the whole of Scotland and the North of England got hit by the blizzard, so we're not the only ones cut off.'

He promised Rhona he would be over to try to pull her car out as soon as he'd tended to his sheep.

'If you want to wait at the farm, Ellen will keep you company.'

Rhona thanked him for the offer but declined, thinking of Chrissy, back at the cottage. She decided to take the opportunity to ask the farmer about the man in the snow hole.

'Alan MacNiven? Can't say I know the name.'

Thanking him, she headed back as swiftly as the snow would allow. Although her feet were reasonably dry, the wellington boots were a little too large and had begun to rub at her heels. She would be glad to kick them off. As she came in sight of the cottage she was pleased to see plumes of smoke coming from the chimney. Chrissy certainly wasn't skimping on the fire.

She left the boots at the front door, delighted by the wave of warmth that greeted her entrance. Chrissy was sitting on the sofa by a blazing hearth, checking her mobile, no doubt for the hundredth time.

'Any luck?'

'Mr Jenkins will come and pull us out as soon as he deals with his livestock.' Rhona realised Chrissy looked perturbed. 'What's wrong? You're not getting contractions?'

Chrissy shook her head. 'I found something.'

'What?'

'The kid left a message.'

'A message? Where?'

'The broken tumbler on her bedroom carpet? I tasted the liquid that had been inside—it was just sugary water. Not lemonade or Coke. I kept wondering why Emma would drink sugar and water, then I remembered.'

'Remembered what?'

'There was a notebook on the desk. Emma had written a poem in it. There was a pen and a *toothpick* near by.'

'What's special about a toothpick?'

'Did you never make invisible ink when you were a kid?'

Rhona shook her head.

'You use a toothpick to write the secret message in sugar water, usually between normal writing. If you heat the paper you find the message.' Chrissy handed her the notebook. 'Look between the first and second line of the poem.'

The area Chrissy indicated was pale brown in colour in contrast to the white page. She was right. There was something scrawled there. Rhona read out the chilling words.

He's here. I think he wants to take us away.

Rhona felt terrible. The message had been left for her and she'd missed it. Thank God for Chrissy's keen eye.

'When we were in the wood, Emma asked what I did. I told her I looked for evidence that was invisible to the human eye, and she asked if it was

226

like invisible ink.'

'Smart kid,' said Chrissy.

Rhona studied the message. 'She says *he*. Who does she mean?'

'It sounds like she didn't know him.'

'Or she thought we would know who she meant? The only person we're aware of from Claire's former life is someone called Nick, and according to McNab, Emma liked him. We have to speak to McNab about this.'

She tried her mobile again, swearing at the *no signal* message still showing.

'I'm going to walk down and start digging out a car.'

'I'm coming with you.'

40

He was pleased with his work so far, very pleased. The underwater team had searched the loch in the woods and found nothing, because what they sought was here.

One end of the workbench had been cleared and was now serving as a mortuary slab. The freezing air in here was as good as an icebox. Really the weather had been a godsend. A Christmas blessing. He smiled at his own little joke.

The remains had shrunk inside their plastic covering, leaving the binding loose. Maybe he should have brought it back here sooner, but he hadn't wanted to desecrate either of the graves.

Anger bubbled up inside him. Desecration, that's what it was. The girl had lain in peace for all those years. He would have buried the boy beside her, but at the time foresters had been working near by and he couldn't risk it. He'd settled for the loch.

They should both have been allowed to rest in peace.

It was the woman's fault. Her reckless driving had started all of this. Had it not been for her, both of them would have remained undiscovered for ever.

He looked out at the snow-covered garden. Pretty as it was, it would make a burial service difficult. He had already chosen a suitable place among the trees, but would have to wait for the weather to change. He was only sorry that he couldn't bury them together.

He locked the workshop door and went inside the house. The sudden warmth quickly brought colour to his cheeks. He entered the kitchen and switched on the radio. He wanted to listen to the service of carols and readings as he prepared lunch.

He set about scraping the surface of the parboiled potatoes with a fork, sprinkled them with salt and slipped them in below the sizzling turkey. He had already opened the red wine and left it to take the air. Touching the bottle, he was pleased to find the temperature about right.

He hummed along with the carols as he set the small table in the dining alcove, laying out two places. The young prison guard had called and had been invited round for Christmas day lunch, an invitation he had eagerly accepted.

He laid out the holly-patterned napkins and chose the balloon glasses for the wine. Now it only remained for him to prepare the remaining vegetables. He washed and peeled the Brussels sprouts, slicing a diagonal cross in the stem, then prepared the parsnips. He was very fond of roast parsnips. He poured a glass of wine and opened a second bottle with a smile.

As he sipped, he contemplated the forthcoming activities. He had planned to show Daniel his workshop, but that wasn't possible now. Instead he had brought in some pieces of finished glass for him to admire. The panel depicting the child was the centrepiece, of course. He was particularly pleased with the milkiness of the hair and the ruby-red glass he'd used for the blood droplets. He wondered momentarily whether Daniel would discern the true picture hidden in the swirls of colour and shape. The idea excited him.

He glanced at the clock. Daniel had agreed to work Christmas morning. Allowing for transport difficulties in the snow, his arrival was likely to be mid-afternoon. Everything would be ready and waiting. There was just one more thing to do.

41

Chrissy had insisted on digging out the forensic van, despite Rhona's attempts to stop her. Rhona had found a shovel in the garden shed, rusted, its handle thinned by wear. She'd used that one, leaving Chrissy with the pristine model that formed part of her 'emergency' collection of utensils.

The snow, although deep, was light and easy to

shift. Once all four wheels were free, she tried the engine. It fired on the third attempt. Behind her Chrissy was doing the same with the van. Rhona let the engine run for a while, then switched off and went to check on Chrissy.

'I'm going to take a look farther on,' she said.

'I'll go with you.'

The next section of track was impassable by car. After that things began to look better for a while, the snow shallow. Unfortunately a few yards later they encountered a waist-high drift of some length. Walking the road in daylight only served to reinforce the danger they'd been in the previous night.

One thing was certain, they were going nowhere without the farmer's help.

'Maybe I should walk to the main road.'

'And leave me here?' Chrissy sounded incredulous.

'There's more of a chance of a signal once I'm out of the glen, and I might get a lift.'

Chrissy wasn't convinced.

'We have to let McNab know what we've found.'

'Then we'll both go to the main road.'

'What if the landline's restored more quickly than the mobile? If I'm still at the road end by the time you're dug out, we'll go together.'

A two-pronged attack made sense.

'OK,' Chrissy conceded.

They parted company. Rhona walked on a few yards, then turned to watch the small bundled figure trudging back towards the cottage. Chrissy wouldn't be alone for long, she consoled herself. Mr Jenkins was bound to appear soon.

By car, the track had seemed a fair distance. On

foot it was endless. Even with the help of a tractor, getting a vehicle to the road would take some time. Climbing out of the valley, she was rewarded by a buzz from her mobile, indicating the arrival of a message. McNab's voice sounded terrible. He asked her to phone him right away.

His phone rang five times. Rhona was anticipating a switch to voicemail when McNab came on the line.

'Where are you?'

'Trying to get away from the cottage. We got snowed in last night.'

'Shit!'

'Emma left us a message.' She gave him a quick summary of their findings, including the fact that Emma didn't seem to know her abductor.

'You and I both know the odds are against it being a stranger,' he said.

'Then who?'

McNab was at as much of a loss as Rhona. 'We've nothing on Claire's life before she left Glasgow. We're still trying to find out which primary school Emma went to before they moved.'

Claire had covered her tracks well, which did suggest she'd been hiding from someone.

'If someone was looking for Claire and they knew about her mother's death, they could have turned up at the funeral,' suggested McNab.

'And followed Emma to the wood?' Rhona suddenly wished she'd brought this possibility up with Claire. Maybe then Claire would have told them whether someone was harassing her.

There was a baffled silence.

'I've been checking the Mollie Curtis file,' said McNab eventually. 'Guess who did the groundwork on that?'

'Who?'

'Slater. That's what led to his promotion.' His tone was loaded.

'What are you suggesting?'

'Nothing, but I'm working on it. Can you hitch a lift back to Glasgow?'

'I'm trying to.'

'Call me when you get here. I'm going to visit Mollie's killer.'

'But it's Christmas Day.'

'So I'll take him a present.'

'Maybe you should take Magnus with you.'

There was a grunt of disapproval.

'He's good at reading people. He could just observe.'

'It's Christmas Day. He'll have plans.'

McNab hung up before Rhona could respond. His obvious agitation worried her. Something bad had happened, something he hadn't told her about.

Ten minutes later she was in sight of the main road. Snow piled up by a plough blocked the end of the drive. She climbed up the hard-packed mound. There were no vehicles in sight, but she could tell by the tyre tracks that someone had travelled along the cleared road recently. She had to wait twenty minutes before a car came into view. She waved it down.

42

The baby-faced guard on reception wasn't impressed by McNab's appearance or his ripe smell. McNab had got used to both by now. Bar going home to change, he'd accepted he couldn't do anything about it and there were more important things than taking a shower and putting on clean clothes.

McNab waited as the guard re-examined his ID. If he'd compared his face to the identity photograph once, he'd done it ten times.

'Fuckssake,' he hissed under his breath.

'What did you say?' Righteous indignation spotted the boy's plump cheeks.

'You do realise you're hindering a murder inquiry.'

A deeper flush crept over the guard's cheeks, and he waved McNab through. The visiting room was dotted with families celebrating Christmas prison-style. By rights the meeting should have taken place in an interview room with McCarthy's brief present, but McNab had sold this as a friendly visit on Christmas Day.

He hadn't had time to study the Mollie Curtis case in detail, but seeing Slater's name in the file had coloured his attitude from the outset. If Slater had been anything like the boss, McNab could have talked over his concerns surrounding the case, including the guy on the road and the possibility that someone had followed the kid in the woods, but Slater wasn't DI Wilson. He was a whole different species.

McCarthy appeared five minutes later, walking into the room and taking a quick look around. Baby-face pointed in McNab's direction. A few words were exchanged, and McCarthy looked quite pleased. He obviously liked having a visitor on Christmas Day, even if it was a police officer. Or maybe *because* it was a police officer. He came over and took a seat across the table from McNab, who showed him his ID.

McCarthy smiled. His teeth were weird, coated with yellow. McNab inadvertently licked his own clean.

'What happened to you?'

'Walked into a lamp-post in the blizzard last night.'

McCarthy shook his head in sympathy. 'You look fucking awful. Eyes like slits.'

'Thanks.'

It was the pot calling the kettle black.

'I knew you would come. Soon as I heard you'd found the grave.'

'Whose grave?'

'Mollie Curtis.'

'The girl you killed?'

The prisoner shook his head vehemently. 'I didn't kill her.'

'You confessed to it.'

McCarthy leaned towards McNab. His breath smelt terrible. 'I didn't kill her and I didn't bury her. Forensic will prove that.' He said *forensic* as if it were the word of God.

'Forensic found her blood on your clothes, along with your semen. Forensic put you in here.'

'She cut her finger. I put a plaster on for her.' McCarthy sounded aggrieved.

'Then you jerked off?'

McCarthy glared balefully at him.

'I didn't hurt Mollie. I didn't kill her.'

McNab drew back to get out of range of the man's red gums and rotting teeth. 'Want to know how we found her?'

McCarthy's eyes narrowed.

The news bulletins hadn't mentioned Emma, and McNab didn't know why he was mentioning her now. 'A wee girl told us where she was.'

McCarthy's mouth puckered like a cartoon character's. 'A wee girl?'

'She said she heard a voice calling to her from the woods. The voice led her to the grave.'

McCarthy's face was turning a similar colour to his teeth.

'I've heard people who are murdered often come back to haunt their killer,' said McNab.

'I *didn't* kill her.'

'Then you've got nothing to worry about.'

But McCarthy clearly was worried.

'Thing is, the girl also heard a second voice.'

'I didn't kill the boy either.'

A shiver descended McNab's spine.

'What boy?'

He watched as the shutters came down on McCarthy's eyes. He'd assumed the look of a child confronted by an angry adult. His voice became a whine. 'Did you bring me a Christmas present?'

'How about early release?'

McCarthy licked his yellow teeth.

'Tell me about the boy.'

*　　　*　　　*

235

McNab examined the visitor list. Apart from himself, a prison volunteer came once a fortnight. That was it. McCarthy had no one who cared whether he lived or died, or cleaned his teeth.

He fired change into the coffee machine and watched as muddy liquid filled the paper cup. McCarthy had rabbited on about CSI and finding forensic evidence at the grave that would clear him. No matter what McNab said, he couldn't get him back on the subject of the boy.

He racked his brains but failed to recall a link with another missing-kid case. Slater would be the one to ask, of course. He contemplated phoning his new boss at home on Christmas Day and enjoyed the fantasy while it lasted.

The caffeine and sugar buzzed around McNab's brain and reminded him how hungry he was. He needed food, and he needed to properly study the notes on the Curtis case. He checked his phone in case Rhona had called while he was incarcerated, but there was nothing. He drank the remainder of the coffee then dragged his sorry body back on its feet.

Glasgow was getting back to normal after the blizzard, or as normal as Christmas Day could be. Snow swept from the roads was piled in the gutter. No longer deep and crisp and even, it now consisted of hardened grey lumps. McNab picked his way through it and managed to flag down a lone taxi. He was compelled to show his badge before the driver would allow such a bedraggled and bloodied passenger to enter his pristine cab. They indulged in some desultory chit-chat about the weather and Christmas in general.

'I can't stand turkey, myself,' the taxi driver told

him. 'So I work and the wife entertains the relatives. That means we're both happy.' He forbore asking why McNab looked as though he had been beaten up. No doubt he'd seen worse in his time on the job.

As he stepped over the threshold of his flat, McNab's legs almost gave out. Fit though he was, being manhandled by Solonik and flung in a skip was taking its toll. He made straight for the whisky bottle and poured a decent shot. He drank it swiftly and poured another, taking it to the shower with him. He dropped his clothes on the floor and climbed under.

The shower felt like hot needles against his bruises, but gradually warmth spread through his shattered, chilled body. He held his face up to the spray, filled his aching mouth and spat the bloodied water out. After a full ten minutes he stepped out, reached for the glass and drank the second whisky. Now that he was warm outside and in, the pain was receding a little. He dressed, then looked up the pizza carry-out number and ordered a pepperoni and a margarita. The inflated Christmas Day prices would have bought him a week's supply of food. While he waited for the pizzas to arrive, he checked out the contents of the fridge for a starter. He was starving, but couldn't face the single soft tomato and square of blue-tinged Cheddar—all that remained from his last shopping trip.

When the buzzer went he released the lower door, assuming it was the pizzas. But the pizza man wasn't his only visitor. When McNab opened the door Rhona looked even more horrified than the guy holding the eagerly awaited boxes. Only then did McNab appreciate just how bad he looked.

'What the hell happened?'

'Let me eat first, then I'll tell you.'

McNab paid the gobsmacked delivery man and ushered Rhona and the steaming boxes into the kitchen.

'Open those while I get the whisky.'

When he reappeared with the bottle, she had set a couple of plates on the table.

'Want some?' He waved the bottle at her.

She nodded and he fetched fresh glasses from the cupboard. He numbed his sore mouth with whisky then set about the pepperoni pizza. A lifetime had passed since he'd eaten roasted piglet at the Russian Restaurant. In retrospect he wished Grogorovitch had poisoned him instead of putting him in the hands of Solonik.

They ate in companionable silence, taking slices from alternate boxes. When McNab had taken the edge off his hunger, he gave Rhona a run-through of the events in the restaurant and afterwards. He avoided telling her about Solonik's party pieces, although he suspected she could read between the lines. Repeating even a sanitised version of the story made him nauseous.

'There was another guy in the room with Solonik but I never saw his face, just heard his voice. He didn't sound Russian; his voice was neutral, well educated, without an accent. I don't think he was in the car when Solonik picked me up. They put something over my head so I don't know where they took me.' McNab knew he should be asking himself the usual questions. *How long did they drive for? Were there any sounds that could help pinpoint the location?* But when he tried to think back, his mind shut down.

'Have you reported this?'

He shook his head. 'I'd rather Solonik and his boss considered me dead for the moment.' He could hear his heart pounding so loudly it sounded as though the organ had taken up residence in his ears. He felt again the excruciating pressure of Solonik's nails on his eyeballs. McNab raised the glass to his lips and forced the whisky down his tightened throat.

'I shopped Brogan to save myself. Only that didn't save me. The illegals did.'

'Brogan should never have got involved with the Russians,' said Rhona.

'Maybe he had no choice.'

'There's always a choice.'

McNab was well aware of that. He'd chosen to point the finger at Brogan in an effort to save himself.

Rhona was observing him with concern. 'You think it was Misha that told them you were at the restaurant?'

He didn't like her use of Grigorovitch's first name. His response was sharp.

'Who the fuck else would it be except *Misha*?'

His tone had stung her. McNab wanted to apologise but couldn't bring himself to. He tried to take another slug of the whisky but could barely raise his arm from the table. His body was seizing up. He would have to move now or he was finished.

He dragged himself to his feet.

'What are you doing?'

'McCarthy mentioned a boy. He said, *I didn't kill*

the boy.'

'What boy?'

'Exactly. I tried to get more out of him but he clammed up. Said he wanted to talk to his prison visitor.'

'Emma said there was another body.'

'And nobody believed her, least of all me.'

McNab was thinking about Emma. Those big trusting eyes.

'What if we're wrong, and Emma's disappearance does have something to do with finding the remains?' Rhona said.

'Exactly what I was thinking.'

43

Daniel had been surprised when he asked him to leave as soon as the meal was over, but there had been little choice, not after the phone call. It would not be appropriate for Daniel to be seen here. As a prison visitor he was well regarded. Entertaining young prison officers in his home might be hard to explain.

He recorked the unfinished second bottle of wine. Disappointment at the shortening of Daniel's visit had been replaced by excitement. He feared nothing from the police visit. He had no reason to. They were coming to see him either because of his voluntary connection with McCarthy or concerning yesterday's letter to the governor.

He'd told DS McNab to come at around six. That gave him plenty of time to clear up after the meal and remove the item from the workshop.

As he washed the dishes, he mulled over what this meeting might bring. He'd always known that his proximity to McCarthy, the endless hours listening to the moron's attempts at conversation, would pay off eventually.

If DS McNab had done his homework he would be aware just how reliable he was. Prison visitor, Justice of the Peace, member of the Children's Panel. All the people he had helped, especially the children. And he'd done his best to help McCarthy. Much more than others in his position would have done.

He rinsed the wineglasses and put them to one side. The truth was he welcomed this visit and was prepared for it. And now that any possibility of being recognised had been circumvented, he felt quite calm about it. No, not calm, more quietly exhilarated.

Daniel had complained a little. Said he'd had too much wine to drive home. But he'd remained adamant. When the young guard looked like arguing, he'd revealed the source of the phone call. He had been taken aback by that. Apparently DS McNab had visited McCarthy only that morning and Daniel had been his point of contact. The policeman had looked a mess, according to Daniel, as though he'd been in a fight.

They had said their goodbyes at the door. Daniel had hung back, obviously keen that they should make further arrangements before his departure. He had not obliged. They had had lunch together. Daniel was interested in his work and he had been kind enough to show him it. That was all.

Now he looked out on the darkness of the

garden, imagining the distant trees. It would have been better if the funeral had already taken place, but there would be time enough when the snow melted.

He dried his hands and put on a jacket against the cold, before he opened the back door and stepped out into the starry stillness.

The temperature in the workshop was well below freezing. Moisture had leaked from the plastic wrapping and frozen hard on the surface of the workbench and the floor below. He contemplated bringing out a kettle of boiling water and rinsing it clean, then decided not to. The boiling water would only freeze and make the floor slippery.

The bundle was light in his arms. He went through the little room at the back where he stored his forensic materials, and opened the door to the cellar.

44

'If there was a guy on the road, why didn't he call an ambulance or the police?'

McNab was right. Any decent person would at least call for help, unless he was somewhere he shouldn't be.

'And when the remains were discovered . . .' said Rhona.

'He could be placed by Claire at the scene.'

They'd been going round and round like this for what seemed like hours. None of it made any sense. Not if McCarthy was guilty of the crime he was locked up for.

They'd already been through the Mollie Curtis file. Slater, a DS at the time, had been the one to nail Colin McCarthy for the murder. The evidence he'd compiled on the case was comprehensive, so it was no wonder he was convicted, even without a body. The only anomaly was his lack of prior convictions. A female neighbour of his had complained that McCarthy had exposed himself to her, but the accusation was made only after Mollie's disappearance.

McCarthy had been ideal suspect fodder. A loner, regarded as odd, even a bit simple. No doubt the local kids made fun of him. He was 'of low IQ and easily led', according to the psychologist who'd interviewed him, but she had offered no reason as to why this should make him a killer. It appeared that McCarthy had moved from a single incident of exposure (assuming the woman's accusation was true) to killing a child in a matter of weeks. Not impossible, but certainly unusual. Child killers usually turned out to have a long list of prior convictions, often for sexual offences. His confession had been the clincher, even though he'd tried to retract it later. And Mollie's blood had been on his clothes.

There had been nothing in the file about a missing boy.

McNab checked his watch and logged out, drawing himself painfully to his feet.

'Let's see what this prison visitor, Hugh Swanson, has to say.'

*   *   *

McNab sat stiffly in the passenger seat. At first

he'd wanted to drive but had eventually conceded defeat and let Rhona take the wheel. His attempts to get in the car would have been comic had they not looked so agonising. Every turn in the road made him grit his teeth.

Mr Swanson had readily agreed to their visit despite it being Christmas. Apparently he'd even sounded keen. 'Another sad bastard with nothing better to do than work on Christmas Day,' was McNab's take on it.

The dual carriageway was relatively quiet. The remains of the snow had turned to a thin film of slush that splattered their windscreen with each passing car. Twenty minutes later they were free of the city and passing through open farmland.

'Leave this to me,' McNab told Rhona as they drew up at the front door.

She was tempted to tell him that his face was more likely to scare Swanson than she was, but let it go.

He knocked a couple of times, then they heard the sound of carpeted footsteps in the hallway before the front door was opened.

Rhona noticed that Swanson coped well with McNab's battered face. He was obviously a polite man, someone who didn't gawp at the afflicted. He looked to be in his late fifties or early sixties, sturdily built, his hair going thin on top. He regarded them with a pleasant smile.

'Mr Swanson? I'm DS McNab, and this is Dr Rhona MacLeod from Forensic Services.'

Swanson gave Rhona an appraising look and held out his hand. 'Delighted to meet you, Dr MacLeod. I take a keen interest in your area of work. Fascinating, isn't it?'

244

'Sometimes.'

'Oh, I know the television programmes exaggerate things somewhat, but I enjoy them nonetheless.'

He ushered them through the hall and into a fair-sized sitting room, comfortably furnished and very tidy. Rhona thought briefly of her own flat. Minimalist as she was, she had never achieved this degree of neatness. Swanson indicated they should take a seat. He offered them coffee or tea, but McNab declined.

'I'm sorry to take up your time on Christmas Day, but I wanted to ask you a few questions about Colin McCarthy.'

'Ah, Colin.' Their host looked suitably concerned.

'I believe you're a regular visitor of his?'

'I've been a prison visitor for about ten years. Colin is one of my clients.'

'Has he ever spoken to you about his crime?'

'Frequently.'

'What has he said?'

'That he's sorry.'

'Sorry he did it?'

Swanson nodded. 'It troubles him a great deal.'

'Really. When I interviewed McCarthy today he insisted he did not murder Mollie Curtis.'

'Colin wishes he hadn't killed Mollie. Sometimes he even convinces himself that's true.'

He clasped his hands together, drawing Rhona's attention to them. They were small and chubby. Both index fingers sported a waterproof plaster.

'McCarthy has confessed all this to you?' McNab asked him.

He nodded. 'Many times.' Then he looked

245

puzzled. 'But you must be aware of his original confession, Sergeant?'

'Which he subsequently retracted.'

'I'm afraid there is no doubt that Colin murdered Mollie Curtis. And now there is the other issue I spoke of in my letter to the governor.'

'What issue?' snapped McNab.

Swanson looked confused. 'I thought that was why you were here, Sergeant. I wrote to the governor on Saturday after I visited Colin. The poor man was in a dreadful state. He'd been told you were coming to interview him. I tried to reassure him, of course, but finding those remains had brought it all back.'

'McCarthy told you the remains were Mollie's?'

Swanson shook his head. 'No.'

'Then what was the issue that compelled you to write to the governor?'

The man took a moment to compose himself. 'It might mean nothing, but Colin began to talk about a boy. I was concerned he might have harmed another child. One we don't know about.'

A thin film of sweat glistened on McNab's bruised brow. He leaned forward, his mouth a taut line. 'What *exactly* did McCarthy say?'

Swanson thought for a moment. 'That the boy wasn't his fault. When I asked what he meant, he wouldn't tell me.'

'Has McCarthy any friends on the outside?'

'Not to my knowledge, and I've been visiting him from the beginning of his incarceration. I am his only visitor, that's why I can't stop going, although sometimes I would like to. Colin is psychologically damaged and simple in the extreme, Detective Sergeant. Not the easiest of clients.'

Swanson was fiddling with the plaster on his left hand.

'Cut yourself carving the Christmas turkey?' asked Rhona.

He shook his head with a smile. 'A hazard of the job, I'm afraid. I work with glass.'

Rhona felt McNab give a start beside her.

'Engraving?' She kept her voice even.

'I specialise in stained glass, repairing church windows mostly, but I also create my own designs.' He looked pleased by her interest. 'It's a passion of mine, actually.'

McNab made a sound that might have been construed as indifference and made to rise, as though the interview was over.

'My father was a keen photographer of church windows,' Rhona improvised as they moved towards the door. 'Are you working on anything at the moment?'

'An American benefactor has donated money to the local church for the restoration of a window. I've agreed to carry out the work.'

'How interesting. I'd love to see it.'

Swanson seemed pleased by the idea. 'If you don't mind a freezing workshop, I could show you before you leave?'

Outside, the temperature had dropped and the moon shone in a black liquid sky. The snow crunched under their feet as it froze hard. Swanson unlocked the workshop door and flicked on a light.

The workshop was as neat as the house and as cold as a morgue, Rhona thought as she stepped over the threshold. A three-metre workbench was backed by a wall rack filled with art glass. The

247

bright overhead light reflected off a patchwork of colours; blues and reds, oranges and greens.

'It's over here. Be careful, it's a little slippy. I spilt some water when I washed the window.'

He led her to a stained-glass panel lying on the left-hand section of the workbench. It depicted a figure kneeling in prayer. Above its head was a smaller figure made up of red fragments.

'I'm not sure who the main character is, but the smaller one is probably meant to represent a seraph. In the Bible, seraphim are the highest rank of angels. They're associated with burning, so are always depicted in red glass.' Mr Swanson was evidently enjoying himself.

Rhona surveyed the panel admiringly. 'I suppose every picture tells a story?'

'Yes. That's what makes the work so interesting.'

A second work lay next to the panel. This one was more abstract, with no clear central image. The swirls of colour were powerful and at the same time slightly unsettling.

'What's this?'

'One of my own designs.'

'It's quite beautiful,' Rhona said honestly. 'Particularly the opal glass segment. What does the image represent?'

Swanson shrugged his shoulders. 'Nothing in particular. I just like mixing colours.'

She sniffed the air. 'The scent of putty always reminds me of my childhood.'

'Linseed oil is used in the cement for the windows,' he explained. 'You smell of it for hours even if you wash your hands well. Good job I don't have a wife to complain about it.'

Swanson led them outside and closed and locked

the workshop door. McNab thanked him for his time.

'You're very welcome, although I fear I wasn't much help.'

'On the contrary. If McCarthy reveals anything more during your visits, you'll let us know?'

'Of course.'

When they reached the car, McNab opened the door, then turned back, as though he'd just remembered something.

'I suppose you know how we discovered Mollie's remains?'

Swanson shook his head.

'A car went off the road near by. One of the occupants of the car was a child. She found the skull when she wandered into the woods.'

'How awful.' He looked genuinely distressed.

Rhona wondered what McNab was playing at. The police had gone out of their way not to tell the public about Emma.

'I don't know if you caught the news bulletin about a woman and her young daughter who disappeared from their home some time on Friday night in suspicious circumstances?' McNab continued.

'I think I do remember something . . .'

'That was Emma, the girl who found the skull.'

Swanson now looked horrified. 'You don't think their disappearance has anything to do with finding the remains?'

'What makes you say that?'

The older man floundered a little under McNab's penetrating gaze. 'I just thought when you mentioned the girl's part in discovering the body, then her disappearance . . .' He tailed off.

'Claire Watson reported seeing a man on the road prior to the crash. She thought he'd come from the woods.'

'Really? Is that important?'

'It might be, if McCarthy had an accomplice.'

'With the greatest respect, Detective Sergeant, McCarthy was and is a loner.'

'That's what bothers me.'

Rhona could see that McNab had rattled the man.

'I don't understand, Sergeant.'

'Colin McCarthy can't drive, Mr Swanson. So how did he transport Mollie's body to those woods?'

45

Swanson waited until the car's headlights were out of sight before he went inside and locked the door. The anger he'd held in check now rose to consume him. He gave it free rein, relishing every violent image of what he could and would do to both McNab and the woman. They thought they were so smart, springing information on him, trying to catch him out. There was nothing, nothing to connect him to the remains in the wood. There was no one to connect him to that night. Not any more. He had absolutely nothing to be concerned about.

That DS was a sly bastard. Bringing up the subject of the bitch and her daughter's disappearance like that. His answer replayed itself in his head and he smashed his hand down on the nearby coffee table. That was the forensic woman's fault. She'd tricked him by pretending to be interested in his work. And he'd allowed her to enter the workshop. He'd shown her the window. He thought about her reaction. The stupid bitch hadn't a clue what was hidden in the picture. And even if she had made out the shape of a child, there was nothing wrong with that. He suddenly recalled the intensity of her gaze. She was a forensic scientist and they noticed things others didn't. But there was nothing to notice. Nothing but glass and the smell of putty.

The thought came to him that she had remarked on the putty smell. *It reminds me of my childhood*, she'd said. Was the remark significant? He quickly dismissed the idea. She had been trying to put him at ease. Trying to make him like her, while the man hovered in the background with a bored look on his face. The DS wasn't interested in the workshop, he just wanted to bring up the subject of McCarthy not being able to drive, hinting that McCarthy must have had an accomplice.

Maybe he was hinting that he had helped McCarthy?

The notion entered Swanson's mind and took root. That was why they were here. They thought he'd helped McCarthy dispose of the body. He remembered how frequently he'd stressed that no one visited McCarthy, that he had no friends on the outside except him! They'd tricked him, put words in his mouth.

He went through to the kitchen, helped himself to a glass of red wine from the unfinished bottle and sat down at the kitchen table. The warm, full-bodied liquid swam through him like a surge of

251

new blood, quelling his agitation. There was nothing to tie him to the murder of Mollie Curtis. Besides, he had just helped the authorities by exposing the possibility that McCarthy might have killed another child.

He mulled this over. Maybe the shock of McCarthy's revelation had upset him so much he wanted to stop his prison visits. A man could only take so much. Visiting a murderer who confesses to further crimes would traumatise anyone.

Maybe he should take a short holiday to recover.

A visit to Venice to study the stained-glass windows? He began to turn the idea over in his head and the more he thought about it the better the plan seemed.

He glanced at the window, where frost sparkled on the glass. It was getting colder by the minute. The forecast had promised sub-zero temperatures to follow the blizzard, lasting through to the New Year. He smiled and took another mouthful of wine, his stomach rumbling a little.

He retrieved what was left of the Christmas pudding from the fridge and slipped it in the microwave to warm, then added brandy butter, watching it soften and run down the sides. He carried the bowl through to the sitting room, switched on the computer and settled down to check availability of flights to Venice.

46

'Sanctimonious bastard!' said McNab. 'Turn left at the crossroads.'

'Where are we going?'

'Somewhere I can get a drink.'

A few miles farther on they found a cluster of houses and a small hotel with its lights blazing. Through the dining-room window they could see people enjoying an evening meal.

They abandoned the car in the first available parking space and headed for the front door. The bar was hot and crowded but moments after they arrived a group were called through to the dining room. Rhona slid into the empty space they provided.

'What do you want to drink?' he asked.

'Coffee.'

He raised an eyebrow but didn't comment. They couldn't both drink alcohol and McNab needed an anaesthetic more than she did. He arrived back minutes later with a large whisky and a cup of coffee.

'Was it true?' she said as he sat down opposite her.

'What?'

'What you said about McCarthy not being a driver.'

'It was in the case file.' McNab swallowed a large mouthful and winced as the whisky stung his tender mouth. 'They assumed McCarthy had buried the body locally.' He examined the amber liquid left in the glass, swirling it in anticipation.

'Painkillers would work better.'

'This is my painkiller.' He drained the glass.

'Michael,' she remonstrated.

'D'you realise you only use my first name when you're telling me off about something?'

'That's not true.'

He met her eye. 'Yes it is.'

'Slater won't listen to you if you're drunk.'

McNab set the empty glass on the table.

'Slater won't listen to me anyway.'

'If McCarthy can't drive then he had an accomplice. There were traces of stained glass in the grave, remember? Swanson works in glass. Maybe he helped McCarthy.'

'Swanson's a do-gooder, a pillar of society. On the boards of various charities, the Children's Panel, a church elder who restores stained-glass windows. I just don't see him and McCarthy as partners in crime.'

'What about the putty smell in the woods?'

McNab gave a sigh of exasperation.

'Did *you* smell putty?'

'No, but . . .'

'The fragment of glass isn't enough. It could have got there in lots of ways.'

'How?'

'Dropped by someone walking in the woods.'

'It was under the body.'

'Dropped there before there was a body.' McNab acknowledged her frosty look. 'OK, you're the forensic expert, what is it you want me to do?'

'Ask Slater for a search warrant for Swanson's place.'

'You are joking?' He regarded her disbelievingly.

'You heard the way he reacted to Emma's dis-

254

appearance.'

'He put two and two together, probably my fault.'

'You don't believe that?'

'I don't know what I believe.'

'So you're just going to get drunk and forget about Emma and Claire?'

McNab grimaced as though she had hit him full on his bruised face. 'If I call Slater with this story on Christmas Day he'll have me suspended along with the DI.'

Rhona wasn't convinced he'd given up. She'd seen him like this before. Like a wave crashing on the shore, he went full at it before retreating, steeped in doubt.

'What if I call Slater?'

McNab looked surprised. 'It won't do any good,' he warned.

She went to look for a quiet spot to make the call. She needed to make the request sound as though it was just the next step in the forensic investigation, and feed Slater the likelihood that the body was Mollie Curtis. She would then remind him that McCarthy didn't drive so he would have needed an accomplice to transport the body to the woods. That would give her the opportunity to bring up the glass fragment and the fact that McCarthy's only contact outside the prison happened to work in stained glass. Suggesting a forensic examination of Swanson's workshop would be the next obvious step.

Mrs Slater answered the phone, sounding festive. Rhona introduced herself then asked to speak to the DI.

'On Christmas Day?' his wife remonstrated.

When Slater came on the line she apologised for disturbing his Christmas, then told him about Mollie.

'Couldn't this have waited until tomorrow?'

Rhona ran through the scenario anyway. A deathly silence followed.

'Who is this contact?' Slater snapped, eventually.

'His name is Hugh Swanson.'

'The prison visitor?'

'Yes.'

'Who is also a Justice of the Peace and a member of the Children's Panel?'

She remained silent.

'And you call me on Christmas Day to ask me to authorise a search warrant for this man's home based on a fragment of glass?' Slater was having difficulty controlling his temper.

'That's not all. DS McNab visited McCarthy . . .'

'He did what?'

Rhona rushed on. 'McCarthy talked about a boy. He said the boy wasn't his fault. Apparently he had also mentioned a boy to Swanson. And, if you remember, it was Emma that alerted us to the possibility of another body, a boy, being secreted in the woods.'

'Who spoke to Swanson?' Slater's tone was icy.

Rhona didn't answer.

'We'll discuss this at the strategy meeting tomorrow morning. Good night, Dr MacLeod.'

The phone clattered down.

McNab looked up as Rhona entered. She slipped in opposite him.

'I think I may have got you into more trouble.'

McNab grinned.

'Forget it. Something interesting happened while

you were away.'

*   *   *

'Anya is Misha's sister. When I described the burned guy to her last night she turned white and puked. Misha made the excuse that the description sounded like a cousin who was in fact alive. I didn't believe him. I think Anya was closer to the dead guy than that. I gave her my card, asked her to call me when she felt up to talking about it.'

'And she did?'

'But not about the skip fire. She heard on the news about Claire. She says she knows her. She sounded really freaked about Claire's disappearance.'

'Has she any idea where Claire might be?'

'She wouldn't say on the phone. She asked to meet me outside Jury's Inn on Clyde Street in half an hour.'

McNab was back on the crest of a wave. Either the whisky had taken the edge off the pain or the possibility of finding Claire had kicked him back into action. Considering what he had been through over the last forty-eight hours it was a miracle he was still functioning at all.

As she drove back towards town Rhona wondered whether meeting anyone from the Russian contingent was a wise move after what had happened the last time. When she broached the subject with McNab, he brushed aside her concerns.

'We drive up, Anya gets in the car. We drive away.'

It sounded too easy. She told him so. 'Solonik

257

thinks you're dead. Maybe he's getting Anya to check out if it's true?'

'She could have done that without mentioning Claire.'

*   *   *

As they crossed the Clyde, Rhona saw a small group of guests vacate Jury's to light up outside the main entrance. She swung left on to Clyde Street. There was no one waiting for them at the allotted spot. Rhona cursed under her breath. A complete circle of the one-way system might take ten minutes with the lights against her.

'Pull on to the pavement!' McNab commanded.

To their left was the docking place for the ferry that travelled upriver to Braehead shopping centre. The Clydeside walkway that ran alongside was in shadowy darkness, split at intervals by brighter light. Rhona pulled abruptly off the road and killed the engine, ignoring the angry horn blast from the car behind. McNab opened the door.

'I think you should stay in the car,' she urged.

'If she doesn't see it's me she won't come out.'

He stepped into a pool of light. At first there was nothing then Rhona saw a movement in the shadow of the walkway and a slight figure came into view. It was a young woman, long dark hair framing her face.

'Anya?' he called softly.

She came forward, tentatively at first. Rhona heard her register the state of McNab's face and saw her hand rise to her mouth in shock.

'Get in the car.'

He held the rear door open. Anya walked swiftly towards them and slid in the back. McNab closed the door then got in beside Rhona, stifling a groan.

'Go!'

'Where?' Rhona said.

'Head for your flat, but make it the long way round.'

He watched in the rear-view mirror as Rhona indicated and drew out. She did as he'd requested, winding her way up through the city centre in the general direction of home. After five minutes McNab seemed satisfied that no one was tailing them.

'Find somewhere and pull in.'

*   *   *

'What happened to your face?' Anya's voice was low and accented, her tone concerned.

'Your brother told someone I was asking awkward questions. They picked me up when I left the restaurant.'

She looked shocked. 'Misha wouldn't do that.'

'You and I both know that Misha's either mixed up with the Russian lot or he's shit scared of them. Which is it, Anya?'

There was a moment's silence. 'The man who died was called Alexei Petrov.'

'Who murdered him?'

'I do not know.'

'Anya,' McNab warned. 'If they were prepared to torture and kill a police officer, what do you think they would do to you or Misha?'

They waited while Anya struggled with herself. 'His name is Nikolai Kalinin. But he would not have killed Alexei himself. There is a man called . . .'

'Solonik?'

'Yes.' Her voice was a whisper of fear. 'That is why I called you. I think Solonik took Claire. Claire came into the restaurant one day about six months ago. We chatted. I hadn't been here in Glasgow long and she became my first real friend. Then she met Nikolai. I didn't know then what he was like, or I would never have introduced them.' Her voice faltered. 'Nikolai became Claire's lover. She even told him about Emma. Then she stopped coming to the restaurant. She didn't answer my calls. I saw her one day on the street a month ago. She looked terrible. I asked her what was wrong.' Anya paused, tears in her eyes. 'She wouldn't tell me. Then Nikolai turned up at the restaurant and demanded to know where she was. I couldn't tell him because I didn't know.'

'And he believed you?'

'He threatened to kill Misha and I still couldn't tell him.'

'Where can we find Kalinin?'

She produced a piece of paper. 'When he orders food from the restaurant we deliver it to this address.' Her hand shook as she passed the paper to McNab. 'If he finds out I've spoken to you . . .'

'He won't,' promised McNab.

They dropped her round the corner from the restaurant. As she walked away, Rhona thought how diminutive she looked. Diminutive but courageous. Anya Grigorovitch had taken a big gamble speaking to them. Rhona only hoped they could repay her trust.

'What if Anya's right and Kalinin has Claire?'

she said.

'There's one way to find out.'

47

'Slater won't argue on this one,' said Rhona. 'He wants Kalinin. Call the station, bring in some help. You can't walk in there on your own.'

They were outside the address Anya had given them. A refurbished building in the Merchant City, it rose through four Victorian floors to a modern glass penthouse with a bird's-eye view of the city.

McNab wasn't listening. 'Food'll be here shortly.'

'This is madness. You can't do this on your own.'

'I'm counting on Kalinin to think exactly that.'

She gave up for the moment. She knew him well enough to know he wouldn't be persuaded once he had made up his mind.

When a van with the restaurant's logo pulled up alongside, McNab got out and approached the driver. There was a muffled conversation, then a carrier bag exchanged hands and the van took off. He brought the bag back. The food smelled delicious.

'What happened?'

'I told him I would take it up.'

'You showed him your badge?'

McNab shook his head. 'He took me for one of Kalinin's lot. Must have been my good looks.' He could see Rhona was worried. 'It'll be fine.'

She shook her head. 'Give me the bag.'

'I don't think that's a good idea.'

'Kalinin doesn't know me.'

The man on the desk was in his thirties, and looked very pleased with himself in his smart uniform. Rhona showed him the bag and told him it was for the penthouse flat.

'You're new.'

She smiled. 'Special delivery.'

He grinned. 'Fancy a drink when you're finished?'

'Depends how long I'm up there.'

'I'm not going anywhere.'

She felt his eyes on her back as she walked to the lift. Rhona gave him a little wave as the doors closed, muttering *Conceited arse* through clenched teeth. She pressed the penthouse button and the lift moved swiftly into action, a robotic female voice reciting the floor numbers as they swept past. Eventually there was a ping and the doors slid open on a glass-walled vestibule.

Rhona stood for a moment on the marble tiles, composing herself before she knocked on the only door. She heard footsteps inside and made herself visible through the spyhole. The door was opened by a man in a smart suit. He definitely didn't fit the description McNab had given her of Solonik. This man was tall and heavily built, with black hair and a pockmarked complexion. He eyed her, then the carrier bag.

'Your food order,' she said helpfully.

He looked puzzled and muttered something in what she took to be Russian. She stepped inside as though that were the norm and walked confidently onwards, chattering brightly about serving up. She suspected from the man's reaction that he understood little of what she was saying.

The penthouse was spacious, open-plan and

apparently empty. Rhona went directly to the kitchen area and plonked the bag on a pristine surface. As she began unpacking a voice called from somewhere out of sight and was answered by the man who'd opened the door to her. The result of the interchange was the arrival of another man.

'I didn't order any food.'

The owner of the cultured voice matched McNab's description of Nikolai Kalinin. He was tall, handsome and well groomed, with no trace of an accent.

'I'm sorry,' she said, puzzled. 'I'm sure this was the address I was given.'

He was studying her intently from across the intervening counter, more amused than angry. Rhona suspected Claire's first impression of Nikolai Kalinin had been much like her own—a good-looking, polite guy with a sense of humour.

'I don't think we've met before?'

'Misha's a friend of mine. I offered to help tonight because he was so busy. Looks like I messed up.' Rhona met Kalinin's smile with one of her own. 'Shall I take this back?'

He checked out the contents of the bag, now laid out on the surface.

'All my favourites, I see.'

'Yes, but if you didn't order them . . .'

'I will enjoy them nonetheless.'

Rhona acted relieved. 'Thanks. You've saved me from embarrassment.'

'Good. Have you many more deliveries to do?'

'Yours was the last one.'

'So you can relax now?'

'Not if I go back to the restaurant.' She laughed.

He was scrutinising her. 'Do you like Russian

263

food?'

'Yes, I do.'

'What do you say to sharing some of your mistake with me?'

'I couldn't . . .'

'Or perhaps you've eaten already?'

'No.' If you didn't count sharing McNab's pizza.

'Why don't you dish up two plates and I'll organise some wine to go with it. Misha's an excellent cook, as I'm sure you're aware.' He nodded at the other man and they left the room together.

The original plan had been to have a swift look round for any indication that Claire might be resident in the flat. Dining with Kalinin could give her a better opportunity to do this but it also meant the Russian would have more time to pick her story apart. She met Kalinin at the door.

'Not leaving?'

'Actually I was looking for the bathroom. If I'm going to stay and eat, I'd like to clean up a bit.'

'Of course.' He pointed in the opposite direction. 'Through the door at the far end of the main room, then third on the left.'

The route he'd indicated led into a square vestibule with three doors. The third lay partly open and was obviously the bathroom. Rhona ignored it and reached for the handle on the first door.

It swung open on a luxurious bedroom dominated by a king-size bed with a leather headboard. Above was a mezzanine gallery which had double doors leading to a balcony. There was no outward sign of a woman's presence in the room.

Rhona quietly closed the door and tried the second handle. This room was smaller and stuffed with computer equipment and what looked like a row of security screens high on the wall. Rhona spotted a view of the reception area and several of the outside of the building. McNab and the car were nowhere to be seen.

A loud grunt startled her as a large seated figure, partly hidden by equipment, turned. She watched mesmerised as the man rose to his feet, exposing a pair of enormous hands. This had to be Solonik. She muttered a string of words that included *sorry* and *bathroom* and swiftly exited.

Once inside the bathroom she locked the door and stood with her back against it, fear rippling through her body. What if Solonik had seen McNab take the food from the van and give it to her? What if they'd already picked up McNab?

Rhona took a deep breath and tried to still her nerves. McNab hadn't parked at the entrance and neither had the van. It was perfectly possible that the interchange would not have appeared on camera, but she had to be sure. She extracted her mobile and called McNab's number. It rang unanswered.

She heard Kalinin's voice in the hall and ended the call, flushed the toilet, then turned on the tap full. While she washed her hands, she checked the bathroom for signs of a woman and found none. In fact none of the rooms she'd seen suggested Claire or Emma's presence. If Kalinin was responsible for Claire's abduction, it seemed he hadn't brought her here.

When she returned to the main room, Kalinin had set out the food on a table next to the window.

'I thought you'd got lost.'

'I did a bit.' She smiled. 'What a lovely flat.'

He acknowledged the compliment, then beckoned her over and pulled out a seat.

'This is very kind of you, but I'm not sure I should stay. Misha will wonder what's happened to me.'

'Then call him and set his mind at rest.'

Rhona checked her watch. 'I don't suppose he'll notice if I'm not too long,' she conceded.

He showed her the bottle of wine he'd selected to go with the meal.

She refused with mock reluctance. 'I'm driving, remember?'

'You could walk, it's not far.'

'I'd better not abandon the van.' Even as she said it, Rhona wondered whether Kalinin was already aware that there was no van. If he was, it wasn't obvious from his expression or his voice.

'Then one of my men will drive you.' His smile suggested he was used to getting his own way.

She took her seat.

'So, Misha's friend,' he said as he poured the wine. 'Are you going to tell me your name?'

She lifted her glass and sipped some of the pale golden liquid. 'Rhona.'

'Ah, Rhona.' He nodded as if in approval. 'And how long have you and Misha been,' he paused, '*friends*?'

She lifted her spoon. 'Not long. A few weeks.'

'And yet I have never seen you at the restaurant?' His voice was playful.

Rhona paid close attention to her borscht. 'I'm not there very often.'

She looked up to find him observing her intently.

266

'Why don't you tell me what you really want?'

Kalinin was no fool. He knew she wasn't here simply to deliver food he hadn't even ordered. Stay as close as possible to the truth, Rhona reminded herself. A good friend would be worried about Claire's disappearance, even perhaps to the extent of contacting her former lover.

'Actually, I'm not a friend of Misha's, I'm a friend of Claire Watson's. I used the excuse of delivering a meal to ask you if you know where she is.'

She had surprised him, maybe even astonished him. Whatever he'd expected her to say, it had had nothing to do with Claire. Kalinin appeared to master his emotions before answering.

'Claire and I parted company some weeks ago, as you are probably aware.' His voice barely concealed his anger. 'I have not seen her since. You can search the apartment if you wish, but then again you may already have done that.' This time his smile was not so benign.

Rhona tried to rise from the chair but Kalinin reached forward and caught her right wrist, forcing her back down.

'We haven't finished our conversation yet, *Rhona.*'

He came to stand over her, maintaining his vice-like grip, slowly twisting her wrist away from her body. She gasped as a line of fire ran up her arm. He grabbed her other hand, prised it open and forced it on to his crotch. Rhona felt the beat of his blood under her palm.

'What, no begging me to stop?'

When she didn't answer, he forced her face hard against his chest. The suffocating scent of his cologne turned her stomach and she began to panic. She was back in that place again: the crushing weight of the Gravedigger pinning her down.

'Shall I tell you what I should do to you for coming here? Or perhaps you have discussed me already with Claire?'

Rhona struggled for breath, her mouth and nose smothered by him. Suddenly he released the pressure on her head and tipped up her chin to stare down into her face. There was a flush on his cheeks, but his eyes were cold.

'When you find Claire tell her I have not forgotten her betrayal, nor will I.' He pushed her abruptly away.

She dragged herself to her feet. This time Kalinin did not prevent her. As she walked towards the door Rhona was aware that he might yet dispose of her as easily as he had disposed of Alexei. One word to Solonik would achieve that. For all she knew he had already disposed of McNab.

When she reached the hallway, Solonik's huge bulk barred her exit. He awaited orders from his master. Rhona tried not to look at the massive hands that had snapped Anya's lover's neck, then thrown him like garbage into the skip. The hands that had pounded McNab's face.

Kalinin's barked order, when it came, was in Russian. Rhona expected Solonik to grab her, but instead he opened the door, his face impassive. She stepped into the glass hallway and reached the elevator. As the lift dropped, she leaned against the wall, her heart racing at the possibility of escape. When she emerged at the bottom the guy

268

on the desk smiled a welcome.

She walked straight past him.

'Hey, where are you going?'

The last word she heard was 'slag'.

Outside, the freezing air cut through her. She glanced wildly around, looking for McNab's car, then walked swiftly away from the building, conscious of the click of her heels on the frosted pavement. Late on Christmas Day, the area round the apartment block was deserted. All Kalinin had to do was have Solonik pick her up by car and take her somewhere away from here. Somewhere no one would hear her scream.

The revving of an engine sent her running for the nearest corner. She turned swiftly left, hearing the wheels' attempts to grip the icy surface as the vehicle followed. The pavement here was covered with the hard-packed remains of snow. Momentum drove her forward, the soles of her shoes skittering across the icy surface. She was in one of the narrower alleys that allowed access to the back of what had once been mercantile buildings. Rhona prayed it would not turn out to be a dead end.

The car slipped past her and turned abruptly left, blocking her flight. She was aware of a figure jumping out and shouting as she turned a full 180 degrees and began her retreat.

The chase was over in seconds. Rhona felt a heavy hand grab her shoulder. McNab was breathing heavily, his multicoloured face like something out of a horror movie.

'Where the hell are you going?'

* * *

269

Now McNab was driving and Rhona was the one slumped in the passenger seat.

'You're shaking.'

'I'm cold.'

He turned the heater up full blast, but the flow of hot air didn't help. Shock had set in, making her shudder uncontrollably.

'I'm taking you home.'

She didn't care where she went as long as it was warm. The inner-city streets were deserted apart from a gritter distributing salt. McNab hadn't asked what had happened inside Kalinin's apartment, no doubt waiting until she was ready to broach the subject. Rhona didn't trust her teeth not to rattle together if she opened her mouth to speak.

When they reached her apartment, he took the key from her and let them in. The cat rushed to greet them, winding round her legs, purring loudly. Rhona asked McNab to check Tom had food while she took a shower.

She let the water run as hot as she could bear it. At first it made no difference, then gradually she felt warmth replace the icy grip on her limbs. She closed her eyes, trying to block out the memory of Kalinin's cold stare and vice-like grip. No wonder Claire had run from him. No wonder she had gone into hiding. According to McNab, Emma had not been afraid of Nick. No doubt Kalinin had enjoyed his hold over the mother, while playing the nice guy to her daughter.

Eventually Rhona stepped out of the shower and redressed, putting on an extra layer. The flat was warmer now, so McNab must have found the thermostat. She also smelt coffee. When she entered the kitchen, he was slipping something into the microwave.

'It was a toss-up between chicken and vegetables and vegetables and chicken,' he said gravely.

Rhona smiled. 'I should have taken the Russian food with me when I left.'

McNab looked relieved. 'You're ready to talk?'

They carried the food through to the sitting room. He lit the gas fire while she curled up on the couch. She was hungry, but when she took a forkful of food it tasted like cardboard. She moved it about the plate for a bit, then abandoned it for the coffee. She told McNab her first impression of Kalinin.

'Nice?' McNab was incredulous.

Rhona persisted. 'He had a *nice* smile. He didn't moan about the food arriving even when he didn't order it, in fact he made a joke about it.'

'Mmmm.' He sounded unconvinced.

'I could see why Claire might have liked him—at the beginning.'

They both fell silent at that.

Rhona related how Kalinin had attempted to persuade her to stay and eat with him.

'Not a good idea.'

'By then I was pretty sure he didn't believe the story about the food. When he asked outright why I was really there I told him I was a friend of Claire's and asked if he knew where she was.'

McNab almost choked on his chicken.

The sudden memory of Kalinin's vice-like grip assailed her but she forced herself to continue. 'He didn't like being questioned about Claire, but eventually told me she'd left weeks ago and he hadn't seen her since.'

'And you believed him?'

'Yes. There was no sign of Claire or Emma in the apartment. I checked all the rooms when I went to the toilet. There was a computer room with security screens. Solonik was in there. One of the screens showed the entrance to the building, and your car had gone. I thought they'd picked you up.'

'I shouldn't have let you go in there.'

Rhona shook her head in irritation. 'You didn't *let* me. I chose to. I think we can be sure now of one thing. Kalinin didn't abduct Claire, so who did?'

48

Chrissy stared across the back garden at the dark outline of the distant woods. She had seen something, she was sure of it. She pulled on a coat and boots and went outside. The winter light had faded fast, dropping its blanket of darkness. As the sky had cleared and the temperature plummeted, the moon and stars had arrived, their reflection on the snow making it seem almost as bright as day.

The farmer had come by an hour earlier, declared it impossible to get her car as far as the main road before tomorrow and asked whether she wanted to spend the night with them at the farm. Chrissy had turned down his offer, wanting to be at the cottage should Rhona get through on the landline or even come back to check on her. Mr Jenkins wasn't too happy about leaving her on her own, but she declared that she was used to being alone and it wasn't a problem. Mollified but not entirely convinced, the farmer promised to be back at first light.

After he'd left, she had built up the fire and raided the fridge. In between times she'd checked her mobile and the hall phone then turned on the television and watched the news of the effects of the blizzard, relieved that the forecast was for severe frost but no further snow.

Chrissy pulled up the hood on the jacket, her breath condensing like a white balloon as she trudged towards the trees. Moonlight gave an eerie translucence to the snow and gave the approaching trees a spectral quality she found slightly unnerving.

If there was someone here, there will be footprints. She spoke out loud, in defiance of her uneasiness. She walked the boundary of the trees, looking for some indication that the movement she'd seen from the kitchen window had been a human being and not just a deer. She found the snow undisturbed apart from clusters of tiny bird-like claw prints.

Satisfied for the moment, Chrissy turned and faced the cottage. From where she stood it looked like a picture postcard, surrounded by snow, outlined against a dark sky filled with stars, smoke drifting lazily upwards in the still night air. She shivered, feeling the intense cold bite at her nose and cheeks. This was silly. There was no one daft enough to be out here except her. Even the farmer had given up for the night and gone home to his supper.

Chrissy headed back to the cottage, vowing to close the curtains, lock the doors and ignore any further daft notions that someone might be observing her. The smell of the warming casserole met her inside, reminding her how hungry she was. She dished up a plate and carried it through to the sitting room.

The cottage settled into silence, punctured only by the crackling of the fire. Exhausted by her constant toing and froing, Chrissy disposed of her plate and lay down on the sofa, her mobile set to loud near by.

*   *   *

The baby's concerted kicking woke her. Chrissy rolled on to her side and cradled her belly, feeling a tiny heel stretch the skin.

'Hey. How about sleeping when I sleep?'

She was rewarded by a larger movement, as though in response to her request, and pulled the heavy grey blanket to her chin, conscious of a drop in temperature. The fire needed more wood, but for the moment she couldn't bear the idea of leaving her warm cocoon. Eventually she stretched out an arm and checked her mobile in case it had rung when she was asleep. There was nothing to indicate a missed call or text message.

Chrissy flung back the blanket and heaved herself up. Sleep had made her heavy and sluggish, the baby pressing low in her abdomen. She grunted as she dropped to her knees in front of the fire, grateful she had made the effort to bring in a good supply of logs.

As she reached for one she heard the distinct sound of a foot crunching on snow. She froze, her hand on the log. A second footstep followed the first. She let go of the log, eased herself on to her feet and extracted a poker from the fireside set.

She may have been wrong before, but she wasn't now. There was definitely someone or something moving about outside the cottage. The most likely explanation was a deer, as McNab had mentioned one grazing in the back garden. Chrissy held her breath, conscious of the baby jerking and kicking as though it shared her dismay.

There was no light in the room apart from the glowing remains of the fire. To anyone wandering about outside, the cottage would be in darkness, little to no smoke coming from the chimney, either deserted or its occupants asleep.

Chrissy's heart hammered in her chest. All the doors were locked. She had checked them before she lay down. No one could get into the cottage.

But someone had got in, a small voice reminded her. And that someone had taken Claire and Emma away. Chrissy ran the layout of the cottage through her head. Was there somewhere she could hide? She discounted the idea almost immediately. Once inside it would be obvious to an intruder that the cottage had an occupant and it would only be a matter of time before they found her.

Chrissy made for the back door as quietly as she could. The heavy jacket she'd worn earlier was hanging up near by. Still clutching the poker, she pulled on the coat and slipped her feet into the boots. As she did so she heard a movement outside. She stood rigid with fear as someone launched their full weight against the kitchen door, shaking it in its frame. The next attempt came seconds later. Under such a determined onslaught it was only a matter of time before the door gave

275

way.

She reached for the bolt and eased it open just as the intruder returned for their third try. Bolt drawn, the door flew open easily.

As the figure stumbled past, Chrissy brought the poker down as hard as she could. There was a crack as iron met bone. The man staggered and dropped. She raised the poker again.

'No!' A voice called out in pain.

Chrissy flicked on the light switch.

MacNiven was on his knees, his head in his hands. Blood from the reopened head wound had splattered the surrounding tiles. He looked up at Chrissy, his eyes cloudy. 'I thought you'd gone.'

'You thought wrong.'

Chrissy let her poker hand fall by her side as MacNiven slid unconscious to the floor.

*   *   *

She began to search him, finding nothing that could serve as a weapon. His body was deeply chilled, his lips blue. She suspected he was on the verge of hypothermia. Had she been able to, she would have phoned for an ambulance. Instead she found a length of plastic washing line and used it to bind his hands and feet together, before washing the wound and reapplying a dressing. Then she covered him with a blanket and sat down to await his return to consciousness.

The guy was fit and resourceful, as evidenced by the snow hole, but the plummeting temperature had forced even him inside. MacNiven, if that was his name, hadn't come to attack her, he had come for shelter. Chrissy studied his unshaven face and grimy skin. He was living rough, that much was obvious.

His translucent lids rippled as his eyes moved behind them. Chrissy watched as his limbs twitched and his breathing became more rapid. He was dreaming, or more likely having a nightmare, imagining he was running from something.

Then he screamed. The blood-curdling sound of it made the hair stand up on the back of her neck. His eyes flew open and he was looking, not at her, but at something that terrified and sickened him. He shook his head wildly, then tried desperately to take his bound hand to his face.

'Fucking guts. Wipe off the fucking guts!'

Chrissy grabbed a towel and knelt beside him, wiping his face as though there was something on it. Gradually terror eased from his face and tears ran down his cheeks. His hands began to jerk in their bindings.

She grabbed his head and cradled it against her. 'It's OK, Alan. It's OK.'

He looked up at her, glassy eyed. 'I'm not Alan, I'm Fergus. Fergus Morrison.'

*　　　*　　　*

Morrison glanced down at Chrissy's swollen belly. 'Nae chance of a fag, eh?' He'd discarded the Queen's English, ever since he'd revealed his true identity.

'There's red wine?' she offered.

'Aye, go on, then.'

Chrissy poured him a tumbler. It took both hands to raise it to his lips.

'Afghanistan,' he said in reply to her unasked

question. 'Ma mate and me were in this compound. A mortar came. Blew him up.' He wiped his face. 'Ah can still taste his guts.'

They were in the sitting room, the fire rebuilt. His face had lost its ashen colour, but the shaking was barely under control.

'We knew by a blood test the body in the skip wasn't you.'

'The dog tag?'

Chrissy nodded.

'I needed to buy time tae get away. Those fucking hands. They snapped his neck. Just like that. He was talking, begging. I couldnae understand, but he was shit scared. The big guy threw him in the skip.'

'Who else was there?'

'A tall guy in a fancy overcoat. He was the one that gave the orders. When they left ah took ma chance. He was deid anyway. Ah gave him ma tag and set the skip alight, then headed south. I've been hanging round the cottage for a while. There's tins of food in the shed. I've been living on them.'

'How did you hurt your head?'

'That happened before the skip. Wrong place at the wrong time.'

'When Rhona asked you about the woman and her daughter who lived here . . .'

'Ah panicked when you mentioned the polis.'

'You did see something?'

He nodded. 'There was a car parked a bit down the lane. Ah memorised some of the number plate. We were taught to take a note of all vehicles. That wis supposed tae keep us alive. Fuckin lot of good it did Gary.' He took another mouthful of wine, both hands gripping the glass. 'When ah came back later, the place was in darkness, the car gone.'

'Did you go in?'

He shook his head. 'Ah took a couple tins and left. If ah'd known it wis goan tae snow like that ah'd have stayed put.'

49

He looked through the spyhole. The child was asleep, curled in a fetal position in the corner. He had designed the hiding place well. The floor was covered with a plastic mattress, the temperature kept even and comfortably warm. There were suitable books, a supply of water and some food, fresh fruit and a bar of chocolate. The girl had eaten nothing, but she would eventually. By the time he returned she would be very pleased to see him. She would let him do anything he wanted to her without making a fuss.

He didn't like fuss. He didn't like mess.

There would be a mess when he came back but a hose-down with warm water would fix that. The girl was his Christmas present to himself and good presents were worth waiting to unwrap. He went back to his laptop and double-checked his booking. The flight would land him at Marco Polo airport in time to deliver his bags to La Residenzia and have lunch at the Corte Sconta. Two days to savour church windows, then home.

From his own window, he looked out on a brilliant moon. The bare arms of the trees at the foot of the garden seemed to stretch upwards like dancers towards the stars.

Another little star for his garden, but not yet, not before he made her dance.

50

'Chrissy?' Rhona could hardly speak, she was so relieved. 'Are you OK?'

'I'm in labour.'

'You're not!'

'Of course not. I bet on the ninth of January. I intend to win my bet.'

'Where are you?'

'Still at the cottage but no longer alone. Remember the snow-hole guy? Well, he came back. Turns out he's Private Fergus Morrison. He witnessed the skip murder and I think I've persuaded him to turn himself in.'

'She's located the missing soldier,' Rhona told McNab.

Chrissy wasn't finished. 'He's been hanging about the cottage, sleeping in the shed, working his way through Claire's store of tins and,' she paused for effect, 'he saw a car the night Claire disappeared.'

McNab was watching Rhona's excited face, trying to make out what was being said on the other end of the phone.

'He remembered part of the registration number.'

Rhona rifled in her bag for a pen.

'Go ahead.' She wrote it down. 'You're a star.'

'Too right I am.'

When Chrissy rang off, Rhona related the news to McNab. 'It's a part number, but it might be enough.'

He called the station and asked for an ID on what they had.

'If it was that sanctimonious wee git . . .' he hissed under his breath.

'We'll pick him up and get a warrant to search the place. All legal and above board,' she said.

'Maybe we're too late. Maybe that's why he was so bloody confident.'

'Maybe he had nothing to be guilty about?'

McNab was making for the door.

'Where are you going?'

'If the car turns out to be his, we're already on our way.'

* * *

Twenty minutes later they had a possible ID on the owner of the car.

'It's not an exact match with the registration number you gave me, but it's close.'

'Name?'

'Swanson.'

When the officer tried to give them the address, McNab cut him off. 'I know where the bastard lives.'

He stuck the light on the roof, turned on the siren and drove like hell.

Swanson's house was in darkness. On the way there McNab had appeared oblivious to Rhona's remonstrations that they should at least inform Slater what they were about to do.

'Maybe he's gone to bed?'

'It's not that late.'

There was no car parked outside.

'He's not here,' said Rhona.

McNab pounded on the door anyway. They could hear the sound echo in the hallway. No lights came on and there was no sign of anyone stirring inside.

'If he was here he would have answered by now,' said Rhona. 'Maybe he was spooked by our visit and ran?'

He shook his head. 'He knew we had nothing. He wasn't worried, only irritated.'

'So where is he?'

McNab glanced at his watch. 'It's still Christmas Day. Maybe he's out visiting friends?'

She didn't fancy the prospect of sitting in the car waiting for Swanson's return. Not in these temperatures.

'D'you think you could get us into the workshop without breaking the lock?'

He grinned. 'A woman after my own heart.'

*   *   *

Ten minutes later McNab pushed open the workshop door and stood back to let Rhona enter. She flicked on the overhead bulb and was stunned again by the myriad of glass colours glinting in its light.

The church window still lay on the bench but Swanson's own design had gone. She glanced about but could see no sign of it. The surface exposed by its removal was covered by a thin film of ice. The workbench was pale in colour, the ice brown. Rhona chipped a piece free.

'Remember Swanson said he'd washed the window and the water had frozen? Look.'

She shone her forensic torch on the surface of the ice, highlighting clusters of tiny feathery brown particles. 'The pattern of peat in water is quite distinctive. On Skye, our water came from a loch and was brown because of the high peat content. When you made ice cubes, they looked like this.'

'What are you saying?'

'That Swanson lied about this water and I'm wondering why.' Rhona slipped the ice into a container.

She selected a piece of red glass.

'If Swanson tends to stick to the same supplier, the constituents of this could prove a match for our fragment.'

McNab had moved towards a door in the wall that backed on to the side of the house. There was a key on a hook near by. He slipped it in the lock and turned it. She heard him give a low whistle as the door swung open.

'Lookee here, Dr MacLeod. Someone's after your job.'

Forensic evidence bags of varying sizes and material were neatly stored on shelving. There were containers for swabs, latex gloves, blood detection kits, just about everything you would need for evidence collection.

McNab shook his head in disbelief. 'He said he was a CSI fan but this is weird.'

'Not as weird as this.'

She indicated a row of evidence bags laid out on a table, the labels itemising the contents.

'Tissues, lipstick, hairbrush, sweets, shoes and an envelope addressed to Mrs Watson.'

'That's the address we got from the hospice for the granny.'

'He must have thought it was Claire's home address,' Rhona said.

The final three bags contained an earring, a child's pencil and a sympathy card. Rhona extracted the card with gloved fingers. Inside was a message of condolence and a promise to be at the crematorium at the allotted time.

*   *   *

McNab had no qualms now about breaking in. Using a glass cutter from a rack of tools in the workshop, he cut a circle in the kitchen window and made his entrance.

He made for the stairs while Rhona walked round the lower rooms. There was nothing unusual. No locked doors, nothing to suggest that Swanson had brought Claire and Emma here. She followed McNab upstairs to the bedroom. The stained-glass window they'd viewed in the workshop hung at the foot of the bed. Several other designs, similar yet different, were displayed round the walls.

Swanson had suggested the work wasn't a representation of anything in particular but Rhona wasn't so sure. At a distance the swirling shapes took on a more concrete form.

'I think that's a picture of a young girl,' she said suddenly.

McNab came over.

'The opalescent glass is her hair. See there, the small red sections look like drops of blood.'

They cast horrified glances round the other

284

pictures, trying to find images hidden in the patterns.

'What has he done?'

'I think we should call Magnus,' said Rhona.

This time McNab didn't argue.

51

He took the motorway to Glasgow then headed south on the A1. The flight from Newcastle airport was ridiculously early, but it would be worth it to be in Venice by midday.

The gritters were out in force. The icy conditions reminded him of the film of water on his workshop table and he was irritated with himself for not cleaning it up. Despite his annoyance, the cold crispness of the surrounding countryside brought him pleasure. That and the anticipation of seeing Venice again.

He turned on the radio. The BBC was replaying the earlier service of carols and readings. He hummed along with his favourites, learned in childhood and never forgotten.

He allowed himself to think about the room and the sleeping child. It had been so long, he'd almost imagined it never happening again, then suddenly the possibility had arisen when he wasn't seeking it. His patience and self-denial had been rewarded. It was a pity that he had had to leave her so soon, but it wouldn't be for long.

For a brief moment he pictured McCarthy. He saw the puffy face, the red gums, the disgusting teeth. He would never visit McCarthy again. He would explain to the governor that the visits were causing him too much distress. He had done his bit, well beyond the call of duty.

He followed the signs for the airport and headed for long-stay parking, eventually finding a free space in the far bottom corner of the car park. The walkway to the terminal was frosted and icy in places. He took care, placing his feet cautiously, anxious not to fall. Age did that to you, he mused, made you more careful about everything.

The check-in desk was open. He joined the short queue and mentally sized up the passengers bound for Venice with him, finding no one of interest.

The young woman manning the desk had a thick Geordie accent to match her make-up. She smiled brightly at him, asking the usual silly questions about someone else having access to his luggage. If he'd said yes, he doubted she would have noticed.

Once through security he made for the café and ordered a full English breakfast and a large mug of coffee, his last fast food before the delights of Venetian cooking.

52

It would soon be light. A thin red streak marked the horizon. In the pre-dawn, the vested officers looked like yellow spectres moving among the trees. Rhona was reminded of that other night, when a little girl found a skull in the woods. She prayed that whatever special ability Emma possessed, it wouldn't be the reason she died.

They'd searched the house and workshop

thoroughly. Apart from the exhibits in the forensic room there was no further evidence to link Swanson with Claire and Emma's disappearance. Swanson hadn't returned and they had no idea where he was.

As the sun rose the extent of Swanson's garden became more apparent, his attention to detail evident in the ornamental layout, trim paths, shrubberies and neat greenhouse. At the foot of the garden was a small orchard of apple trees and the skeletal forms of bare birch and rowan trees.

Magnus arrived with the dawn. Rhona was surprised how pleased she was to see the tall figure ease himself from the car and walk towards her. Magnus looked stressed, and she wanted to apologise for not telling him about Emma's disappearance earlier. She shouldn't have let him discover it via a news broadcast. She knew if she tried to apologise he would dismiss it, saying he wasn't officially involved with the case and didn't have to be included in the latest developments. But she knew he'd be thinking of what had gone wrong the last time and how he had failed them.

'Anything?' he said hopefully.

Rhona shook her head.

He took a deep breath. 'Show me the workshop.'

The powerful fluorescent strips seemed to excavate every corner. In the stark light Magnus looked even worse. Rhona had grown used to McNab's pummelled face as the bruises developed in colour from mottled purple to a frightening yellowish-green. Magnus hadn't been beaten up but his eyes were bruised too, from lack of sleep or from worry.

His eyes swept the room. He stood for a moment

then took a deep breath, assimilating and analysing what his strong sense of smell was picking up. He approached the work table and touched the icy film, then tasted his finger.

'He doesn't store any gardening stuff in here? Soil bags, fertiliser, anything like that?'

'No.'

'This area smells of something peat-based. The ice tastes of it too. How did the water get here?'

Rhona described their visit to the workshop with Swanson, his enthusiasm about stained glass and the delight he'd taken in showing off his own design.

'He said he washed the window and the water froze.'

Magnus shook his head. 'Something lay here. Something in a state of decay.'

She explained that Swanson had been at Claire's mother's funeral and had probably followed the three of them to the wood.

'Then I think there's a possibility he removed something from the loch and brought it here.'

Neither of them voiced what that something might have been. Emma may well have been right.

'Show me the back room.'

She led him through to Swanson's lab.

He surveyed the pristine whiteness, the neat rows of materials. He approached the exhibits Swanson had collected on his victims, picking them up one by one to study. Rhona saw distress on his face as he examined Emma's pencil, the half-eaten packet of sweets. Swanson's hoard consisted of the casual items of Claire and Emma's lives, abandoned, lost, unmissed; yet now they were all that remained of the missing mother and child.

'I'd like to look at the house now.'

Magnus paced through the downstairs, then climbed to the upper level. He checked the spare room first. It looked unused, the bed unmade, the duvet and pillows folded neatly at the foot.

Swanson's room was a different matter. It had the same neatness and order, but Rhona sensed Swanson's presence, even now when it was empty. Magnus stood in the centre, viewing each of Swanson's pieces in sequence. The colour and intensity of the stained-glass images seemed even more powerful to Rhona now as he examined them.

'He's talented,' he said. 'A patchwork of colour. Beautiful and yet somehow also disturbing.'

It was exactly how she had felt when Swanson first showed her his work. She indicated the one that had been in the workshop.

'Can you see anything in the pattern?'

Rhona watched as realisation dawned on his face. He swung abruptly round to look at her.

'That's an image of a child.'

'I think they all are.'

*   *   *

Magnus stood in front of the open wardrobe.

'He organises his clothes, shirts, sweaters, everything, by colour, like the stained glass.' He flicked through the shirts. 'Three of each shirt except blue and white.' He checked the drawers. 'Socks and underwear also arranged by colour, three of each except blue.' He thought for a moment. 'My guess is Swanson's gone on a short trip.'

289

Rhona understood. 'He's taken enough clothing for two days.'

*   *   *

It was strange to have the three of them together again. McNab looked sullen but was not openly hostile. Magnus's pronouncements on the contents of the wardrobe had prompted him to alert the airports, although if Swanson had departed immediately after their visit, he might already have left the country.

Magnus questioned McNab closely, about his meeting with McCarthy, their talk with Swanson, asking them to go over what each had said in detail. He particularly wanted the man's precise responses, his facial expressions, the tone of his voice, his mannerisms. Rhona wished Magnus had been there, instead of encountering everything second hand. She suspected McNab felt the same, although he would never admit it.

'If we accept Swanson was complicit in Mollie's death and Claire saw him that night, then he would see her as a threat. Once the link between the crash and finding the skull became clear, she was in real danger. I suspect the fact that Claire had a child came as a pleasant surprise to him.'

Rhona shuddered at the thought.

'His penchant for children might dictate he keep Emma alive, at least for a while. It would be easier for him to hide her here on the premises.' Magnus looked over at McNab.

'We've searched. There's nothing,' he replied sharply.

Rhona flashed McNab a warning look, willing

290

him to cooperate.

'I thought there might be a cellar,' he conceded, 'but I can't find any access to one.'

'If Emma is here, he has to keep her warm for her to stay alive,' Magnus said.

Light dawned in McNab's eyes. 'And for that he needs power.'

As the lights and sockets were switched off, the steady hum prevalent in every modern home gradually faded to nothing. In the torch's beam, the electricity meter slowed its whirring movement almost to a standstill—but not quite. McNab had the junction box exposed. As silence descended he flicked each of the switches in turn. Turning off the final switch brought the meter to a halt.

*   *   *

It was McNab who discovered the cable. It ran along the underside of the workbench, down the leg and from there through the wall behind the stained-glass store to the forensic room. It took longer to work out how to access the cellar. The external wall of the cottage was over two feet thick, but the section behind the shelves of evidence bags contained a narrow stairwell to an old root cellar. Without following the path of the wire they would never have found its access point.

McNab went down the narrow stone steps first, calling Emma's name into the frigid darkness. Rhona followed, the strong scent of decay catching the back of her throat. She heard him curse as he stumbled over something in the dark, saw his torch beam circle a mound on the floor.

The plastic-wrapped parcel was partially open.

291

Water had seeped from it to form a pool of ice in the sub-zero air. What they were looking at had to be the remains Swanson had retrieved from the loch.

'Over there!'

McNab swung the torch as directed.

Rhona had spotted what looked like an item of clothing in the nearby shadows. Close by were the remainder of Claire's clothes strewn about as though removed in a frenzy. As they approached, the torch beam found Claire's naked body. She lay on her side, curled up as though in sleep.

Of Emma there was no sign.

*   *   *

Rhona asked Magnus to carry Claire's body upstairs to Swanson's bed as carefully as he could. In advanced cases of hypothermia you had to be gentle—no rubbing the limbs, nothing that would send a cold rush of blood to an already struggling heart.

Rhona pulled back the duvet.

'Lay her in the centre and take off your own clothes. All of them,' she told Magnus.

Rhona fetched the duvet from the spare room, then quickly undressed to her underwear.

'We have to warm her with our own bodies.'

They slipped under the covers and positioned themselves against Claire, front and back, skin on skin.

'Her torso and neck area. That's what we have to get warm.'

Rhona felt Magnus's long arms stretch out to encircle them both. She shivered as heat flowed from her to Claire's icy limbs, but Magnus's body heat was plentiful.

When they'd checked for life signs in the cellar, Claire's pulse had been weak, her breathing shallow, the pupils dilated. If her body temperature dropped any lower, she wouldn't survive long enough for the paramedics to arrive.

In the muffled darkness of the cocoon created by their naked bodies, Rhona listened to Magnus's steady breathing and felt his breath on her hair. They didn't speak, focused as they were on bringing Claire back to life.

*   *   *

McNab watched as Magnus dipped his head at the top of the stairs and manoeuvred Claire's inert body carefully through the narrow gap. Claire, he knew, was as near death as it was possible to be. He could do nothing about that now. He had to think only of Emma. If Claire was here, there was a chance Emma was somewhere close by.

The cellar was fully lit now. The arc lamp threw shadows against the wall, illuminating long scratches on the surface as though Claire had fought to escape her silent freezing grave.

A faint scent of stagnant water came from the bundle that still lay on the floor. He suspected, as had Rhona, that this was the second body removed from the loch before the divers had arrived. Emma had been right and he'd treated her eager disclosures as irritating lies.

McNab paced the dungeon-like room. He could see nothing that suggested another space beyond what they had already discovered. He retraced his steps to the wire's entry. Perhaps there had been an electric point here at one time, but this place was not using the power that was making the meter turn.

He went back into the house. Men were searching every room, carefully, methodically, with a sense of urgency to match his own. Frustration welled up in him. Maybe they were wrong about the power supply. Maybe Swanson had simply taken the child with him. If so she could be anywhere, if she was still alive.

A call came from the sitting room.

'He's gone to Venice.'

Swanson's computer was switched on, details of his early morning flight on the screen.

'One return ticket only.'

'When is he back?'

'Forty-eight hours from now.'

*　　　*　　　*

The German shepherd entered by the front door and stood sniffing the air. They had nothing of Emma's to give it, but it was a general-purpose dog, trained to search for humans inside and out. The dog team had arrived shortly after the paramedics, who were already upstairs with Claire.

The dog moved swiftly through the house, tail waving and muzzle twitching enthusiastically. It wanted to find someone as much as they did. McNab stood near the front door waiting for the shout, but none came. When the dog descended the stairs, the handler shook his head, indicating they had found nothing.

McNab followed them outside. They headed for

the workshop. As the Alsatian worked the air, he was suddenly conscious of the smell of putty. It reminded him of Swanson and the sanctimonious look on his face as he'd trotted out that stuff about seraphim. And all the time Claire was freezing to death in his cellar. If Swanson had been in the vicinity McNab would have killed him with his bare hands and to hell with the consequences.

And what about Emma? What had the bastard done to Emma?

The police dog was sniffing its way round the workshop, but without the urgency that would suggest it had picked up an unexplained scent. The handler moved with it into the forensic room. Through the workshop's open door McNab was keeping half an eye on the waiting ambulance. It didn't look as though Claire had been brought down yet, and he didn't want to contemplate what that meant.

The dog was back in the workshop now and making for the door. The handler mouthed 'sorry' before heading into the garden.

It looked as if Swanson had hidden the girl somewhere else. They would have to widen their search. The adrenalin was beginning to drain from his body, leaving a battered, exhausted shell. He gave his head a shake, knowing if he allowed his eyes to close he would fall asleep right there.

Maybe they had no choice but to await Swanson's return. They could put him under surveillance, follow him to Emma's hiding place. But what if he never went there? Could they make him talk? McNab suspected he would never give the girl up, dead or alive.

He went outside, anxious to be away from

Swanson's things—the coloured glass, the cloying putty smell, the stained-glass window awaiting repair, with the blood-coloured seraph looking down on its supplicant.

There was a flurry of activity by the greenhouse. McNab felt his chest tighten as someone shouted and a uniform waved him over. They had found something. His heart took off, pounding his chest. He found himself praying that it would be the child. That she would be alive.

The group of anxious faces parted to let him through.

The trapdoor was obvious now that it was open. McNab wondered how he had missed it before, tucked below the bench of wintering geraniums. The morning sun was already warming the glass roof, accentuating the smell of damp and soil. He crouched by the opening.

A set of wooden steps led downwards. McNab eased himself through and flashed his torch around. The space below was about a metre square, earthen sides prevented from caving in by wooden props. A pale grey fibreglass container sat partially exposed above the surrounding soil. It was onion shaped with a lidded top, a spyhole in the centre, a soft pink light filtering through the glass. McNab swore as he realised what he was looking at.

The bastard had buried her in a septic tank.

When McNab pulled open the lid, heat and the scent of sweat and fresh urine escaped, catching in his throat.

'Emma?'

There was no answer.

He dropped inside, feeling warmth encase him.

He landed on a soft spongy base. A plastic bottle of what looked like water rolled away from his foot to clunk against the curved side of the container.

Then he saw her, naked, knees curled to her chest, white-blonde hair covering her face. McNab had never been in the presence of something so openly and achingly vulnerable and so infinitely precious. His own heart had ceased beating, waiting to learn if this child was alive.

He crawled towards her, afraid to call her name again in case there was no response. He gently touched her shoulder, and the skin beneath his fingers was warm.

'Emma? It's me, Michael.'

He gently moved her hair to one side. Her small face was dirty, the cheeks tracked with tears. Then the blue eyes flickered open and Emma smiled at him.

'I knew you would come.'

53

Swanson shivered as cold December air met him at the top of the plane steps. Venice had been cool and damp, but not like this. He smiled. Despite the cold he had much to look forward to.

It wouldn't take long for the house to warm up. There was food in the fridge and he had brought a couple of bottles of Venetian wine back with him.

The drive from the airport was uneventful. He turned on the radio, choosing Classic FM over a news and weather bulletin. The fields he passed were still white with snow, so the forecast for low temperatures until New Year were proving accurate.

He wondered how long he would keep the girl. For the holiday period, at least. He smiled to himself. She would be grateful to see him again. She wouldn't have liked being alone, but he hadn't left her in the dark. He would have to wait for a thaw to bury the boy's remains. Perhaps he could bury them together. That gave him a week with her.

He turned into the drive, a little surprised to see a light at the sitting-room window. Had he left it on? He'd departed in a hurry so it was perfectly possible.

He was more perturbed when he did not need his key to open his front door. He was on the point of dialling 999 when a police car entered the drive and drew in behind him.

Then the detective sergeant emerged from his sitting room and beckoned him inside.

54

Claire had believed herself dead, her hallucinations the afterlife—or more likely purgatory, because Emma wasn't there with her.

But she hadn't died. More than a week had passed since that night when they'd brought her back to life. *Haemodialysis*, the doctor had explained; they'd taken the chilled blood from her body, warmed it and put it back.

She had the forensic woman and the psychologist to thank for her life. The doctor had been blunt about it. Had they not acted promptly to raise her body temperature, her heart would have gone into cardiac arrest.

Claire recalled the day they'd come to take Emma to the woods. How she'd hated them for doing that. How she'd despised Emma's stories and drawings. She'd believed she'd hidden herself and her daughter from evil, only to find it had followed them.

Emma was facing the window, her drawing book on her lap, selecting coloured pencils from a long clear plastic folder. Claire no longer feared her drawings. Fear was born of fear, and she refused to be frightened any more. DS McNab had promised her she had no reason to fear either Hugh Swanson or Nikolai Kalinin. Neither of the two men would trouble her or her daughter again, he would make certain of that. Claire wanted desperately to believe the man who had saved her daughter's life. What if she'd awakened from sleep to find the opposite had happened? The fear she was trying to banish slid its cold fingers round her heart once more and squeezed tight. Claire wondered whether a life without fear was possible or probable, after what she had done.

Her small daughter's back was arched in concentration, her dedication to the drawing process evident. This was how Emma would always be. Intensely engaged in everything. Sometimes frighteningly so.

'There.' Emma had finished and was ready to show her mother. She strode over to the bed, her face still creased in concentration. She handed Claire the picture.

It was Fern Cottage in summertime. Splashes of

yellow climbing roses round the door. A cottage garden full of colour and life. A butterfly the size of a bird. Window boxes stuffed with red, pink and blue flowers. She'd told Emma they could make a garden like this when summer came, and Emma would have her own space where she could grow anything she wanted.

'It's lovely,' Claire said, and meant it.

Seeing her daughter's smile now, Claire hardly dared think of what the child had endured. A special team had worked with her after her rescue. Emma had asked that Professor Pirie be there too. Through their delicate questioning it emerged that Swanson had not harmed Emma other than to strip her and lock her in her prison. Magnus believed that, for Swanson, keeping the child hostage, controlling and observing her, together with the anticipation of what he would do when the time came, was part of his obsession.

Perhaps Swanson had been saving Emma, or simply didn't have time to hurt her before Rhona and DS McNab spooked him enough to leave the country. Claire didn't care which it was.

She glanced at the clock. DS McNab would be here soon. This hospital room that had been her safe haven would be abandoned and she would have to face the world outside. She had promised herself she would tell the policeman the truth, the whole truth. And she would tell it in Emma's presence. The child deserved to know the real reason for the nightmares and the drawings.

*　　　*　　　*

McNab glanced in the rear-view mirror. Emma

300

was humming to herself, her face animated. She'd already told them she was glad to be going home. Claire, he wasn't so sure about. He stole a glimpse at her pale face, her tight mouth that seemed to be on the cusp of saying something.

The cottage, he knew, had been cleaned and set to rights. Mrs Jenkins had seen to that. Claire's blood had been washed from the walls, but the memories of what had happened there would remain.

They drove past the scene of the crash. The snow had melted, exposing the bog-like terrain of grass and heather that led to the trees. The place was visible for a moment then gone, as though their time there had never happened.

The track to the cottage was muddy and slick with water from the melted snow. Here and there a fence post had staggered under the weight of snow and now hung at an angle, wire drooping.

As the cottage came into view McNab noticed smoke coming from the chimney. Mrs Jenkins had been true to her word: the place would be warm and ready for Claire's return. The poor lassie, the woman had declared over the phone, had only to call her if she needed company or help.

McNab stood back to let Claire turn the key and push open the door. As her mother hovered, Emma rushed past and headed upstairs. Claire gave him a nervous smile.

'It'll be OK,' he said.

In the sitting room the fire was blazing, the Christmas tree still in place, lights twinkling. Below it was a pile of presents. Claire surveyed it all in amazement.

'We found the presents you'd hidden from

Emma when we searched the place. I presumed you'd want them out for your homecoming. There's a couple from me and the rest of the team.'

He saw tears fill her eyes and quickly turned away. 'I'll make us a cup of tea.'

*   *   *

In the end Claire waited until they were alone. Emma's excitement was too intense, her enthusiasm for her belated Christmas almost too wonderful to watch. When she finally headed upstairs to play with her presents, Claire broached the subject.

'There's something I have to tell you. Something you, the police, need to know.'

She watched his face, trying to read its expression, aware that what she was about to say would change his opinion of her for ever.

He was waiting for her to continue. Claire knew he probably expected some revelation about Kalinin, something that she had been involved in, unwittingly or otherwise. In a way he was right.

'I know why Emma drew that picture. The one with the little boy buried under the tree.'

He was going to interrupt her, tell her not to worry about Emma's strange ability to foretell such things. Claire held up her hand.

'Emma saw me bury a child below a tree. That's what she remembers.'

He had such nice eyes, but now they were cold and questioning.

'I was pregnant. I didn't tell Nick because I had no idea how he would react. At twelve weeks a baby is fully formed. Did you know that?' She couldn't see McNab through the film that clouded her eyes. 'He had this thing he liked to do to me. I knew it might hurt the baby so I refused. He was very angry and did it anyway.' She paused, searching for words. 'The baby came that night, so quickly I barely got to the bathroom in time. There was so much blood.' She gripped her hands together. 'We were staying in a different flat then, not the place you visited. There was a back garden with a pine tree. I buried him under that tree. I was so frightened that Emma might wake up, that Nick might come back. I dug a hole and slipped him down inside. Emma must have woken up and followed. Suddenly she was there beside me.' She shook her head. 'I'll never forget her face when she asked me what I was doing. I told her that her little brother had died and gone to heaven. We never spoke of it again. I spent my time planning our escape. I brought her safely here, then she found the skull and it all came back.' Claire had run out of words. She bowed her head, unable to meet those eyes.

'You didn't do anything wrong.'

'I killed my baby.'

'No. If anyone did that, it was Kalinin.'

'I should have called an ambulance. Maybe they could have saved him.'

'He wouldn't have survived.'

He sounded so certain she almost believed him.

'We'll get him back for you. You can bury him properly.'

Claire looked up, hardly daring to hope. His eyes were full of warmth and compassion.

55

McNab called Rhona on his way back from the cottage.

'We have to make sure Kalinin doesn't find out about this. I have a feeling his lawyer could make things difficult for Claire,' she said when he'd told her the whole story.

'Kalinin caused her to miscarry.'

Rhona agreed, but from a professional viewpoint the baby would have to be exhumed and a pathological estimate of its gestation period established. She didn't mention it now, but Claire might have given birth to a viable baby. They only had her word that she was three months pregnant when she miscarried.

'When's your meeting with Slater?'

'In half an hour.'

'And what has he said up to now?'

'Gave a little *well done* speech to the assembled team on the Russian case.'

'What about picking up Swanson?'

'He was a bit more low key on that.'

'I bet he was.'

'Slater built a decent enough case against McCarthy. When someone confesses like that . . .'

'Bill would have kept on looking for the body, especially when McCarthy retracted.'

'Maybe.' There was a pause. 'I phoned the boss. He's back from Orkney. Asked him to meet up for a drink soon. Fancy coming along?'

'I'd like that.'

'How's Chrissy?'

'Crabbit as hell.'

'Ready to drop?'

'Determined to keep it in until the ninth. That way she wins her bet.'

'I'm taking her out tonight.'

'Where?'

'The Poker Club. Posh frock. The works.'

'Is that wise?'

'Brogan's in the clear. No reason not to.'

'You're not in his bad books?'

'Brogan and I go back a long way. That's why he called me and put us on to Solonik, which led us to Kalinin. Kalinin's banged up and Solonik's left the country, so it worked for Brogan and it worked for us. Time for us both to celebrate.'

'What about the soldier?'

'We have him in a safe place until he gives his evidence.'

She still wanted to urge him to be careful, but knew he wouldn't appreciate her counsel.

'When are you headed for the club?'

'Eight o'clock. If you fancy coming along, give me a call.'

*   *   *

Rhona and Chrissy stood together by the last unearthed grave in Swanson's garden. There were five in total. There would have been seven had Swanson been able to inter the boy's remains and Emma's. He'd buried the bodies in an upright position, their heads towards the sky.

Chrissy had insisted on being party to the excavation, although she couldn't stay on her knees for long. The remains, Rhona knew, could

305

have been there for decades. Swanson was in his fifties. How long had he been abducting and killing his victims? As far as they were aware he hadn't lived anywhere else other than the family home. Born to middle-aged parents, an only child, he had lived with them until they died. His father had gone first, his mother four years later.

To all intents and purposes Swanson had been a model, caring son and an asset to the community. He'd also been involved in repairing church windows the length and breadth of the UK. Ideal for picking up stray children and bringing them back here to die.

Chrissy groaned as she got to her feet.

'A twinge?'

'I wish it was. I'm fed up waiting.'

'I'll remind you of that when you're doing night feeds.'

They made their way to the van and stripped off their suits. New Year had come and gone with the snow. The surrounding fields looked grey and damp, stripped of their white blanket, a leaden sky above completing the picture.

'D'you want to come home and eat with me?' offered Rhona.

'OK, but I have to warn you I'm headed out later.' Chrissy looked smug.

'Really?' Rhona pretended innocence.

'McNab and I are playing poker.'

*   *   *

McNab arrived towards the end of the meal, sending Chrissy scurrying off to get ready. Rhona opened the door to him, raising an eyebrow at the outfit.

'Very smart.' She waved him inside. 'Very James Bond.'

He looked uncomfortable. 'Too much?'

'Not at all.'

He joined her at the table, eyeing up the last slice of pizza. She gestured that he should help himself. His face was no longer multicoloured and the swelling round the eyes had subsided, although the scratches were still visible. It gave him a rakish look Rhona quite liked. McNab caught her observing him.

'What?'

'Nothing.'

'Sure you don't want to join us?'

'I'm rubbish at cards. My face gives me away.'

He smiled. 'That's true. You never were much of a liar.'

They exchanged awkward glances.

'Sorry.'

'Don't mention it,' Rhona said. 'Sometimes you know me better than I know myself.'

'I was about to say the same about you.'

'Well? What d'you think?' called Chrissy from the doorway.

McNab's mouth fell open at the elegant black dress, which did much to disguise her advanced state of pregnancy. He rose to his feet and gave a long, low wolf whistle.

Chrissy surveyed the penguin suit. 'You don't look too bad yourself.'

McNab offered his arm. She took it with a flourish.

'Remember, tonight's winnings go to my baby fund. Agreed?'

'Agreed.'
Rhona watched them leave, arm in arm.

56

'He'll be here.'

'You'd better be sure of that.'

Brogan poured another shot of vodka, ashamed of how his hand trembled. His father would have hated him at this moment. Hated his cowardice, his willingness to sell out, his abandonment of his father's certainty that the underbelly of this city belonged to them.

It was all gone, or fast going, everything his father had worked for, everything that had paid for his son's fancy education. An education the old man had expected him to make use of in this brave new world, but an education that had instead made his son weak.

Brogan slipped his hand under the table and rubbed his shin, feeling for the knife he kept there for emergencies. Once they did what they came here to do, would he still be alive? There was no guarantee of that, not after what had happened.

He stood up.

'Where do you think you are going?'

'For a piss, then to the lobby. I'd better be around when he shows.'

Kalinin nodded, his cold eyes blazing.

The piss hit the pan with force, urged on by a mix of fear and exhilaration. When he finished, Brogan pulled the knife from the shin strap and examined it. It had been his father's weapon of choice. Swift, deadly and silent. Brogan touched the point to his finger, drawing blood. It was the point that counted, not a keen blade. The point pierced the skin, allowing the blade to enter. After that it was skill and knowledge. You aimed for an artery, or up and under the back ribcage to the kidneys. Or, better still, straight through the heart.

Brogan had stood here once before, planning what he would do to get Solonik off his back. He'd been naive enough to believe the plan had worked, until McNab had blabbed and they'd come looking for him. He sighed and headed for the lobby.

57

'Very posh.' Chrissy gazed up at the pillared entrance.

'Somerset Maugham once described Monaco as a sunny place full of shady people,' offered McNab.

She threw him one of her looks. 'And your point is?'

'The Poker Club has very nice lighting and is also filled with shady people.'

A smile spread over Chrissy's face. 'Like us, you mean?'

'Definitely like us.'

McNab felt light hearted or light headed, he wasn't sure which. The chat with the boss had helped. Things weren't resolved on that front, but the Christmas break in Orkney had done the old man good. McNab was also secretly nursing a notion he might get him to change his story when it came to court, or at least let him share the blame for the assault.

The glass door opened magically in front of them and they stepped into the marble lobby.

'Wow. This just gets better and better.' Chrissy took in the magnificent mahogany staircase and the crystal chandeliers. 'How the other half lives, eh?'

'The shady half.' He was enjoying himself. As well as his chat with his boss, the meeting with Slater had gone better than expected. Slater knew when the cards were stacked against him. They were even now. The DI could no longer slag McNab off for fucking up with Henderson, because the whole team now knew Slater had been fucked by Swanson.

McNab felt a tingle in his fingers and decided Chrissy could look forward to a nice little nest egg for baby McInsh from his winnings tonight.

'We're going to hit it big,' she said, echoing his thoughts. 'I can feel it in my waters.'

He cocked an eyebrow at her. 'Just no *breaking* waters.'

Paddy Brogan was coming down the stairs, a benevolent smile on his face. He shook McNab's outstretched hand. 'It's good to see you, Detective Sergeant.'

'Plain Michael will do tonight.'

Brogan turned to Chrissy.

'Chrissy's the one who figured out your message,' McNab explained.

Brogan gave her an appreciative look. 'I hear you're a poker player?'

'Taught by the best.'

'Then welcome to the Poker Club.'

310

McNab had to admit Chrissy did have a face for poker. No doubt about it. You could read nothing from it, and he had been trying—hard. He wasn't sure whether she was winning honestly or using some of her dark arts. He'd warned her in the taxi not to cheat. Brogan might be all smiles at the moment with Kalinin out of the way, but he didn't get where he was by letting the punters shaft him.

He lifted the glass and drained it. The twenty-year-old malt was going down very smoothly and Brogan had obviously left instructions that his guest was never to nurse an empty tumbler for long. Good whisky had brought a mellow feeling absent from his life for too long. His only regret was that Rhona wasn't there. He allowed his mind to stray to her for a moment. What had happened that night had been a revelation, he suspected, for both of them. No playacting, no competition.

And it would never happen again.

McNab felt his mood begin to slip and strove to return to his earlier elation. Tonight wasn't about him, he reminded himself. It was about Chrissy and the baby.

He focused on the game and his hand. Did he feel lucky enough to raise his bet? He stole a look at Chrissy. Most people had tics or mannerisms that gave them away. Your body informed the world what you were thinking, Magnus was right on that front. You only had to observe long enough and have the tools to interpret the signs.

Her face and body told him nothing. In the heat of the room, her skin colour had remained constant, even and softly pink. No sudden neck flushes, no nervous twitches, just a studied calm. She hadn't avoided looking at him, but there had been no message transmitted by eye contact.

McNab took his hat off to her. Chrissy would likely clear them all out, himself included, before the night was over. He decided to fold and watch her screw her only real opponent, a smart guy in his thirties wearing a TAG watch and smelling of expensive cologne.

There was a hush among the remaining players waiting for the final call. He could sense the majority were on Chrissy's side, if only to see smartarse and his TAG watch get turned over. He was so intent on the game, he didn't see the door open and two people enter.

He should have known something was up the moment he saw her, but Anya was barely recognisable as the woman he had met in the Russian Restaurant and later in the car with Rhona. She was wearing a black evening dress, her long hair fastened up to expose a slender neck. She was with a tall, distinguished man. As they passed the poker table, she glanced fearfully at McNab, then he heard the man order her to the bar. McNab recognised that voice immediately. Kalinin.

A million thoughts raced through McNab's brain. How the hell had Kalinin been released? He knew the guy had hired an expensive London lawyer, but he couldn't see that being enough to set him free—unless the officer in charge had backed down in some way. McNab recalled Slater's parting glance as he'd left the room. Slater wanted Kalinin, wanted the whole damn lot of the

312

Russian gang. He would never jeopardise that, no matter how much McNab had pissed him off. Or would he?

Kalinin hadn't acknowledged McNab yet but the Russian knew he was there, Anya's frightened demeanour had told him that. Which meant Brogan must be in on this. Christ! He had been set up and had been stupid enough to fall for it. Worse than that, he had brought Chrissy into it with him. His mouth was bone dry. It was all falling into place. Brogan's phone call inviting him to play. His wiping out of McNab's tab as a thanks for the police getting the Russians off his back. The bastard had handed him over.

A gasp from the table indicated Chrissy had produced a royal flush. TAG man wasn't pleased but there could be no argument who had won. Chrissy threw McNab a triumphant smile and he jerked his head towards the bar. She didn't know or recognise the two standing there, but McNab hoped his expression indicated that he did. Chrissy took the hint and rose. She arched her back, displaying the full size of her pregnancy, and gave a sigh.

'Sorry, gentlemen, but I think it's time for me to retire. Thank you and goodnight.'

She held out her hand to McNab. He took it and they began walking towards the door. He didn't look back to see whether their exit had been noted.

When they were out of the room and beginning their descent of the staircase, Chrissy stumbled a little, as her heel caught in the deep pile.

'What the hell's going on?' she whispered under her breath, as McNab steadied her.

313

'That was Kalinin and the girl from the Russian Restaurant.'

'I thought Kalinin was in custody.'

'So did I.'

'Did Brogan know he was out?'

McNab didn't want to scare her. 'Maybe.'

They were on the mid-landing now, about to make their way down the final stretch of stairs to the lobby. Below, on their right, the bar buzzed with talk and laughter and the constant chink of glasses.

'What about my winnings?'

'I'll pick them up tomorrow.'

The doorman was tall and broad. Even in evening wear he looked like a boxer, his thick neck straining the white collar and bowtie. He stared at them blankly, then opened the door. McNab stood aside to let Chrissy through.

The steps were deserted, the street in front of the club devoid of cars. He took her arm and began to walk her swiftly away from the entrance. Despite his attempts to appear calm, he sensed she was picking up on his fear.

They were at the corner now. McNab could see the glint of the river, the glass windows of Jury's Inn in the distance. He pulled out his mobile.

'There's a taxi,' Chrissy said. 'Stick out your arm.'

The orange light was headed across the bridge in their direction. McNab stepped out on to the road to wave it down.

58

Rhona tried McNab's number again with no luck. He must have switched off for the duration of the poker game. She considered calling a taxi, then decided to head out and pick one up on the main thoroughfare.

Anya's call had come out of the blue. In a whisper, she'd told Rhona that she'd tried McNab but the mobile went to voicemail. In the background Rhona had heard running water and the click of heels.

'What's wrong, Anya?'

'Kalinin's been released on bail. He came to the restaurant. He was very angry. He knows I told you where he lives.'

'Anya, listen. I'll contact DI Slater . . .'

'No. If you tell the police they'll kill Misha.'

Rhona was at a loss. 'Where are you now?'

'In the ladies' room at the Poker Club. Kalinin brought me here. He has something planned, I don't know what.'

Rhona felt the ground open under her feet. 'McNab's at the Poker Club.'

There was a whimper on the other end of the line.

'I have to call the police, Anya, in case Kalinin harms you or McNab. Do you understand?'

*   *   *

Rhona waved down a taxi and showed the driver her ID. He took her request seriously, running three amber lights and a red on his way downtown. En route, she called the station and got through to Janice.

'Kalinin was released on bail two hours ago.'

'And no one thought to tell McNab?'

'DI Slater said he would.'

'Seems he forgot.'

What had Slater been thinking? Kalinin had taken care not to show his face to McNab, but McNab had identified him by his voice. Kalinin would be even angrier now. Rhona explained her concerns for McNab's safety and advised they send back-up.

'Something's happened?'

'Anya Grigorovitch called me. Kalinin's at the club and so is McNab.'

The taxi was passing Jury's Inn, crossing the river, near to the spot where she and McNab had met Anya.

Rhona recalled how cheerful he'd been when he'd left her flat earlier than evening. The wink he'd thrown her when they'd left.

59

McNab watched as the cab light went out and the vehicle made a wide U-turn, having caught sight of a fare on the other side of the road.

'I'll phone for one.'

He tried to keep his voice level, but Chrissy was no fool. She knew enough about Kalinin to know they would be better off out of there, and fast.

'Stand back out of sight,' McNab ordered.

She retreated into the shadow of a nearby doorway.

A computerised voice answered his call, and he gave his location and rang off. He glanced back towards the club. The entrance area was deserted. No one had followed them out. Maybe he was overreacting? Kalinin was way too smart to jeopardise his bail by attacking him. Maybe he'd just wanted to scare him.

Maybe he had turned up at the club to put the frighteners on Brogan, not knowing McNab was there. Chances were Brogan had been as freaked as he had. But why was Anya with Kalinin when she'd professed to be terrified of him? An alternative scenario occurred to him. Had Anya set him up when she gave him Kalinin's address? Maybe Kalinin had expected McNab to appear that night with the food? He dismissed this idea. Anya hadn't been at the Poker Club through choice, not the way Kalinin was treating her.

A taxi was coming his way, orange light off. He prayed it was the one he'd ordered.

'Chrissy!' he called softly.

He stepped out of the shadows, just as a second vehicle turned on to the main thoroughfare. It had probably come from the car park at the rear of the Poker Club. It was a limo, long and dark with smoked windows—Brogan's best. It drew alongside McNab and, as the back window whirred down, Brogan's voice called out to him.

'Heard you and the girl cleaned me out?' Brogan sounded cheery for a man who had lost a considerable amount of money.

'We did OK,' McNab conceded warily.

He heard the click of Chrissy's heels as she came

317

to join him.

Brogan gave a strangled laugh. McNab turned to tell Chrissy to get back, then saw the terrified look on her face. He swung round. The front passenger window was open and the face he feared most stared out at him. It was the one and only time he had seen Solonik smile. There was a semi-automatic pistol clasped in the Russian's hand.

McNab turned and launched himself towards Chrissy, trying desperately to put himself between her and Solonik. The first bullet struck a nearby wall and ricocheted off, sparking the pavement, just as he reached Chrissy and pushed her down.

The second round came a fraction of a second later, pumping between his shoulder blades with the force and power of one of Solonik's fists. For a moment McNab imagined he was back in that room with those fists raining down on him, then his legs softened and he collapsed face down on the icy pavement, air rushing from his lungs as if from a punctured balloon.

He heard Chrissy scream as he slumped alongside her, then the roar of the car as it took off. Then his world began to revolve in a whirl of startling images and frantic sound.

McNab wanted to tell Chrissy to fetch Rhona. He needed to speak to her. He needed to tell her something. Something important. He tried to form Rhona's name, but his mind was drifting. He was suddenly on a fairground ride, travelling rapidly through the decades of his life. Michael Joseph McNab; the child, the adolescent, the man. He was outside himself looking on, painfully observing his own clumsy endeavours, his stubbornness, his stupidity.

He wondered fleetingly whether he would ever be able to make things right.

* * *

Rhona jumped out of the taxi and pushed her way through the gathering crowd. Chrissy had McNab's head in her lap and her cheeks were streaming with tears.

'What the hell happened?'

'They shot him.'

'Michael!' She dropped to her knees and began searching for the wound. There was nothing on his shirt front, no freckled pattern indicating residue, no evidence of an entry point. Below him blood pooled on the pavement.

Rhona rolled him over. The back of his jacket was soaked, a hole punched through the silky black material. She slipped the jacket off his shoulders. The bullet had entered his back but hadn't exited the body. Designed to create maximum damage, it had disintegrated internally.

'Jesus Christ, Michael, why won't you ever listen to me?' She wadded his jacket and pressed it hard against the bullet hole. Chrissy was sobbing beside her. She wanted to yell at her to stop, that McNab was not going to die.

The blood had stopped pumping, which meant one of two things. Either she had plugged the wound or his heart had stopped. There was a gurgle as McNab tried to suck air into his damaged lungs. Rhona placed her mouth on his, tasting blood, willing his chest to rise.

For a moment the green eyes flickered open and he smiled at her as though they were a million miles away from this place and nothing bad had happened. It was the smile he'd often bestowed on her, the smile she'd chosen to disregard.

'I love you, Dr MacLeod.'

'Please, Michael, no.'

Rhona drew him to her as his eyes emptied of life, willing her own heart to beat for the both of them. She rocked him there, feeling his warmth against her, the roughness of his face in her palms. She bent and kissed the auburn hair, whispering a thousand sorries for what she had said and not said, hoping that wherever he was he would hear her.

60

Rhona hesitated at the door. Stepping inside would be like going back in time. She had worked here as a student, serving behind the bar. The place had an illustrious history. In the seventies it had been the meeting place for Celtic Football Club. Back then, Kenny Dalglish had been a promising young player, and his future wife's family had run the place. All the Celtic greats had spent time here, including the greatest of them all, their manager Jock Stein. No wonder this was Bill's favourite watering hole.

Next to the entrance was a plaque, which ignored former famous customers in favour of the resident ghost. Rhona took a deep breath and opened the door. The spacious room was the same yet different. The long bar had changed its position, but the place was familiar enough for memories to come flooding back. She stood for a moment savouring them, then looked round for Bill.

He was sitting on the left in the far corner. He hadn't seen her come in, so she had the opportunity to observe him unnoticed. He sat alone, a pint of beer on the table in front of him. Many of the other clientele would be policemen, like him. The nearby estate of Simshill was often referred to as Policehill.

Rhona bought a drink and carried it to Bill's table. She was shocked to see how much older he looked. Old age came swiftly to people in his job. No wonder so many tried for retirement as soon as possible. Being a policeman was a bit like being in the army; hang around too long and you were asking for trouble.

Who would blame Bill for getting out? Maybe she should do the same. Be her own boss, choose her cases, as Roy Hunter had suggested. If Bill wasn't going to be around any longer, she wasn't sure she wanted to be either.

Bill freed up a space for her beside him.

'Hey,' she said.

'How are you doing?' He examined her face.

'Not so good.'

He nodded.

They sat in silence, their drinks untouched. There was so much to say and yet no words to say it. She fished in her bag and passed the photographs to Bill.

'They called him Michael.'

The baby's skin was the colour of creamy milk chocolate, his eyes a surprisingly dark blue. He was staring wide eyed at the camera or at his father who, according to Chrissy, took a photograph ten times a day.

Bill made a small sound of appreciation in his throat.

'Chrissy's coming home in a week,' she said.

'And Sam?'

'Now the charges of abduction have been dropped, he can return and finish his medical degree.'

'A happy ending, then?'

'More like a hopeful beginning.' Rhona looked down at the image of a smiling Chrissy. 'I've really missed her.'

Bill threw her a concerned look, knowing that Chrissy wasn't the only person she was missing.

Rhona had promised she wouldn't ask Bill outright. It wasn't her business. She had no right to attempt to persuade him, yet at the same time she would never forgive herself if she didn't try.

'Don't go, Bill. Don't leave.'

He didn't answer. His face was shadowed by sorrow. He was in as dark a place as she was herself.

'We can't let him down. We have to make it right.'

'It can never be made right.' He shook his head.

'We can try.'

His eyes swept the room. The bar was lined with regulars, mostly groups of middle-aged men talking. A gaggle of young women sat at a nearby table nursing vase-size glasses of white wine, their loud laughter indicating how much they'd drunk already. A couple of young guys with carefully constructed hair stood in conversation near the door. In the blink of an eye, Rhona spotted something change hands between them.

'I've been coming in here for thirty years,' Bill said. 'Now when I come I sit with my back to the wall. I drink my pint and I make a point of not noticing what goes on around me.' He looked at her. 'There comes a day when you give up the fight and start to live.'

'But not today.'

He gave her a half-smile. 'You sound like Margaret.'

Rhona lifted her glass. 'I'll drink to Margaret.'

'You women ganging up on me?'

'Don't we always?'

Bill was silent for a few moments, then asked about Swanson.

'He's denying everything. Says he didn't know about the remains in the garden. Insists they must have been there before his family bought the bungalow. Nonsense, of course, and easily disproved. He also maintains he had nothing to do with Mollie's death. On our side, we can prove the red glass in the grave matches the type he buys. We also have a couple of fibres from Mollie's grave soil that match a rug in his house. Swanson doesn't know about that.' She paused. 'It was a good idea of yours to have Magnus talk to McCarthy. It seems Swanson has been feeding McCarthy false memories, constantly reinforcing his supposed guilt.'

Everyone knew Swanson was guilty of all five murders, but proving it wouldn't be so easy. They would have to concentrate on the ones they could prove, like the body he'd taken from the loch.

'What about the wee girl?'

Rhona shook her head. 'She's taking the business with Michael very much to heart.'

323

The business with Michael. Why could she not say the words?

In the mess after the shooting, Nikolai Kalinin had simply disappeared, as had Solonik. The police suspected they had gone south, been hidden by Prokhorov, then been smuggled back to Mother Russia or to supervise other operations. There were plenty to choose from. The Riviera, South Africa, the United States. Kalinin would fit in anywhere. McNab had almost nailed him. Almost but not quite.

The door opened and a man walked in. Tall, auburn haired, broad shouldered. He glanced towards them and for a moment Rhona believed it was him. She imagined Michael looking over, giving them a wave, miming to ask whether they wanted a drink. He would approach the table and bestow his smile on her. This time she would return it. This time she would acknowledge the man who had loved her.

Having searched the room, the auburn-haired man turned on his heel and let the door bang shut behind him.